OH, HAPPY DAY!

A Selection of Recent Titles by Nicola Thorne

* *available from Severn House*

OH, HAPPY DAY!

Nicola Thorne

This first world edition published in Great Britain 2002 by
SEVERN HOUSE PUBLISHERS LTD of
9–15 High Street, Sutton, Surrey SM1 1DF.
This first world edition published in the USA 2003 by
SEVERN HOUSE PUBLISHERS INC of
595 Madison Avenue, New York, N.Y. 10022.

British Library Cataloguing in Publication Data

Thorne, Nicola
  Oh, happy day!
  1.   Great Britain - Social life and customs - 20th century - Fiction
  2.   Domestic fiction
  I.   Title
  823.9'14 [F]

  ISBN 0-7278-5903-X

Typeset by Hewer Text Ltd.,
Edinburgh, Scotland.
Printed and bound in Great Britain by
MPG Books Ltd., Bodmin, Cornwall.

Dedicated with love and gratitude to
Sybil Brooke

One

The bridal couple stood on the steps of the castle, Maisie with her veil thrown back, revealing her face radiant with happiness. Brides on their wedding day are traditionally beautiful. Even the homeliest, plainest face is transformed, the dumpiest figure flattered by the art of the beautician, the skills of the dressmaker. But Maisie had no need of such artificial aids: her beauty was real, made, if anything, even more ethereal by love.

The folds of the skirt of Maisie's ivory-satin wedding dress fell gracefully to the ground, a short train carefully arranged behind her. Beside her, Ed Hallam, her handsome bridegroom, looked resplendent in naval uniform. At the feet of the couple, angelic in white, crouched the small pages and bridesmaids, and to one side, just behind the groom, stood Ed's niece Jenny who had the important role of chief bridesmaid.

Below in the drive the wedding guests jockeyed for position with their cameras, snapping away, each anxious to capture the moment for posterity, for a treasured place in their albums. Peg Ryland would always remember that moment, frozen, as it were, in time, as she tried to snap the perfect picture of a beloved brother and his beautiful bride. It had been such a lovely day: the weather perfect, the ceremony at the church in the castle grounds solemn and beautiful.

Afterwards the bridal party wended their way slowly up

towards the castle, the young attendants bearing her short train, the wedding guests following, a chattering, laughing, happy crowd of people, some overexcited, overloud, of all ages, all shapes and sizes, dressed in their best. Some of the outfits of the ladies were outlandish. Many looked as though they might have been got out of mothballs. Some men wore morning dress but most wore suits, shirts with stiff white collars and ties; hair plastered back, shiny jaws freshly shaven.

It was an extraordinary mixture of people, for it was not a society wedding even though it had been held in a castle. Ed Hallam was a local man whose father had been gardener to the father of the present Lord Ryland, whom his sister Peg had married. By contrast, Maisie had been a dancer in a London nightclub and her friends stood out by the fashionable, extravagant and sometimes exotic nature of their dress.

Peg lowered her camera as the group on the steps broke up and Ed and Maisie, shepherding the little ones before them, descended the steps and wandered towards the marquee on the lawn, to which many of the thirsty wedding guests had already repaired. Waiters carrying trays of glasses of champagne were already circulating among them. Peg's eldest son Jude had been one of the pages and had conducted himself beautifully together with Maisie's niece and nephew, Samantha and Paul. Jude ran towards his mother, who lifted him up and gave him a kiss.

'I think he's sleepy,' she said to Jenny, brushing back his hair. 'Are you sleepy, darling?' Vigorously Jude shook his head and struggled to get down, anxious to play with his new friends.

'Didn't they look lovely?' Jenny spoke a little wistfully, Peg thought, as they gazed towards the bridal pair now chatting to a group on the edge of the lawn. 'Maisie is *so* beautiful.'

'You're beautiful too,' Peg insisted gently. 'One day it will be your turn.'

Jenny's face lit up. 'And will I have my wedding at the castle?'

'Of course.'

'And who will I marry, Auntie Peg?'

Peg gave her a mysterious smile. 'Oh that, as yet, we don't know.'

'Some lucky man.' Hubert Ryland came in at the end of the conversation and ruffled Jenny's hair, which was a mass of blonde curls.

'Don't *do* that, Uncle Hubert!' Jenny said sharply, moving away. 'You'll spoil my hair.'

'I only meant . . .' Hubert began apologetically, but Jenny abruptly turned her back on him and flounced away.

Hubert attempted to hide his anger and embarrassment by lighting a cigarette.

'She has a temper that one,' he said, blowing smoke into the air, like an engine letting off steam.

'She's very young. She's at that age,' Peg said placatingly.

'I can't understand Jenny. Never could.' Hubert shook his head, looking at the back of the retreating young girl. 'Her moods are so unpredictable. She reminds me vividly of my brother Lydney, who had sudden outbursts of temper too. The funny thing is' – he paused and stroked his cheek reflectively – 'she has always reminded me of him.' He looked sideways at Peg. 'You remember Lydney, don't you?'

'Hardly. I was quite young when he died.' Peg's expression was guarded.

'But you must have seen him about the place – very tall, fair . . .'

'Oh yes, I certainly remember him.' Peg turned, almost, it seemed, with relief towards Maisie's sister Joan who had come up to take charge of the children, now abandoned by the chief bridesmaid whose little charges they had been.

'What's the matter with Jenny? She seemed to go off in a huff.'

3

'I ruffled her hair,' Hubert said. 'You'd think I'd tried to murder her.'

'Oh but hair is very *important*.' Joan, who was an older version of Maisie and almost as pretty, gave a knowing smile. 'Isn't it, Lady Ryland?'

'You must call me Peg – after all, we're nearly related – and my husband is Hubert.'

'I'm sure I'm quite confused,' Joan confessed in bewilderment. 'My sister marrying into a titled family, in a castle and all!'

Peg felt that now was not the time to attempt lengthy explanations about who was related to whom, how and why. The history was a complex one and Joan had only arrived the day before to meet Maisie's new family. Her children's outfits had been made in London by the dressmaker who had made Maisie's wedding dress.

'Maisie looked beautiful,' Hubert intervened gallantly. 'And you were a dancer too, Joan?'

'At one time.' Joan bristled slightly. 'I had to give it up when I got married.'

'Come and have some champagne.' Peg took her arm. 'Darling,' she said, looking over her shoulder at Hubert, 'can we leave the little ones in your care? I want to introduce Joan to some members of the family.'

It was true there were a lot of them. There was Addie, Jenny's mother, with her little son Arthur, who had also been asked to be a page but his mother had declined because he was delicate and an excessively nervous child. He now clung to his mother's skirt, finger in his mouth, so perhaps the decision had been a wise one. There was Verity, the elder sister, in appearance rather stern and formidable but with the kindest of hearts, a superintendent of nurses at a large hospital in Bristol. There was Stella, Peg's half-sister, who the year before had been struck down by polio and walked with a brace on her leg, aided by a stick.

Oh, Happy Day!

There was Frank Carpenter, Peg's stepfather, in short
sleeves and sweating in the large marquee, busily supervising
the bar. All of them greeted Joan warmly and she began to
feel at ease and relaxed amidst this array of strangers.

'And this is Violet, my sister-in-law,' Peg said after the
round of introductions. 'You must be feeling very bewildered
by now.'

'They're ever so nice,' Joan said a little breathlessly.
'Though I'm not sure I'll remember all the names.'

'This is Maisie's sister,' Peg said, bringing Joan forward,
'mother of the little page and bridesmaid.'

'How do you do?' The Honourable Violet Ryland extended
a gloved hand, peering at Joan from under the brim of a large
picture hat. Then she turned away, rather abruptly, as though
her attention had been diverted by someone else.

'Sorry,' Peg said apologetically. 'That was a bit rude.'

'I expect she's seen someone she knows.'

'I expect so.'

'A bit hoity-toity, is she?'

'A bit.'

'I expect it was strange' – Joan paused and looked at Peg
keenly – 'marrying a lord?'

'Very strange,' Peg agreed. 'But he wasn't a lord when I
married him and didn't expect to become one for many years.
His father was in very good health and was relatively young.'

'Heart attack was it?' Joan grimaced sympathetically.

'He had a riding accident. Hubert and I lived in France and
expected to be there for a very long time.' Peg shrugged. 'But
of course he had to return and look after the estate.'

'It certainly is a lovely place you have here.' Joan looked
appreciatively around. 'Beats the East End any day. I suppose you wouldn't know the Whitechapel Road, would you,
Lady Ryland?'

'I know it very well,' Peg said with some asperity, guessing
what Joan was trying to lead up to. 'I worked as a journalist

5

in London and lived in Clerkenwell. In fact I once . . .' Peg stopped, thinking it might seem provocative to tell Joan how she had once been involved in a fracas at a political meeting in Whitechapel and could have lost her life.

Joan, though, was curious to know, and pressed her: 'You once what?'

'I once covered a political meeting there that ended in a fight.'

'It's not always like that, you know.' Joan's tone was defensive. 'People have their views about the East End – that is, if they don't live there – but they're not always true. There is a great sense of community among East Enders.'

'Oh I know,' Peg said hurriedly; 'this was just before the General Strike, a very restless time.'

A waiter hovered at her elbow and Peg took, with relief, a glass of champagne, inviting her rather prickly guest to do the same.

'It will soon be time for lunch,' she said. 'I'd better go and see what's happening in the kitchen. Come and talk to my sister Verity. She lived in London too.'

'I think I'll look for my mum,' Joan said, peering round. 'Too much of this stuff' – she indicated the glass in her hand – 'and she'll be well away.'

Verity, as the eldest sister by several years, always took her responsibilities seriously, invariably thinking it incumbent upon her to take care of anyone adrift; but on this occasion the party was quite clearly divided into two groups: the locals, who were by far the most numerous, and Maisie's crowd from London plus a few of Ed's shipmates, most of whom had lost little time in chatting up Maisie's female friends, who were, almost without exception, strikingly good-looking with figures to match. When asked by her sister, Verity was quite happy to take care of Joan, who was, however, becoming agitated about her mother.

'Your mother's perfectly all right,' Verity said reassuringly, indicating a group sitting on chairs in the shade by the side of the main marquee. 'She seems to have made quite a hit.' And indeed, Mrs Reed's laughter could, at that point, be heard echoing across the lawn as a waiter poured champagne into her empty glass.

Dora Reed was a rather stout, slightly dishevelled-looking lady dressed in a tight-fitting costume with a straw hat, which by now sat perched on the back of her artificially blonde hair. However, despite the obvious ravages of time, it was not difficult to see where her daughters had got their looks from.

When Joan, followed by Verity, reached her, Dora, her face flushed, eyes overbright, looked at her daughter defensively. 'It's quite all right, love,' she said, putting her glass to her lips; 'never enjoyed meself so much in me life.'

'Oh *Mum*,' Joan said, detecting the signs of early inebriation, 'don't you think you've had enough?'

'I certainly do not,' Dora said firmly, stretching out her glass for a refill from the obliging waiter hovering next to her with a bottle in his hand. 'Don't have a do like this every day, do we? In a castle, hey? Your sister landed on her feet, my girl. Pity you couldn't have done the same instead of a worthless—'

'Oh *Mum*,' Joan said crossly, 'I knew you would overdo it and you have.' She bent down towards her mother in an attempt to relieve her of her glass; but Dora, struggling indignantly to her feet, gave her a violent shove and then fell back in her chair, losing her hat in the process, which tumbled the ground revealing a head of bright-gold hair with deep, crinkly permanent waves.

'I'm sure your mother is fine.' Verity, in the nick of time, had caught Joan, who floundered in her arms like a beached fish.

'You mustn't worry about your mother, love. We'll look after her. What's the point of a party if you can't have a drop

7

to drink?' A rather portly man with dyed-black hair parted in the middle and a curled waxed moustache, a large cigar in his mouth, put his arm familiarly round Joan's waist, helping to steady her and, in the process, gave it a tight squeeze. Whereupon Joan rounded upon him, giving the offending arm a sharp slap.

'Don't be like that, love!' The man, rubbing his arm, looked aggrieved. 'I only meant to help. No need to give yourself airs and graces just because your sister has married a nob.'

'Don't you talk to my daughter like that,' Dora said aggressively, rescuing her hat from the ground and dusting it carefully before sticking it back firmly on her head.

'I do *not* have airs and graces,' Joan retorted. 'I just don't like being fondled by someone I don't know. Or care to know,' she added, pushing him further away.

'I was not fondling . . .' the man began, and then they all stopped as Maisie, still clutching her bouquet, appeared in their midst, a little out of breath as though she had been running.

'Is anything wrong?' she asked, looking anxiously at her mother. 'Mum, have you been drinking too much?'

'No I have not!' Mrs Reed said indignantly, 'and I'll thank you not to talk to me like that, my girl.'

'She's afraid you'll show her up,' said a voice in the group, 'now that she's married into the aristocracy.'

'Ed is *not* an aristocrat,' Maisie retorted, looking angrily at the speaker, 'and I'll thank *you* to mind your own blinkin' business.' When she was aroused, her vowels became pure cockney, like her mother's.

Then she looked sharply at the man who had put his arm round Joan's waist. 'What's up, Sam?'

'Nothing's up,' Sam mumbled. 'Just a bit of a misunderstanding.'

He wore a well-cut grey morning suit with a mauve cravat

secured by a grey pearl tiepin. An array of diamond rings glittered on his fingers and he smelt strongly of pomade.

'He squeezed my waist,' Joan said. 'I told him not to be so familiar.'

Sam drew out a handkerchief and mopped his perspiring brow. 'I meant no offence. Your sister lost her footing and I tried to help.'

'Tried to help yourself, you mean,' Joan retorted.

'Sam was once my boss.' Maisie gave her a meaningful look. 'He owns one of the most popular nightclubs in London.'

'It doesn't mean he can fondle me.'

'I was *not* fondling,' Sam said heatedly, agitatedly brushing the front of his jacket. He was a small, compact man, and both Joan and Maisie towered over him. 'I am a happily married man with four children. You completely misunderstood the situation.'

'Said I had airs and graces because of *you*.' Joan was loth to let the matter drop. 'I want to see this through,' she added as an afterthought.

'What through?' someone else muttered.

'She wants an apology.' Dora reached for another glass from the waiter, who was still hovering, obviously enjoying the spectacle, which was unusual in that it offered a departure from the rather formal, dressy affairs, echoing to the braying of well-bred voices, that usually took place at the castle.

Maisie, goaded by her mother's behaviour, reached over and, deftly retrieving the glass from her, emptied the contents on to the ground.

'I don't want you making an exhibition of yourself,' Maisie hissed; 'this is Ed's family home – people he has known all his life. I don't want anyone to think *my* family don't know how to behave.'

At that point Dora once again eased herself from her chair, lurched slightly and then steadied herself.

9

'Will someone please take me home?' she demanded. 'I have the feeling people like us are not wanted here.'

'That is *ridiculous*, Mum.' Maisie pushed her gently back into her chair. 'We're going to have lunch soon and there will be speeches and I want it to be a happy day. My wedding day, after all.'

Dora staggered to her feet yet again, linking her arm through Joan's to steady herself. 'I don't care,' she said firmly. 'I don't want to stay, and nor does Joanie.'

Sensing an ugly situation getting out of hand, Verity looked despairingly around and saw Hubert coming purposefully towards them. He seemed to have sensed from the agonized expression on Verity's face that something was gravely amiss and, looking at Dora propping herself against Joan, had quickly assessed the situation as one in need of his attention.

'Just the people I was looking for,' he said with a smile. 'Luncheon is about to be served and I wondered if the mother of the bride would do me the honour of allowing me to escort her to the marquee?'

'Oo my lord,' Dora gulped, nonplussed.

'There, Mum' – Maisie was all smiles – 'I knew it would be all right.'

'Your husband, madam, is looking for you,' Hubert said amiably. 'I was just about to go and tell him that I'd spotted you and you hadn't run away.'

'Oh lordie,' Maisie cried shrilly and, picking up her skirt, ran across the lawn into the arms of her puzzled-looking groom.

Hubert turned to Dora and took her hand. 'May I escort you, dear madam?'

'Isn't he a love?' Dora murmured to her daughter, and tucked her arm confidently through his.

The marquee had been beautifully decorated with white lilies and orchids from the castle greenhouses, and at the long top table the bride and groom sat with their families on either side. Dora, mollified by all the attention she was receiving, seemed suddenly to have sobered up, awed perhaps by the presence of a real live lord beside her. Waiters and waitresses moved effortlessly around the tables, serving course after course of delicious food prepared by Mrs Capstick, who had ruled in the castle's kitchens for many years and, assisted by two chefs brought in from outside, had been cooking for days.

Looking at the assembled company, Peg thought back to the old days, when there had been a rigorous separation between the gentry and the ordinary people, usually estate workers. The time had been when the classes never mixed and no one had thought it in any way extraordinary. Peg herself, when young, had accepted the situation as it was as if it had been ordained by God. She had looked up to the Ryland family as her natural superiors; she felt that people like Frank and Mrs Capstick still did and had never accepted her new place in the hierarchy, as if she were an interloper. In a contrast with the past, today, apart from Violet, who she felt had come rather reluctantly, and, of course, Hubert, there were no gentry here. She certainly wasn't gentry and never would be. The common people, the ordinary man in the street, personified by Ed, had indeed taken over.

She had no idea why Hubert had taken in Maisie's mother and now seemed so solicitous towards her. They had not had a chance to discuss the situation, but he appeared to have recovered from his contretemps with Jenny, who was sitting next to one of Maisie's friends from London, a good-looking man with a natural smile who seemed to be paying her a lot of attention. Jenny looked older than fourteen and, with her beauty and vivacity, attracted the men like flies, as her family were just beginning to realize. Peg had seldom seen her in this context, but she knew there was rather a wild side to her,

11

which had surfaced today in her encounter with Hubert, and which she knew worried her mother, Addie.

Peg turned and smiled at Hubert, who was studying the speech he was due to give in a few minutes.

'All right, darling?'

'A bit nervous,' he confessed.

'You'll be splendid.' She gently nudged his ankle under the table. 'How's the mother-in-law?' She raised her eyebrows in Dora's direction.

'Fine. I'm trying to make sure she sticks to water. There was nearly a scene.'

'Oh!'

At that moment the toastmaster approached deferentially, murmured a few words in Hubert's ear and gently banged his gavel on the table.

'Ladies and gentlemen, please be silent for the host, Lord Ryland, who will toast the health of the bride and groom.'

His name, he said, was Alfonso, but everyone called him Al. He said his parents were Spanish and he had been born in Spain but thought of himself as English; but he did look very foreign: tall and slim, with shiny jet-black hair sleeked back, long sideburns and large, brilliant-blue eyes. He had high cheekbones, a quick, engaging smile and beautiful teeth. He was like some rare, exotic bird, quite unlike the men and boys Jenny knew, and ever since they'd been seated next to each other he had fascinated her. He'd also travelled a lot on the continent as a dancer, and regaled her with the stories of his adventures. He looked at her in a special way, was very courteous towards her, and she knew she looked good in her bridesmaid's dress, soft, flowing blue voile over a satin underskirt with a pleated bodice, a high neckline and three-quarter mutton-chop sleeves. There was a blue band round her golden hair and she wore tiny pearl earrings, which had been Ed's gift to her as chief bridesmaid.

They talked exclusively to each other and when the music started were the first to join the bridal couple on the floor. Naturally Al was a good dancer and at one point in the evening everyone around them on the dance floor stopped and watched them, because Jenny, though not nearly as practised or skilled as Al, had natural rhythm and proved herself a good dancer too. Most of it was instinctive, as she'd seldom danced with a member of the opposite sex except at staff parties at the hall, where she kept on getting her feet trodden on by overzealous farm hands. Their synchronization was perfect and when they came together again Al held her just a little closer, a little more intimately than before.

Jenny was aware that people were watching her – not only her family but all those she'd known since she was a child; and, after all, she had lived here since she was born. But she didn't care. Al mesmerized her; she had become alive.

When the music stopped and Al, face flushed, put out his arms again invitingly, she shook her head.

'I'm thirsty,' she said.

'Then let's go and get something to drink.' Al looked disappointed but steered her carefully into the corner of the marquee where the bar was still presided over by Frank.

'You dance beautifully,' he whispered. 'You would be stunning if you ever decided to do it professionally.'

'This is my stepfather.' Jenny nudged Al towards him. 'Uncle Frank, this is Al, who used to dance with Maisie.'

'Oh really?' Frank gave him an appraising, slightly disapproving glance. 'What will you have to drink?'

'Half a pint of beer would be nice,' Al said, his cockney vowels just like Maisie's though there was a touch of Spanish in them too. He mopped his forehead with a large white handkerchief. 'It's very hot in here.'

'Lemonade for me, please, Uncle Frank,' Jenny said. 'We're just going to go outside and cool down.'

'It's a bit chilly outside,' Frank warned; 'don't get cold and don't go too far.'

'Don't worry, I'll look after her.' Al carefully steered Jenny out of the marquee past the dancing couples, but Frank looked after them with a worried frown.

'That's your stepfather, then?' Al said as they paused outside in the cool air. 'He seems nice. You call him uncle, not father?'

'Always have,' Jenny said; 'I don't know why. My brother and sisters are all so much older than me that I call them uncle and aunt too. I grew up like that. I don't know when or how it all started. Verity, the eldest, was over twenty when I was born. She'd been right through the war. It's a strange family, but you see my mother married three times. She was very pretty.'

'Is your mother here?'

'My mother's dead,' Jenny said. 'I was brought up by one of my sisters, Addie, who left her husband. I call her Mummy. She's very nice. I think she's still in the marquee where we ate, gossiping to her friends. She wore a large pink hat.'

It was now evening. The wedding breakfast and speeches had seemed to go on for hours. The bride and groom had left for a secret destination soon after the dancing had begun.

'Do you ever come to London?' Al asked, leaning suggestively towards her. 'If so I'd like to see you again.'

'Oh no!' Jenny shook her head, amused at the thought. 'Besides . . .' She was about to say she was still at school but on impulse decided not to. Al was very nice, handsome and amusing, and there was something so enchanting about this evening, the interest Al was taking in her, treating her not as a child, as everyone else did, but as a grown-up. 'Besides . . . well, if I do . . .'

'Look me up,' Al said. 'The Monkey Club on Frith Street, Soho. I'll give you the address before I leave. Perhaps you could write to me?'

'Is that where Maisie dances?' Jenny asked quickly, avoiding the question.

'One of the places. She danced in quite a few.'

'Was she good?'

'Very. She's fallen on her feet all right has Maisie,' Al said, looking around appreciatively at the castle ablaze with lights, illuminated against the sapphire evening sky; and at that moment he saw Frank standing at the door of the marquee, beckoning to them.

'I think we'd better go in,' he said; 'your dad seems anxious about you.' He lightly put his arm round her waist as they drifted slowly towards the marquee where, soon after being shepherded in by Frank, they began to dance again, but this time keeping well apart.

Eventually, when Al left with the group of friends with whom he had come, Jenny felt a pang of sorrow, because she knew that, when she was old enough to go to London on her own, he was sure to have forgotten all about her.

Ed raised his glass towards his new bride.

She lifted hers and without a word they toasted each other; then, looking surreptitiously round the restaurant, which because of the lateness of the hour was nearly empty, they kissed.

They had driven fifty miles since stealing away from the castle, leaving the revellers dancing to the music of two bands, one indoors and one out, enjoying themselves so much that they were scarcely aware that the bridal pair had slipped away. Only a few who had been tipped off, like close family, had seen them off. Joan, who was divorced, had caught the bride's bouquet and had promptly handed it to Jenny, who had accepted it with glee.

In the corner of the dining room of the hotel, overlooking Poole harbour, a tired waiter leaned against a dresser, arms akimbo.

Maisie wore a white-linen suit, its simplicity making her look even more ravishing than she had during the day. Her stylish broad-brimmed white-felt hat had been left in their bedroom and her shoulder-length pale-gold hair gleamed in the mellow candlelight. Ed had changed into a grey, double-breasted lounge suit with which he wore a white shirt with a soft collar and a blue tie. He had curly black hair and blue eyes, a firm mouth, and his skin was deeply tanned. The two looked at each other adoringly, relishing anticipation of the moment when they would be alone and in each other's arms.

Ed reached out for Maisie's hand, but he was surprised to see her expression had grown thoughtful, even sombre, as a contrast to the euphoric moment they had just shared.

'Penny for them, darling?' he said anxiously.

'It's nothing.' Maisie shook her head and a swathe of long blonde hair momentarily obscured her face. She had high cheekbones, which undoubtedly gave her an air of unattainability, almost hauteur, deep-set blue eyes, and sensuous carmine-coated lips which, when parted, showed very white, even teeth gleaming like pearls.

'It must be something,' Ed prompted her gently. 'Is it something I said? Did?'

'Not at all!' Maisie gasped. 'It's just that . . . well it's just that I felt ashamed of my family. My mother getting drunk. It rather spoilt the day.'

'Oh no, it was a happy day! Such a happy day! Besides, she wasn't *very* drunk. Hubert said she sobered up no end and only drank water.'

'Oh he told you that, did he?' Maisie said waspishly. 'You already discussed my mother's behaviour, did you, without saying anything to me?'

'Well it didn't seem appropriate or very sensible. We didn't "discuss" it in any detail. I simply asked him what had happened. While I waited for you, and Hubert went over, there seemed a bit of a commotion. When you came rushing back to go into lunch you said nothing.'

'That didn't seem appropriate either. I didn't want to tell you that Mum had made a fool of herself or that my sister Joanie didn't seem entirely sober either. She took exception to a helpful gesture from a mate of mine who was once my boss, Sam Hunter, who owns one of the best joints in London.'

'Well that doesn't matter,' Ed said dismissively. 'You're never going back to dancing, that's for sure.'

'But it *does* matter, Ed. It embarrasses me that my family should draw attention to themselves in front of your sister and brother-in-law and their guests, as well as mine. Sam was really hurt about what happened.' Maisie paused. 'But you see, Ed, I suppose I explain it like this: we – my family and I, that is – are not brash and ill-mannered but nervous and insecure in a place like a castle.'

'I understand perfectly. I was insecure too.'

Maisie looked surprised. 'Oh, but not today?'

'Not today exactly, except that I was just as nervous as you, but when Peg first went to live there. We always lived in the shadow of the castle. We were servants, don't forget.'

'I can never see Peg as a servant.'

'Well none of us children were actually servants. Frank was, and my father, who was head gardener; but we lived in that sort of world, below stairs. Our parties were always in the servants' hall. I'd never been upstairs until Peg married Hubert, and of course his father was furious because he had married beneath him.'

'Well then *I* was embarrassed that Hubert had to take my mother under his wing.'

'There's no need to be; I'm sure he didn't mind.'

'I'm sure he did. I also don't think he approves of me. He asked Joan in rather a patronizing way if she was a dancer too. She said he had a funny tone in his voice when he said it. No wonder she had a bit too much, as well as Mum.'

Nicola Thorne

Ed sat back and produced a shiny silver cigarette case from his breast pocket. It was engraved with his initials entwined with Maisie's and the date of the wedding, a present from his bride. He looked at it, then at her and, opening it, passed it to her.

Maisie carefully selected a cigarette, which she held in her long fingers, blood-red nails gleaming, as he lit first hers and then his. Momentarily the smoke from their cigarettes mingled in the air before evaporating towards the ceiling.

'Hubert is a product of his age and class,' Ed said. 'He doesn't mean these things, but it is hard for him to change.'

'I mean, Ed, we are East Enders pure and simple, used to a good knees-up, drinking a lot, not having to be judged and always be on our best behaviour.'

'Nothing wrong with that.'

Maisie shook her head. 'I shall never be comfortable at the castle, Ed – not after what happened today. I shall go back there and stay with you – of course I will; but I will never feel at home there.'

'You won't have to go there if you don't want to. Besides, we'll have our own home soon.'

'But I want to please you, Ed. I *do* want your family to like me and approve of me and I want to try and understand them.'

'When you understand they are *not* noble,' Ed said as patiently as he could, 'you will have achieved a real victory. It seems to be bogging you down.'

He then sat back, smoking thoughtfully, wondering why all this hadn't come out before they were married.

That night, their wedding night, they didn't make love but lay in each other's arms as though locked in their own thoughts, as though some invisible barrier had somehow come between them.

18

Two

Hubert Ryland stood by the window of his study, looking gloomily out across the lawn which, via a series of terraces, sloped gracefully down to the lake. Below him, workmen were busily dismantling the two marquees that had stood on the lawn, supervised by Frank Carpenter, who was nominally his lordship's chauffeur but in fact, by virtue of years of long service, busied himself with a number of tasks about the estate.

Some distance away from Frank, Jenny, with a long stick in one hand and a sack in the other, was busy, together with a number of other helpers, picking up the debris left by the revellers as the night had progressed. In fact, dancing hadn't stopped until well after midnight, and many people had still been lurching about the grounds at dawn. Hubert, anxious about his property, had scarcely had any sleep at all.

It had not been like that in the old days. People had known when to go; they had treated a place with respect. So much had changed since the war.

Hubert sighed and went back to his desk, but he found it difficult to deal with the mass of papers that lay there awaiting his attention. It was true he was tired, but he was aware that there were other reasons for his black mood. He had felt, as the day had progressed, that somehow his home had been taken over by alien forces. A foreign army had invaded and he was not altogether sure that he liked it. There had been something very satisfying and stable about

19

the old regime – the generations of Rylands, who had lived in the castle, who had been born there, married from there and, finally, been buried in the church in the grounds. People's attitude towards them had been one of respect.

Such occasions had been attended by people like the Rylands, of the same wealthy, leisured class, who knew how to behave. In the old days the estate workers had also known how to behave. They had filed into the ballroom and filed out again, sometimes a little the worse for wear, but it seldom showed. There were too many elders about, with grave, reproving faces, who had served the Rylands for generations, for the younger people to misbehave. They did not brawl in public as Maisie's relations had done or leave papers and bottles strewn over the grounds, scraps of sandwiches and pork pies that had not yet been demolished by the birds.

The estate workers living in tied cottages had dwindled in number and many people were now employed from outside. There were itinerant workers who came, stayed awhile, maybe for sheep-shearing or harvesting, or some other seasonal work, and went away again. Invariably they lacked the tradition of the old faithful family servants, the Frank Carpenters and Mrs Capsticks, who had worked on the estate almost from their youth. It was altogether a different kind of person who had formed the majority attending the wedding, and he knew he didn't like it. Did that mean he wasn't the democrat he thought he was? Marrying, against his father's wishes, the stepdaughter of a family retainer, inviting her brother to celebrate his nuptials in the Ryland home – was he the one who had turned the old order on its head?

Then what sort of person had Ed married? He was a university-educated man who had become an officer in the Royal Navy. Yet he was well and truly leaving his origins behind. He had chosen for a wife a nightclub dancer whose family was even commoner than she was.

Hubert put his head in his hands and stared wide-eyed at his desk. Common: he hated himself for even thinking in these terms, but that's what it amounted to. That's what his mother and his sister would have said. Ed and Peg were of solid British yeoman stock, but Maisie and her family were common. The common people had invaded Ryland Castle and, as far as he could see, were there to stay.

The door opened very quietly and Peg put her head round. 'Did someone bring your coffee, darling?'

'No.' Hubert raised his head and attempted a smile of welcome. 'That would be nice.'

'Are you all right, Hubert?' An expression of concern on her face, Peg crossed the floor and put her hand on his head. 'Tired, darling?'

'Very.' Hubert rubbed his face and gave a rueful smile. 'Well we didn't get much sleep.'

'You have a nap this afternoon.' Peg sat down and, impulsively joining her hands in her lap, leaned towards him. 'I do want to thank you, Hubert, for yesterday. I know it wasn't very easy for you and I assure you that I, my family, Ed in particular, are extremely grateful to you for allowing us to have the wedding here.' She rose and walked over to the window, looking out on the lawn still partly covered with debris. 'I'm only sorry everyone left such a mess.' She turned and looked at him, her expression troubled, as though she had known all the time what he was thinking. 'It wouldn't have happened in the old days, would it? Is that what's bothering you?'

Hubert looked startled at the uncanny ability of his wife to read his mind. 'How did you know?'

'I guessed. I was a bit shocked too.' She sat down again. 'In the old days everyone knew their place. Now they no longer do. The gentry piled into the drawing room, the estate workers into the ballroom. No bad thing, was it, Hubert?'

'I didn't say that.' He thought he detected a note of

contempt in her voice. His wife had once entertained very strong socialist views, which he felt had been tempered by time and, inevitably, marriage to him.

'I'm as upset as you are by the row that broke out among Maisie's relations and friends,' Peg went on earnestly, 'and I think it is only due to your timely intervention that a disaster was averted – a real shindig. I am grateful to you. I know Ed is and I am sure Maisie is too.'

'It was nothing.' Hubert airily waved it away.

'But it wouldn't have happened in the old days.'

'The old order changeth,' Hubert intoned. 'We must accept these things. About that coffee?'

Peg went reflectively down the stairs across the great hall, through the green-baize door and into the kitchen, where she found Frank, Mrs Capstick, Jenny and Addie sitting round the table drinking coffee.

'Hubert would like a cup,' Peg said after greeting them. 'I think we're all rather tired.'

'It was worth it, though, wasn't it, for such a lovely day?' Mrs Capstick fetched a cup and began pouring coffee into it; then she stopped. 'I expect His Lordship would like a pot on a tray?'

'I think it would stay hotter that way,' Peg agreed. 'Where's Verity?' she asked her sister.

'She's looking after Arthur. He's not very well and Stella felt a bit off-colour. I think there is some sort of bug around.'

'Oh well, I hope we don't all catch it.'

'Stella overdid it yesterday, I think. She even tried to dance!' Addie sighed. 'She gets frustrated that she can't do more. And she so loved dancing.'

Mrs Capstick finished setting up a tray, placed on it a pot of coffee, milk in a jug, a cup and saucer, sugar bowl and biscuits, and looked across at Jenny. 'Take that up to His Lordship, love. I can see your Aunt Peg is tired.'

'I'm tired too,' Jenny said, pursing her mouth mulishly.

22

'Do as you're told!' Addie commanded and Jenny immediately got up and took the tray from Mrs Capstick's hands.

'Here, let me . . .' Peg said, rising, but Addie firmly put a hand on her arm, holding her back. 'Jenny must do as she's told.'

'Very well.' Peg sat down, biting her lip and thinking back to the scene between Hubert and Jenny the day before.

'There you are, dear.' Mrs Capstick put a cup of coffee in front of her. 'Drink that and you'll feel better.'

Mrs Capstick glanced at the large clock on the wall. 'Dearie me, I haven't started preparing lunch and it's nearly eleven o'clock. I've all those extra workers to feed today. I'd better get my skates on.' She bustled into the scullery, closing the door behind her.

Frank sat back, arms akimbo, watching her go. 'I don't know what's got into Jenny,' he said with a worried frown. 'I've never know her so disobedient or contrary as she's been lately.'

'It's adolescence.' Peg gave a fleeting smile, but her overall expression was serious. She looked at the scullery door through which Mrs Capstick had disappeared. 'Hubert said yesterday that Jenny reminded him of Lydney and had for some time.'

Addie clasped a hand to her mouth, her expression shocked.

'He actually said that?'

'I think it's time I told him.'

'Oh but you can't.'

'She must.' Frank got up and stretched. He was tired too, having had no sleep, so worried had he been about the revellers remaining in the grounds and the damage they might do. He put his cap firmly on his head and fixed Addie with a steady eye. 'She must also know that you're her mother, Addie, her real mother. She's called you Mummy for so long she's almost forgotten she was brought up by Cathy.'

23

'It's never seemed the right time,' Addie murmured, looking abjectly at her hands.

'Well it's the right time now.' Frank walked across to the kitchen door, then turned and stared at her again. 'You don't want her to find out from someone else. There have been too many secrets for too long on this subject and one day they will all come tumbling out.'

Hubert looked up in some surprise as Jenny entered the room carefully balancing the tray.

'Mrs Capstick sent me with this,' she said, putting it down rather clumsily in front of him so that some of the coffee spilled on to the tray. 'Sorry,' she mumbled and grabbed a handkerchief from her pocket in an attempt to mop the mess up.

'Don't use your best handkerchief, child,' Hubert chided her, reaching towards the tray.

'It's not my best handkerchief and I'm not a child,' Jenny said frostily and, after giving him a mulish stare, went on mopping up the spill.

Her cheeks had gone pink and her blue eyes blazed with annoyance and, seeing her so close, Hubert was once again struck by that remarkable resemblance to his brother Lydney, who had been killed in France fifteen years before. His curiosity got the better of a strong desire to send the little minx packing.

'How old are you, Jenny?' he asked.

'Fourteen,' she said without looking up from her task.

'You're a big girl.'

'Yes,' she said. 'Is there anything else you want, Lord Ryland?'

'I don't think so.' Hubert sat back and attempted a smile. 'Unless you'd like to pour me a cup.'

Woodenly Jenny reached for the pot and did as he requested, completing her task without slopping coffee into the saucer.

'Sugar?' she asked.

'Two, thanks, Jenny.' Hubert took the cup and began to stir his coffee. 'I wish you'd call me Uncle Hubert. After all, I'm married to your aunt.'

'That doesn't make you my uncle,' she replied.

'Nevertheless, it's usual to call the spouse of a real aunt or uncle uncle or aunt too. I'd much prefer it if you called me uncle rather than Lord Ryland.'

'I'll see,' Jenny said, treating him to one of her rather unnerving gazes. 'Is there anything else?'

'Perhaps it would help us to get on better.'

Jenny said nothing, but her expression spoke volumes as she let herself out without looking at him again.

After she left, Hubert sat for a long time, his chin propped in his hand, looking out of the window but seeing nothing, the coffee untouched on the table in front of him.

As the elder sister, Verity was loved, and to some extent feared, by her family, but they all looked up to her. Verity had not had the happiest of lives but had somehow contrived to make the best of it, and for this she was greatly admired. Her father had died in an accident when she was eight years old, leaving her mother with three children, one of whom – Peg – was only a baby, and no money to keep them.

Accordingly, Verity had been adopted by her mother's sister Maude and her husband Stanley. They had been comfortably off and had provided her with a nice home near Bournemouth and sent her to one of the best girls' schools. The childless Maude and Stanley had lavished affection on her and the young Verity had wanted for nothing except, perhaps, that particular warm intimacy of close family ties, the loving special embrace of a mother whom all the children had adored.

Accordingly Verity had always felt different from her siblings and had been considered not quite part of the family.

She had trained as a nurse at Charing Cross Hospital and had served as theatre sister there during the war, when she had become engaged to a doctor, who had jilted her two weeks before their marriage.

Being Verity – controlled, self-contained – she had coped with this as well as she coped with everything else: the death of her father, the marriage of her mother to a man they had all come to hate, the early death of that same beloved mother from TB, and her further disappointment in love through an affair with a married man, which had left her feeling ashamed and humiliated. In a sense Verity had always felt an outsider, someone who had been rejected by her mother, even though the circumstances at the time had been such that she could not help herself. She had always struggled to find a sense of belonging.

Verity had survived it all, even the isolation, and because of her strength it was Verity to whom her sisters came when they were in trouble or needed help. She had always felt a special affinity with young Jenny, whose behaviour was now causing her family some concern. There was a wilfulness about Jenny that none of the family, brought up rather strictly, could understand. She had always been so quiet and obedient. What had caused this change in her, this reluctance to conform, a totally inexplicable hostility towards Hubert Ryland? It was true she was exceptionally pretty and, even at such a young age, knew that men liked her – had a sense of her own worth, her own attraction.

Although Verity was rather severe and tolerated no nonsense, had even been feared by those placed under her at the hospital, she had a very gentle side, too, and she was always at her gentlest with Jenny, who in so many ways reminded her of her young self.

Verity had recently bought a house in Bristol, the first home of her own and large enough to welcome any members of her family who wanted to visit her. Indeed, it had been bought with the idea in mind of entertaining her family. It was quite a large house, built of red brick and gabled, with a pretty garden, and when she suggested that Jenny might like to come back to Bristol with her after the wedding and spend a few days of her school holidays there, Jenny was delighted, if only for the chance to get away from the tensions of home.

'It's a *beautiful* house,' Jenny enthused, dancing around the large sitting room with French windows opening on to the garden, 'and my room is so pretty.'

Verity was pleased. She had taken trouble with the guest rooms, which all had different wallpaper and curtains, and the one she had put Jenny in she had taken special trouble over, because she remembered how much her room had meant to her as a young girl; she hoped that Jenny would want to stay with her often.

They had travelled up in the morning in Verity's newly acquired motor car, lunching on the way; now it was mid-afternoon and Verity had just made tea, which they would take on the lawn.

'There's so much to do,' she said, sitting down with a sigh and looking about her. 'The lady who owned this house before me was very old and she let the garden go. In fact there's still a lot to do, but I wanted to get your room just right.'

'It's a *lovely* room.' Jenny gaily tripped after Verity into the garden and, flopping into a chair, eyed the cake on the table though she had not long ago had lunch.

'I hope you'll come and stay with me often.'

'Oh I *shall*,' Jenny said, helping herself to a large slice of sponge cake covered with a thick layer of icing. Then she paused and looked across at Verity. 'Maybe I could come and *live* with you.'

'*Live* with me!' Verity exclaimed. 'Oh I don't think your mother would like that.'

'I don't think she'd mind,' Jenny said offhandedly. 'Be-

27

sides, she isn't my real mother. She prefers little Arthur. She's cross because she says I was rude to Lord Ryland.

'Why don't you like Lord Ryland?' Verity, also helping herself to a slice of cake, looked curiously at Jenny.

'He treats me like a child.' She looked askance at Verity, who now suddenly thought she really did look quite grown-up. 'I know I'm still young, but Lord Ryland is so *patronizing*. I know he's a lord, but I don't like being patted on the head like a dog and talked down to.'

'I'm sure he doesn't mean it.'

'He looks at me so *strangely*. I think there's something odd about him. He stares at me all the time and makes me feel uncomfortable. He wants me to call him uncle, but I can't.' Jenny shook her head and finished munching her cake, then brushed the crumbs off her lap. 'May I have another slice?'

'Of course.' Verity, disturbed by what she had heard, put a large slice of cake on Jenny's plate.

She settled back in her chair and closed her eyes, listening to the sound of birdsong, the sigh of the breeze that ruffled the tops of the trees in her very own garden. It was lovely to have her own home, to have found a measure of peace after the many vicissitudes that had afflicted her in life.

She opened her eyes and gazed across at Jenny, who had linked her hands behind her head and also shut her eyes to the sun. She really was a beautiful child and yet also a disturbed one.

Addie had reported to her and to her half-sister Stella the conversation in the kitchen at the castle the day after the wedding. The four sisters had talked hard and long into the night about what to do. Frank, they decided, was quite right. It was time Jenny knew, and her sisters had given Verity the task of telling Jenny, should the opportunity arise.

'Jenny,' she said softly, 'are you awake?'

'Quite awake,' Jenny replied brightly; Verity thought it was cruel to disturb her contentment, and nearly faltered. But then, the older Jenny grew, the more difficult the task would become and the worse it would be.

'I want to tell you a story,' Verity said after a while, 'and I don't want you to speak until I've finished.'

Jenny's eyes narrowed suspiciously. 'What sort of story?'

'It's about a girl who fell in love with a handsome soldier during the war. She was only seventeen and he was a bit older. He had been sent home from the front after being badly wounded, but was anxious to return to his regiment. He and the girl—'

'What was her name?' Jenny asked curiously.

'I'll tell you in a minute. I asked you not to interrupt.'

'Sorry,' Jenny said, snuggling back into her chair. 'I like stories like this.'

'As I was saying,' Verity went on, 'he and the girl loved each other very much and he vowed to marry her when the war was over. Then they did something they shouldn't have done. It was very silly, but because of the circumstances they decided to pretend they were married already, and after the soldier returned to the front in France, the girl found she was going to have a baby.'

'Oh dear,' Jenny said, looking grave.

'You can imagine how awful this was for a very young girl, especially as the soldier was the son of the man her father worked for, a very rich and powerful man who would undoubtedly have disapproved of his son marrying someone so beneath him socially.'

'What happened?' Jenny said with a catch in her voice.

'Well, the girl had the baby in due course but, sadly, the soldier was killed without knowing that he was going to be a father, or having the chance to tell his parents about the girl he had wanted to marry.'

'He was probably afraid of his father,' Jenny said gravely.

'Probably,' Verity agreed.

29

'What happened when the girl had the baby? Did she give it away?'

'No. She didn't want to because – the baby was a girl incidentally – she loved her so much. So her mother agreed to look after the baby and bring her up as though she was her own until her daughter was able to look after her. You see, in those days it was considered very shameful for an unmarried woman to have a baby.'

'Still is,' Jenny said glumly.

'I agree. Unfortunately the girl married a man who refused to tolerate her daughter, so she was unable to give her a home as she had wanted, and the baby remained with her mother . . . until . . .'

'. . . the mother died.' Jenny continued the story in a calm, matter-of-fact tone of voice. 'And the baby was me. I understand it all now.'

The birdsong seemed very loud in the silence that followed and the sun had momentarily disappeared behind a cloud.

'Why did no one tell me?' Jenny said eventually, her voice strangulated 'Why didn't Addie . . . Mummy . . . the girl in your story tell me?'

'She said it never seemed the right time.'

'So why do you tell me now?'

'Because it *is* the right time. We sisters discussed it well into the night and thought it was time you knew.'

'I think I always knew she was my real mother although we don't look a bit alike.' Jenny gazed into Verity's eyes. 'I look like Lord Ryland, don't I? That's why he's always looking at me, and it was his brother, the one who was killed, who was my father.'

Verity nodded.

'And *that's* why I wasn't told,' Jenny said heatedly, 'so as not to embarrass the Ryland family. I suppose he doesn't know either, or does he?'

'Peg is going to tell him. We all decided the other night this had gone on long enough.'

'I should think so,' Jenny said bitterly. '*Quite* long enough.'

Verity stretched out her hand. 'You *must* try and understand, Jenny. It was a very difficult situation. A lot has changed in the years since you were born. It is a very different world now. Things have changed, above all at Ryland Castle. The old Lord Ryland, of course, didn't approve of Peg marrying Hubert, which was why they went to live abroad.'

'How could *anyone* have believed that . . .' – Jenny faltered over the name – '. . . Cathy, your mother, my grandmother, was also my mother? Surely people weren't silly enough to believe that?'

'The Rylands, of course, knew that Addie was your real mother and a lot of other people might have guessed, but in those days matters like this were kept under wraps. The main thing is, Jenny, that you are and always were loved, very much loved by the whole family, particularly of course Addie, who yearned to be with you again.'

'It didn't make any difference that I always felt somehow I didn't belong,' Jenny said stubbornly. 'It was almost as if I knew I was surrounded by lies. You were all so much older than me and yet you were supposed to be my sisters. I called you all "aunt". It was, and is, a ridiculous situation and I am surprised that you of all people, who are so straightforward, let it continue.' Jenny got up. 'Do you mind if I go up to my room?'

'Let me come with you.' Anxiously, Verity also rose.

'No, I'd rather be alone, Aunt Verity.' Jenny gave a little laugh. 'You really *are* my aunt, aren't you?'

'Yes I am.' Verity put an arm round her shoulders and tried to draw her to her, but the young girl resisted, and all she could feel was a tight, withdrawn little body unwillingly pressed against her that seemed suddenly to have become a stranger.

* * *

31

Verity looked anxiously at the clock in her office. It was still only five: another hour to go before she could leave for home. A stickler for the rules herself, she didn't want to set a bad example by leaving early, but she had been anxious all day about Jenny, hating to leave her on her own.

Instead of the hoped-for discussion the night before there had been a profound reluctance to talk on Jenny's part. She had been listless over dinner, a bad sign, as she was a girl who enjoyed her food.

Instead, Verity talked and Jenny listened, or appeared to listen; but the expression on her face was mulish, unforgiving. She had been deceived, she seemed to be saying, for far too long. There were long, lingering, baleful stares as Verity tried to explain Addie's behaviour. To Jenny it was obvious her mother had preferred her new husband to her. To Verity it wasn't so simple. For one thing, Cathy had adored Jenny and had been reluctant to part with her.

All Verity was suggesting was that it was easy to be wise after the event. At the time, really, one had acted in what were thought to be her best interests; but Jenny didn't seem to agree.

Had it been possible, Verity would not have gone to work, but she had had her leave entitlement and she was someone on whom the functioning of the hospital depended: super-intendent of nurses – a pivotal cog in the wheel of a large city hospital. So, accordingly, after a sleepless night she had left the house at eight, leaving Jenny a note to tell her where food was, hoping that, when she returned home, she would find that a day's reflection had left her young niece in a better mood.

So far there had never been a right time but, Verity thought with the benefit of hindsight, maybe yesterday afternoon had not been it either. Maybe she should have waited a few days, given Jenny a chance to settle down. After all, Jenny planned to be with her a week. On the other hand, Addie had delayed and procrastinated for years and Verity had decided that, if she left it any longer, trying to find just the right moment, the week would be over and Jenny would have returned home none the wiser.

The minutes ticked slowly by. A sister and a staff nurse called in; her deputy came to make her report; the physician-in-charge came to see her; Matron popped her head round the door to see how the wedding had gone. Yet even when they'd all gone it was not quite six and Verity's report was not finished. Diligently she put her head down and got on with the task in hand, and it was after six when she finally left the hospital and drove home as quickly as she dared.

Even as she looked at the house from the road she somehow knew it was empty. True, it was not yet dark and there would be no need for the lights to be on, but there is something about an empty house that seems to proclaim itself, and when she turned the door handle and found the door was locked, she knew Jenny wasn't there.

Hopefully she'd just gone for a walk. The park wasn't very far away. Throwing her hat on to the hallstand and calling out Jenny's name, Verity rapidly mounted the stairs, but the door of Jenny's room was wide open and not only was she not there, but all her things had gone as well, the brush, comb and mirror, the little trinkets and knick-knacks she had so lovingly and carefully spread out on the dressing table the night before. The wardrobe door was half-open, showing that it too was empty; and then on the mantelpiece Verity saw a note addressed to her, snatched it up and tore it open.

'Sorry, Aunt Ver,' it read. 'I have found this news hard to cope with and have gone to think it over. Love, Jenny.'

Gone? But where?

Three

T he taxi stopped outside an Italian restaurant from which came an enticing smell. Jenny sat forward, startled.

'Is this it?' she said, looking once again at the address Al had scribbled on a piece of paper.

The driver pointed to a doorway tucked between the restaurant and a greengrocer's whose wares spilled invitingly on to the street. 'That's number 47.'

'Thank you.'

Her spirits had been rather low since she had made the decision to leave Verity's, and now they sank ever further. It was late afternoon and Verity would be about to arrive home and find that she had gone. Jenny, knowing what pain and anguish she would cause her and her family, had already begun to regret what she had done and had half a mind to ask the driver to turn round and take her back to the railway station.

'Are you all right, miss?' the driver asked impatiently.

'Well if it's the Monkey Club, yes.' Jenny grabbed her bag and got out on to the pavement, which was teeming with people jostling one another as if bent on urgent and important business. Noise was everywhere: people calling, talking, shouting; car horns blaring, their drivers impatient to make their way through the narrow street. Nothing could have been further from the calm, even leisured, atmosphere of Ryland Castle, home and school that she was used to.

She fumbled in her purse for some money and gave him a pound note.

'Thank you, miss.' The driver handed her the change and then looked at her closely.

'Sure you'll be all right?'

'I'll be fine,' Jenny said, taking her bag and turning towards the green door on which there was a plaque that said 'MONKEY CLUB' in bold letters. Underneath was a drawing of a seated monkey covering its face with its paws.

Jenny turned the handle of the door and, slightly to her surprise, it opened, revealing a dark, narrow passage at the end of which she dimly glimpsed another door.

Then she began to feel really nervous, even afraid, and was about to retrace her steps when the door opened and a scantily dressed woman with a cigarette in her mouth came out as if she was looking for someone. She stopped when she saw Jenny and without removing her cigarette said:

'Are you looking for someone, love?'

'Is Al here?' Jenny asked morosely.

'Al?' The woman looked puzzled.

'He's a dancer.'

'Oh Al,' the woman said again, as if she hadn't heard properly the first time. '*That* Al. I don't think he's come yet. It's a bit early. We're rehearsing now and the bar doesn't open until seven. I don't know if Al will be at rehearsals or not.'

'I'll wait,' Jenny said, heart beating fast, and put her suitcase down.

'Is he expecting you?' The woman looked curious.

'I think so,' Jenny said, deciding it was only a bit of a lie.

'You *think* so?'

'Well yes,' Jenny said decisively, 'he is expecting me.'

'You'd better come and wait inside,' the woman said in a friendlier tone. 'I'm Bunty.'

'And I'm Jenny.'

Bunty expertly ran her eyes up and down Jenny as if appraising her. She was about to say something, then appeared to change her mind.

'Come on, I'll find you somewhere to sit. Been here before, have you?' Jenny shook her head and Bunty looked at her once again as if more dubious than ever, then took her through the inner door into a foyer, which had a reception area and a recess for coats. The foyer was decorated with red-and-gold flock wallpaper and had a thick red carpet, badly worn. In fact the initial impression was one of seediness, as if the whole place had seen better days.

Bunty threw open a partly glazed double door that led to the auditorium filled with tables and chairs. At the far end was a stage occupied now by a troupe of women, also scantily dressed like Bunty, and all kicking their legs high in the air to the sound of a pianist thumping away on an ancient grand to one side of the stage. Below, a man was sitting at one of the tables, which he banged in time to the music, calling out instructions in a loud voice.

'And *again* – one, two, three. Higher, girls, higher' – and, hands on their hips, bottoms wriggling, bosoms thrust forward, the girls began to kick in unison very high indeed.

Jenny, scandalized by what she saw on the platform, was nevertheless also fascinated by it and slowly sat down at one of the tables, her eyes riveted by the action on the stage.

'And again – *one*, two, three,' went the man, slapping the table in time to the rhythm. 'Higher, girls, higher.'

This went on for some time until the music stopped. The girls broke line, clearly exhausted, and several lit cigarettes as they flopped on to the floor. The man turned round and looked at Jenny.

'What are you doing here?' he asked abrasively. He was short and thickset and had a day's growth of stubble on his face.

'I'm waiting for Al,' she said.

'Al?'

'Yes.'

'Does he know you're coming?'

'Yes.'

'He should be here soon for the novelty number.'

'All right, I'll wait.'

The man, as if losing interest in her, turned and clapped his hands at the stage. 'Come on, girls. Time's up. Let's go through that once again.' And as they reformed he began again: '*One*, two, three. Higher, girls, higher. Get those legs right up,' and up went their legs until they literally nearly reached the tops of their heads.

Had *Maisie* done this? They were scantily dressed in such brief tops and short skirts that the contours of their bodies left nothing to the imagination. Jenny had had a very different idea of what being a dancer meant, envisaging pictures she'd seen of the Ballet Russe and Pavlova dancing the Dying Swan. It seemed to her that none of these girls – and many of them were very young – wore brassieres, and their breasts, some quite full, flapped up and down in time to the music.

The routine went on for some time and Jenny sat quite mesmerized by what was going on on the stage, not noting the passage of time. Then, satisfied that the routine was right, the producer clapped his hands again and called this time for the speciality dancers.

Immediately a man and a woman appeared from the wings, stamping their feet and waving castanets above their heads. The mood, as well as the pace, changed. The woman was dark and Spanish-looking, fully made up with long eyelashes sweeping her cheeks and black hair fastened at the back of her neck in a large chignon. She wore a tight white bodice and a long black skirt, and the man wore tight black trousers and a white shirt, and it wasn't until he was halfway through his routine that Jenny recognized him.

Then the woman leaned towards him and, with a swift movement, Al divested her of her white bodice, revealing, to

Jenny's shocked surprise, that she was wearing nothing underneath. Al sensuously ran his hands lightly over her pendulous bare beasts, gave another twirl and then clicked away her long black skirt to reveal a black suspender belt attached to long black stockings, and a very skimpy pair of black knickers. Again, in strict tempo with the sounds of the old piano, Al knelt on the floor and, as the woman whirled about him still clicking her castanets high above her head, her teeth bared in a provocative smile, he began to undo her suspenders and, as she daintily lifted each leg, deftly remove her stockings. Finally, with an expertise that surely came from months if not years of practice, he took off her belt and left the woman still twirling around as if oblivious to what was going on, looking amazingly provocative in her wispy black knickers.

All the girls from the chorus had been standing in the wings watching the performance, and when the climax was reached they burst into spontaneous applause, though they had all surely seen it dozens of times before.

Someone stepped forward with a gown for the Spanish dancer, who wrapped it round her body and nonchalantly producing a pack of cigarettes from her pocket, stuck one in her mouth that Al, stepping forward, lit for her.

'Excellent,' the man called. 'Break. Al, you have someone waiting for you' – and he jerked his hand towards Jenny, who was by this time cowering in her seat wishing desperately that she was somewhere else, shocked to the core by what she had seen.

Al looked out into the darkness, then ran lightly down the steps to the auditorium, perspiring heavily. When he saw Jenny, his expression changed to one of shock.

Words seemed to desert Jenny and she sat there staring at him.

'I thought you never came to London.' Al sat down next to her, the surprise still showing on his face. In his hands he held a towel with which he started to mop the perspiration trickling down his cheeks.

'Well I've come,' Jenny replied with a confidence she was far from feeling. 'You told me to look you up.'

'Yes, of course. I'm glad you did.' He gazed at her suitcase on the floor. 'Where are you staying?'

'I thought you might know somewhere, and perhaps help me find a job . . . perhaps as a dancer? You said I danced well.'

He looked so dismayed that Jenny's false sense of confidence diminished even further and she hurried on: 'I know it seems a lot to ask, and I don't want to be a nuisance, but you're the only person I know in London.'

'You want to be a dancer like this?' Al looked at her incredulously. Jenny paused, thinking of Pavlova and the Dying Swan. 'Was Maisie this kind of dancer?'

Al nodded. 'I can see you're surprised. Look' – he gazed at his watch – 'I'm not on until after ten. I'll take you to my room, which is not far from here, and we can talk some more.' He smiled into her eyes. 'Is that all right?'

'It's very nice of you.'

'Not at all.' Al got up and took her case. 'My goodness it's heavy. You've come for a long time, I think . . .'

Al's room was a couple of blocks away. It, too, was approached through a street door, sandwiched between a continental grocer's and a fishmonger's. The building was permeated by a strong smell of fish and his room was right at the top of a steep, rickety wooden staircase. It was a small, narrow room with a tiny window looking over rooftops, sparsely furnished with a small trestle bed at which Jenny looked in dismay.

'Don't worry,' Al said, seeing her expression as he put down her case. 'I can sleep on the floor. Besides, I don't get home until dawn. Seriously,' he said, squatting by her as she wearily sank into the only chair, 'I am pleased to see you, but surprised. You gave no indication the other day of what you were thinking. What do your parents say?'

'They don't know.'

'They don't *know*?'

'Well, not everything.'

'But won't they be worried and upset? Don't you think you should tell them where you are? I don't want to get into trouble with Maisie's family over this.'

'Oh I'll never involve you,' Jenny said reassuringly. 'I have a little money.' She flushed guiltily at the thought of what she had stolen from Verity, even though she knew she would repay it as soon as she could. 'If you can help me get a room and look for a job, I promise I won't be any trouble.'

Al looked at her dubiously. 'Well I suppose you're old enough to know what you're doing.' He examined her face more closely. 'You *are* old enough, aren't you? You look younger now than when I saw you the other day.'

'Well, I'm not twenty-one,' she mumbled.

'I can see that. Eighteen?'

'Just.'

'And you want to be a dancer?'

'You said I had rhythm.'

'That and professional dancing are not quite the same thing.' A note of irritation had entered Al's voice. 'Do you want to be a stripper?'

'A what?' Jenny looked at him aghast.

'A woman who takes her clothes off. You saw my act.'

'No, I don't want that at all,' Jenny replied blushing. 'Those other women – the ones who came on first – do they take their clothes off too?'

'Sometimes, and if they don't, they wear very little.'

'Is that what *Maisie* did?'

'Well she worked there. Decide for yourself.'

Jenny put her head in her hands. 'I can't really believe it. Did *Ed* know?'

'I suppose he did if he met her there. Of course he did. Jenny' – Al got up and crossed to the window – 'I think you should think very seriously about staying on here. Above all you must tell your family where you are and that you're safe.'

'I . . . I'll tell them when I'm settled,' Jenny said. 'But I have to get a job. I don't want them to take me home, and my money won't go very far. A waitress – anything for the time being.'

'Look, I tell you what . . .' Al perched on the side of the bed. 'I take classes at a dancing academy. Sometimes I take a pupil to help with demonstrations. No' – he smiled when he saw her expression – 'nothing like last night, not yet anyway.' He gave her a suggestive smile that might have been serious or it might have been a tease.

Jenny's sense of unease deepened. She realized she really wasn't sure what sort of person Al was.

'I can't tell you how sorry I am.' Verity's eyes were swollen with tears and Addie could never recall having seen her sister so upset, even when Stella had been seriously ill or Mother had died. 'Jenny is so precious to me.'

'I know, I know.' Addie clasped her arm reassuringly.

'I should never have told her,' Verity continued. 'It was not the right moment. At the time I didn't realize it, but . . .'

Now Peg got up and put an arm round Verity's shoulder. '*None* of us would have realized it. As Addie said, there was never a good time to know how Jenny would react.'

'But she's only *fourteen*.'

'She looks much older,' Stella murmured. 'She could pass for seventeen or eighteen.'

'That's what I'm so afraid of.'

'She doesn't look all *that* old,' Addie protested.

'Jenny will be able to take care of herself,' Peg said robustly. 'She has her bad moments, but basically she is very sensible and independent. I'm sure she'll be all right.'

'Supposing we never hear from her again?' Once more Verity gave herself up to tears. 'I shall never be able to live with myself.'

They all fell silent. Verity was usually the strong one. People did disappear and were never heard of again. It seemed incredible that that should happen to Jenny, and yet what had happened was incredible too.

As soon as she had realized Jenny was missing Verity had telephoned her sisters and decided to wait until the next day, in case Jenny came home or tried to get in touch. When this failed to happen, Verity took emergency leave from the hospital and drove straight down to the castle, where they were now. Hubert was away judging a country show and would not be home until evening.

'The police must be told,' Peg said after a pause.

'Oh, do you think so?' Addie immediately looked distressed.

'Of course. She's a minor. She might be in very grave danger.'

'But where could she have gone?'

There was silence again as each addressed the question, but no one came up with a solution. Jenny's life had been so firmly anchored in her home and its surroundings that it was unthinkable she might be being sheltered by a school friend or have gone to one of the Bournemouth relatives.

'I suppose she wouldn't go to Harold?' Stella ventured, referring to Addie's estranged husband.

'*Harold?*' The other sisters turned on her in astonishment.

'Well . . .' Stella shrugged. 'It seems a forlorn hope. She always seemed to get on well with Harold, even though he didn't want to give her a home.'

'Harold is the *last* person she would go to,' Peg said, 'but I don't mind telephoning him if it makes you feel better.'

'She wouldn't go to London, would she?' Stella tried again.

'Why would she go to London?' Now it was Addie's turn to look surprised. 'She doesn't know anyone there.'

'The Rylands have a house there. I think Violet might be staying there at the moment. Besides, anyone she'd gone to would contact us immediately.'

They all shook their heads. The idea was absurd, clutching at straws.

'I'll telephone the police,' Peg said, getting to her feet; but Verity raised her hand.

'Why don't you give it another twenty-four hours? Just to see. We know she has gone of her own accord, and when she stops to think about it, she may decide to come back.' She gazed anxiously around at her sisters. 'We don't want to look silly. Maybe we could discreetly ask among her friends if they have any idea where she might have gone. She can't just have disappeared into thin air.'

When Jenny woke in Al's bed, dawn was breaking across the rooftops in Soho. She lay for a moment adjusting to where she was, and this uncertainty was followed by a feeling of anxiety as she thought about what she'd done and why she'd done it. Common sense told her that she should leave immediately and take the first train home, confess all and ask to be forgiven.

Then indignation took over. Forgiven for what, indeed? Wasn't she the one who was owed an apology for having been deceived about her parentage for so many years? After all, she knew now that she was half-Ryland. How did one whose family were more used to the servants' hall come, without any warning, to accept that? She had always assumed her father was Jack Hallam, who had been gardener to Lord Ryland and had gone off with another woman during the war; that her mother was his wife, Cathy, who had worked hard to bring her up, and that Addie was her half-sister, who had left her husband to take care of her after Cathy's death.

43

Lies, all lies, she thought bitterly, though she could not deny she had had a happy, carefree childhood, loved and protected by a large, close family. She certainly could not deny that or complain about it; but still, that happy life was in a shambles, rudely interrupted by the revelation of years of lies and deception. Her sense of outrage grew, knowing no bounds, as she lay there thinking and strengthening her resolve to give them a jolly good fright before she went home again.

Jenny jumped out of bed and went over to the single window, throwing back the curtain. It was a breathtaking sight for someone used to green fields and quiet country lanes. Soho was right in the heart of London. It considered itself a village, though it was nothing like the sort of village Jenny was used to. The sloping rooftops were interspersed here and there with the spire of a church or the top of a tree. There were chimney stacks of all shapes and sizes, some with thin spirals of smoke drifting out of them. There was a haze in the air as though to herald a hot day. A pigeon on a neighbouring roof cocked its head curiously towards her. She smiled at it, held out her hand and it flew away, flapping its wings in alarm.

From below, the smell of newly baked bread drifted up, and the sound of a horse and cart clip-clopping along the street reminded her of the country, where there were still very few people who had motor cars.

Confronted with all this wonder at a vast city stirring around her, Jenny felt her fear evaporating. After all, had she not embarked on a great adventure?

She heard the door handle turn and, aware that she was standing in her nightgown, took a flying leap back into bed, pulling the sheet up to her throat.

Al appeared round the door, carrying a paper bag.

'Ah, you're awake.' He put the bag down on the rickety table. 'I brought some breakfast. Fresh bread.'

44

'Goody.' Jenny rubbed her hands together. 'I could smell it as I stood by the window.'

'How did you sleep?' Al looked tired.

'Fine. What time is it?'

'Just after six.'

'Do you always work so late?'

'Sometimes.'

'And did you do your . . .' – Jenny paused to find the right word – '. . . "performance" again?'

'Three or four times,' Al said nonchalantly. 'Did it shock you so much?'

'A bit,' Jenny confessed. 'I'm a country girl, you know.'

'And you still want to be a dancer?' Al started slicing the bread with a smile on his face. 'But not a stripper.'

'Not like that.' She threw her hands in the air. 'I don't know how *anyone* could do it.'

'People do it for money, that's how.' Al looked across at her. 'The world is a hard place, Jenny. I don't think you realize how hard. You know' – he spread butter on the piece of bread he'd cut and took it across to her – 'I think you should go home. I don't know why you came, but London is not the place for a girl like you. Not yet, anyway.'

Al watched her intently as she ate the bread. His gaze made her feel uncomfortable. She realized she had not only let down her family and stolen from Verity, but she was also deceiving Al. She had lied to him about her age, her presence in London.

What would Ver and Peg, above all her mother and Frank, say if they could see her now – lying in bed with a man sitting by her side?

Al was studying her face thoughtfully. 'A penny for them?'

'I'm not a very nice person really, Al.'

He looked startled. 'What made you say that?'

'I don't want you to get the wrong idea about me. I'm not as sweet as you seem to think.'

Surprisingly Al put out a hand and gently touched her shoulder. 'On the contrary, you're *very* sweet,' he said bending towards her as though he was going to kiss her. Then he changed his mind and drew back.

'I'll get breakfast,' he said, jumping up; 'and then I must get some sleep. After that we'll go to the dance studio and see how you perform.'

Hubert sat for a long time, gazing thoughtfully into the fire that had been lit in his study, where Mrs Capstick had left him a late supper. Peg had eaten earlier with the children and now sat studying Hubert's face anxiously as she told him the story of Jenny's disappearance.

Hubert seemed in a bad mood, as though the day hadn't gone well. It was not at all an auspicious time to give him more bad news, and she felt she had not told the story well; but it was hardly a subject one could put a gloss on.

'When did all this happen?' Hubert sounded grumpy.

'Yesterday. Verity came this morning first thing.'

'Have you told the police?'

Peg shook her head.

'Why not?'

'I thought I should discuss it with you first,' Peg said tactfully. 'She may come back. I wanted your advice. She obviously went of her own accord. She wasn't kidnapped. I mean, do we want everyone to know, if it can be avoided?'

'Any idea *why* she went?' Hubert looked across at his wife and his enigmatic expression unnerved her even more.

She shook her head, feeling like a person being interrogated for some misdemeanour. She was struck by a sudden chill and pulled her cardigan more closely round her shoulder. She should have told him before, but the time had never seemed right. It had been cowardly not to. What had she feared? It wasn't right now. In fact, it was even

46

harder, but it had to be done. Things like this could not be hidden for ever.

Peg took a deep breath and, rather as Verity had done two days before with Jenny, she told her husband something that had been a well-kept secret for a long, long time.

Four

The policeman, notebook in hand, listened respectfully to Hubert, his attitude one of extreme deference. It was the first time he had ever been called to the castle and he considered it a responsibility, to say nothing of an honour. Hubert and Peg had received him in the library together with Addie and also Verity, whose usual composure was completely lacking. In a few days she had become a bundle of nerves. All her training as a nursing sister, a woman used to taking command, of being in control, seemed to have deserted her. Even now she looked as though she had recently been weeping, her eyes red and her face puffy.

'And you say, madam,' the policeman said, turning to her, 'that you know of no reason for this young lady to run away, other than that she was restless?'

'Not that I know of.' Verity's glance briefly rested on Hubert, who had given strict instructions that the truth was on no account to be revealed. Verity was a deeply religious woman to whom lying was anathema, but in this case she had to agree with him.

Besides, knowing the truth would not help them to find Jenny.

'The search must be conducted very discreetly,' Hubert said; 'we don't want the local people to get wind of the disappearance of this girl, and it must on no account be in the papers.'

'I understand that, my lord.' The policeman snapped his notebook shut. 'We will alert police stations throughout the

48

country, though I understand that some of the young lady's friends have been questioned.'

'Only close friends,' Peg said. 'People we know and trust. We don't want a hue and cry because that will make Jenny unwilling to come back.'

'And she's only fourteen,' the policeman frowned.

'She could pass for sixteen.'

'Or older.'

'And there is no . . . er . . . man friend . . .' The constable tried to put it as delicately as he could.

'Oh, out of the question.' Addie looked shocked. 'She might look older but she is a normal young girl of fourteen, and boyfriends have not yet come into the picture.'

'As far as we know,' the constable murmured.

'We *know*,' Addie corrected him in her best schoolmarmish voice. 'We know that for sure.'

The policeman, who, when a youth, had been taught by Addie, looked suitably reprimanded.

'Very well, my lord, ladies.' He turned to Addie and Verity. 'We shall do our best to find this young lady before any harm should befall her.'

Addie saw the policeman to the door, exchanged a few friendly words with him and went slowly back up the stairs to the library. She felt that she'd grown very old in a short space of time. Verity too had changed, her usual air of calm completely gone.

They had all changed, perhaps Hubert most of all, because, like Jenny, he too had experienced a shock – the knowledge that his much-loved brother had fathered a child and this was the first any of his family knew about it.

Hubert had found that very hard to forgive and considered all the Hallam family culpable, but especially his wife – perhaps her more than anyone.

A profound silence greeted Addie as she re-entered the library.

'That was Charlie Hussey,' she said chattily. 'I taught him when I did my teachers' training. That was when I met Lydney,' she said, looking at Hubert. 'That's when it all started. It was the summer of 1917.'

'Oh please don't . . .' Peg began, but Addie shook her head.

'It's no use sweeping it under the carpet, Peg. What happened happened, and Hubert must know.'

'We only have your word for it,' Hubert said.

'I *beg* your pardon?' Addie looked at him sharply.

'Well, it could have been anybody . . .'

'Don't be so ridiculous, Hubert,' Peg said angrily. 'You know that for a long time you have thought that Jenny looked like Lydney . . .'

'It doesn't mean to say that she is his daughter. It might have been coincidence.'

'I believe you can have a blood test' – Verity's tone was icy – 'if you doubt my sister's word. I don't know much about it, but I can find out.'

'There is no need,' Peg said. 'Hubert knows quite well that Jenny is Lydney's daughter and that Addie is telling the truth.'

'The fact is, Hubert . . .' Addie's face was stony. 'Please don't think we expect anything from you, if that's what you're thinking. We are making no claims on your family. None at all.'

'Oh *please* don't speak like that,' Peg implored her. 'Hubert doesn't think like that at all.'

'Then how *does* he think?' Addie demanded, her cheeks flaming. 'What does he really feel? Why is he being so hostile?'

Hubert heaved himself to his feet and glared at his sister-in-law. He was a tall, thickset man with a thick moustache and, in his way, formidable. There was no doubt that, since he had inherited the title, he seemed to have become more imposing, gained in authority and, indeed, it had been a very heavy responsibility after the halcyon, almost carefree days of his life as a farmer in the Umbrian countryside. Hubert planted both hands firmly on the table and leaned across it.

'I am not being hostile, Addie, as you suggest. But I can tell you how I really feel and what I think.' He paused for a moment and gazed round at them all: Addie and Verity, again close to tears, sitting in leather armchairs on either side of the fireplace; Peg, arms akimbo, standing by the window out of which she kept on glancing as though she wished she could escape.

'I really feel and think,' Hubert continued menacingly, 'that I and my family have been kept in the dark and thus grossly deceived for fourteen years. If my father had known that Lydney had left a daughter, he would have been overjoyed.'

'He would not!' Peg intervened sharply. 'You know that, Hubert. Your father was the most awful snob and he would have been shocked. He would probably have chucked us all off the premises.'

'I don't see how you can say that,' Hubert exclaimed.

'Well I can and do. Look at your reaction, and I have always regarded you as a liberal, enlightened man. What do you think your father's would have been? That's why we couldn't tell you.'

'Would you have told me even now, if this hadn't have come up?' Hubert challenged her.

Peg bit her lip. 'Yes, I expect so. We have all been talking about it, and I knew it was in your mind.'

'It was not in my mind. I just thought Jenny looked a bit like Lydney.'

'Well I felt, rightly or wrongly, that it was very much in your mind. Addie has felt guilty for some time that she had never told Jenny. But really, Hubert darling, it was a very difficult decision to make. You must see that. Besides, what difference would it have made?'

51

'A lot. Lydney's daughter would have had a proper education.'

'Jenny was very well educated, thank you,' Addie retorted indignantly. 'The village school and the girls' grammar are the best schools you could wish for. She has not been neglected in any way. Besides, I share Peg's opinion that your mother and father would have been horrified. Just see what your mother says when you tell her.'

Hubert sat down again and, his chin resting on the tips of his fingers, appeared to ponder the situation.

'I just don't know what to say,' he concluded, 'or what to do, except that I feel very angry indeed and terribly, terribly worried about the fate of a girl I must now acknowledge as my niece.'

Teresa Solario was not Spanish but Portuguese. She looked even more imposing offstage than on. She was a tall, large-bosomed woman whose age it was hard to define. She was fully made up, wore long earrings, with two kiss curls prominently planted on her cheeks, and her magnificent raven hair was worn in an elaborate coiffure secured by a large tortoiseshell comb glistening with artificial diamonds. She wore a tight red dress with a pleated bodice and a large black jabot at her throat. Black stockings and shoes completed the ensemble. Jenny thought it seemed as though she was dressed for a party, but maybe she always looked like this.

'Well,' Teresa demanded after Jenny had had a good look round, 'will you take the room?'

'Oh, yes please,' Jenny said, turning towards her.

'Ten shillings a week,' Teresa said. 'I don't normally let the room, but I'm making an exception for you as Alfonso asked me.'

'It's very kind of you,' Jenny said gratefully.

'When you've unpacked your things, come and have a cup

of tea,' Teresa said graciously, having become increasingly amiable since Alfonso had brought Jenny round and left after a brief introduction. The room in Teresa's house just beside King's Cross station was tiny and was obviously constantly bombarded by noise from the trains shunting in and out of that great main-line terminus. It had a narrow bed, a scrap of rug on a linoleum floor, a dressing table with a badly scratched top and a wardrobe that tilted to one side like the leaning tower of Pisa.

Al had left her case on the floor and gone, ostensibly to an appointment.

Jenny had felt awkward sharing a room with a man, and she knew she was depriving him of sleep. His presence also made her nervous and he was obviously ill at ease with her. They found little to talk about. After this uneasy relationship, which lasted several days, he said that he'd spoken to his partner, who was willing to let a room. As dancers they were not particularly well paid and she was happy to do this from time to time to make some extra money.

Now that she was alone, Jenny sank down on the bed, overcome by a sense of despair. She had to admit that, so far, her London adventure was not a success. She was over-whelmed by it all and knew what consternation she must be causing at home. She had tried to blot it from her mind, but it became increasingly hard the longer she stayed away. She felt that, if she didn't go back soon, she would never be able to face them again and would be forced to disappear for ever.

While Al had slept Jenny had got to know London, exploring a little more widely every day. She thought it was an incredibly beautiful and exciting place, with its tall buildings, streets full of traffic – the bustle of a great city that never seemed to sleep. At night Soho buzzed and the noise came off the streets well into the small hours of the morning.

In the afternoon she had gone to the dance studio session

53

with Al, but even that had been a disappointment, consisting mostly of exercises that reminded her more of gym at school. Al had stood in a corner smoking a cigarette while the students performed, pausing occasionally to bark out some commands. She suspected, from the general air of apathy, that either he was not a very good teacher or they were not very promising students.

She also discovered that Al was moody and at times uncommunicative. She suspected that he had begun to think she was boring and he would be glad to get her off his hands.

Jenny felt very homesick and close to tears. She badly wanted to be back home again and with her mother. She was not short of money. She had taken £50 she'd found in Verity's bureau, money carelessly left lying about, which Verity had clearly thought was quite safe. If it had not been for that chance discovery, the idea of running away would have died on the spot.

Making a determined effort, Jenny shook herself out of her torpor, inspected the bed and saw that the linen was clean, as was the wash basin where she was expected to perform her ablutions. The window was grimy, as though it had not been cleaned for years, and even when she rubbed it she could see very little except a jumble of criss-crossed railway lines.

She unpacked her few things and listlessly passed a comb through her hair. She left the room and went along the landing down the stairs and to the sitting room, the door of which was slightly ajar, where Teresa sat over a tea tray.

'So,' she said, looking up as Jenny entered, 'you want to be a dancer?'

Jenny nodded.

'And what gave you the idea?'

Jenny, fumbling for words, sat down nervously as Teresa went on. 'Was it Alfonso?'

'Oh no. I met him at my brother's wedding to Maisie. He did say I had a good rhythm.'

'Huh, Maisie!' Teresa uttered her name contemptuously. 'She made a good marriage for herself, I hear.'

Jenny wondered why she hadn't been asked to the wedding. Maybe, judging from Teresa's tone of voice, they hadn't got on.

Teresa handed her a cup and, as she passed it across, scrutinized Jenny's face.

'You don't look eighteen to me.'

'*Nearly* eighteen,' Jenny mumbled, taking her cup.

'I'd say you were a lot younger. I hope you haven't run away from home. I wouldn't be surprised if you're still at school. I don't want to get into any trouble here or they'll take my licence away. Besides,' she sniffed, 'Alfonso is no use to you. Don't get ideas.'

Jenny felt bewildered by these remarks.

'I see you don't understand, my dear,' Teresa said with amusement. 'You really are very naive. I dread to think how a few more weeks in the city would spoil a nice girl like you. Besides, Alfonso has to be careful. He's nervous about losing his licence too.' Teresa shook her head and sat back, studying Jenny, who was gazing around her. The sitting room was full of heavy furniture, decorated with brocaded wallpaper and dozens of photographs of Teresa in various exotic poses. None of the men with her resembled Alfonso.

'How long has he been your partner?' she ventured.

'Months.' Teresa shrugged. 'My last one was Italian and he went back to Rome when his wife came after him.' She smiled maliciously. 'She thought there was something between us, but she was wrong. I am very attractive, no?' She put a hand behind her head, striking a pose. Happily, Jenny didn't think she expected an answer. 'As you can see, Alfonso is much younger than me but he is a very good dancer.' She looked knowingly again at Jenny. 'If you were serious about a career, you could do worse than take lessons from him.'

55

'He took me to the studio where he teaches. I must say I found it very boring.'

'But it *is* very boring, darling.' Leaning forward, Teresa stabbed a finger at her. 'Boring and hard work and dangerous.'

'Dangerous?' Jenny repeated in alarm.

'You meet all kinds of people. Some of them are not very nice. You have to know how to look after yourself. Success does not come to everyone. Besides' – Teresa leaned back and gazed at Jenny, her eyes gleaming with speculation – 'I cannot believe this is the sort of work you are really interested in. You want to take your clothes off on the stage?'

'Oh no,' Jenny said with horror.

'Then take my advice' – Teresa pointed towards the door – 'take your bag and go home.' She stared at Jenny again in silence for a few seconds. 'You know, there's something very funny going on here and I don't know what it is. Meanwhile' – she looked at the clock on the mantelpiece, which was covered with a fringed cloth – 'I am going to meet Alfonso to rehearse a new routine. You want to come?'

'Well . . .' Jenny looked dubious.

'Don't be shy.' Teresa waved a hand at her. 'It will be nothing to make you blush.' Then she got up and ruffled Jenny's head the way Lord Ryland had, and Jenny realized she disliked Teresa just as much.

There was no nudity, no suggestion of anything improper such as had shocked her before. Teresa had changed into a long black dress, a mantilla, high-heeled shoes and, carrying a large fan, performed a series of intricate movements while Alfonso swirled about her, and all the time the piano in the background banged away various tempestuous tunes from Spain.

Whatever the nature of their relationship, one thing Jenny had to admit was that they were a very good team. Their skill, their symmetry were amazing. For the first time for days she felt herself relax and began to enjoy herself, tapping her foot in time to the music, imagining the bullfights, the arid plains of faraway Spain, made almost as real to her as the faded film shown in the village hall of Pavlova dancing the Dying Swan.

There was nothing to make her blush in their programme. Teresa remained fully clothed and, after they had rehearsed the routine several times, Jenny stood up and clapped loudly. They were alone in the room and Alfonso and Teresa joined in the play-acting, coming to the front of the stage and making an elaborate bow. Alfonso blew kisses and then, in a theatrical gesture, held out his hand towards her.

'Come, Jenny. Come. I will teach you some Spanish flamenco – much more exciting than what you did at the studio.'

'Yes, come.' Clearly in a good humour at the success of the routine, Teresa, all smiles, also extended her hand and shyly Jenny approached the stage, Alfonso leaning forward to help her up.

With a dramatic flourish Teresa opened her fan and handed it to Jenny as Alfonso took hold of her right arm and positioned it above her head. 'Now, one foot forward like this,' he said, and with a nod to the pianist he walked in measured steps around her while, from the wings, Teresa started clapping her castanets.

Tentatively Jenny put first one foot forward, and then the other. Al put his hands round her narrow waist. She began to feel the rhythm seeping through her body.

'Excellent,' Alfonso murmured in her ear. 'You see you are making progress already. Maybe you have it in you to become a dancer.'

At that point Jenny was aware that the door at the end of the room had opened and two men stood silently in the dark watching them. Nervously she continued her routine as they seemed unobserved by either Teresa, busily shaking her noisy castanets, or Alfonso, concentrating on his pupil.

After a short while the men started to walk slowly towards the stage and, as they emerged into the light, it was possible to see that one was a policeman in uniform. The other Jenny recognized as the large man who had been at Maisie's wedding, whom Maisie had later identified as her former boss, Sam.

Now they were seen by the others on the stage and the sight of the policeman's uniform was electrifying. The pianist stopped playing, Al's hands flew from Jenny's waist and the small assembly on the platform stood as if frozen in time.

Sam was in shirtsleeves and a waistcoat, a florid bow tie at his neck, and removing an oversized cigar from his mouth he furiously gestured towards them.

'What do you think you are up to, Alfonso?' he boomed from below. 'Are you crazy? Don't you know that this young girl is the niece of Maisie's new husband? She is fourteen years old, has run away from home; her family are mad with worry and this policeman has come to arrest you for enticement and abduction.'

Five

A ddie sat bolt upright on a chair in the foyer of the hotel where she had arranged to meet her husband, Harold, for he was still her husband despite the fact that they had been separated for eight years. They had met twice since then – once when he had come to beg her to return to him, and the second time, two years later, when she had asked him for a divorce so that she could remarry. Harold had absolutely refused to entertain the matter and that had been that.

Addie had fallen in love with a worker on the estate, Gilbert Youngman, with whom she had lived until his sudden departure the year before. By nature he had been a wanderer, but when he had met Addie he had wanted to settle down and marry her. However, because Harold refused to let her have a divorce, marriage was impossible, so Addie and Gilbert had lived together and had a child, Arthur, who was now three.

Things might have stayed that way for ever had not Hubert, following the death of his father, become Lord Ryland, when Gilbert had begun to feel that he didn't fit in. Addie's sister was now mistress of the castle; Lord Ryland was her brother-in-law. After a disastrous dinner at the castle, Gilbert had got drunk and disgraced himself, and the following morning Addie had woken to find him gone. There had been no letter, no explanation, no farewell to his son, and she had never heard from him again.

59

Addie looked at the clock above the reception desk. Harold was late, perhaps intentionally. After a while Addie began to wonder if he was coming. She had made her own way to the hotel, not wanting to alert any member of her family as to what was in her mind – especially Frank, who had brought her to the meeting in this same place years before.

Addie went across to the reception desk and said hesitantly, 'Mr Smith hasn't sent any word, has he?'

'No, madam,' the clerk replied politely.

'He's a little late – half an hour, in fact.'

'No message of any kind, madam.'

'I'll wait a little longer,' Addie said with dignity, returning to her seat; but she felt agitated. What if Harold was playing a nasty game with her – agreeing to a meeting only with the intention of humiliating her and not turning up?

When she looked up, however, he was standing at the door of the hotel, hat in hand, smiling at her. He appeared a little out of breath as though he'd been hurrying.

'Addie,' he said, giving a stiff little bow, 'please forgive me. I had a puncture. I was afraid you might have gone.' He then kissed her rather formally and awkwardly on the cheek and stood back to look at her.

'And how are you, Addie? I must say you look well.'

'I am well, thank you, Harold.'

'Is Frank with you?' Harold enquired, glancing around.

'No, I came alone.'

This information seemed to please her husband. 'In that case, I'm wondering if you'd like lunch, Addie?' He pointed to the door leading to the dining room. 'Or have you eaten?'

'No, I haven't.' Addie felt a little light-headed, as though a weight had suddenly lifted. This was a meeting she had pondered long and hard over, had dreaded once she had initiated it, and had had so many misgivings about that she'd thought of cancelling it; and yet her initial reaction was that it now seemed to be going quite well. Harold actually looked pleased to see her.

'Yes, that would be very nice, thank you, Harold.'

Harold took off his coat and gave it with his hat to the cloakroom attendant. 'Maybe you'd also like to leave your coat and hat, Addie?'

'I'll just pop along to the ladies' cloakroom,' Addie replied. 'I'm sure I can leave it there.'

'See you in a minute.' Harold gave her a friendly wave as he watched her go off.

Addie hurried to the ladies' room, removed her hat and coat and realized she was shaking with nerves. Harold's reception had surprised her. He was warm and friendly, not at all the cold, detached man she remembered and had come, indeed, to hate. Perhaps he had reformed, been mellowed by time? Maybe all would be well after all?

Had she made enough effort to look nice, to attract him? Had she taken enough trouble? Anxiously she inspected herself in the mirror, ran a comb through her neatly bobbed brown hair. She knew she was not noted for her looks. Jenny took after Lydney Ryland, not her, but she had good, strong features, a clear, healthy complexion and warm brown eyes that people found sympathetic and compassionate. She had another advantage; she was thirty-four.

Harold was fifteen years older, a man with no obvious physical attraction. He was tall, but with bowed shoulders, as if his height made him self-conscious. He had the furrowed brow of a worrier, was pale-faced, sallow-cheeked. His best feature was undoubtedly his blue eyes, which, however, were virtually obscured behind heavy horn-rimmed spectacles. He had never been a ladies' man and had been a virgin on their honeymoon. She doubted whether he had had much experience since.

But Addie still felt she wanted to impress him and briskly patted her cheeks to bring out her natural colour, straightened herself – shoulders back, bosom out.

When she returned to the reception area the clerk informed her that Mr Smith was in the dining room, where Addie found him studying the wine list. He got up as she came over to him, and watched an attentive waiter pull out her chair and spread a napkin on her lap.

'I thought we might have a bottle of wine, Addie?' Harold sat down again. 'Would you like that?'

'Very nice, Harold.' Addie lowered her eyes on to her hands folded in her lap. Wine indeed! It was just like their honeymoon. It seemed an auspicious start and, indeed, the meal went well. Harold was chatty. He was the headmaster of an infants' school near Exeter – work that he enjoyed. He told her he had thought of applying for another post nearer London, but had decided against it. He had become part of the community.

As he spoke, she remembered how impressed she had been by him when she had first known him: the deputy headmaster of the school where she had been teaching in Dorchester. She had been flattered by his attentions and, although she had never loved him, had agreed to marry him because, for one thing, she was afraid of being left on the shelf like her sister Verity appeared all set to be, and for another and more important reason: her mother approved. Harold was clever, well read, and she had basked in his erudition when they had been on honeymoon exploring the cultural and religious treasures of Europe.

The end of that honeymoon had been a disaster, however, because it had been then that she had told him about the existence of Jenny, in the hope that he would give her a home. It had been a fatal mistake, and the following year she had fled from a cold and barren marriage.

As she listened to him, she found herself mentally reliving the experience of that unhappy marriage and, as they finished eating, the doubt returned about whether or not she was doing the right thing. Addie had only had a glass of wine –

she knew her limitations – but Harold had nearly finished the bottle and there was a flush on his cheeks and a smile of self-satisfaction as he sat back.

'Well, Addie,' he said, 'to what do I owe the pleasure of this meeting? I'm sure there's a reason.'

Addie suddenly felt tongue-tied. Maybe she should, after all, have written. It was so difficult, so awkward, and she had not taken the advice of her sisters – not even told them what was in her mind. Addie's eyes fastened on her hands again and she spoke without raising them.

'I wondered if you would like me to come back to you, Harold?' she said timorously. 'You know – start all over again.'

Peg felt in a state of shock at Addie's news and said little during the course of the meal, which was eaten, as usual, with her and her husband sitting at opposite ends of the long dining-room table. This meant that conversation was difficult anyway – certainly any sort of intimate conversation – with the butler hovering by the sideboard supervising the serving of the meal, which was usually simple: a main course and a sweet, not a banquet.

It was rather silly to eat like this, with Hubert wearing a black tie and Peg a frock, but he said that his parents always had and they should too. One mustn't let standards slip.

He hadn't talked like this when they had first taken up residence at the castle, but the more formal Hubert had ousted the informal one, especially since the events of August, when Jenny had run away and he had been told she was the daughter of his dead brother – his niece.

It is often said of certain significant events that happen in life that afterwards things can never be the same again, and that revelation certainly seemed to have marked a downturn in their marriage.

Yet in many ways, Peg thought, that turning point had

really begun with the death of Lord Ryland and Hubert inheriting the title. Nothing had changed for a while. They had been happy and had had another baby. Hubert had wanted to change things, to modernize, and in many ways he had; but Peg had never thought he was really happy with the social changes, the abandonment of the old way of life in which every one had known their place.

She felt that it had suddenly dawned on Hubert that he had married the stepdaughter of a family retainer and with her had inherited all her relations who, however much they had raised themselves in the world, could never really cease to be what they had been when they were born: lower-class.

No matter that Peg had been a woman of some consequence, a respected and well-known journalist, a woman of achievement. It was her origins that mattered, as they had mattered to his father, who would never receive her after their marriage, which had exiled them abroad.

After dinner, largely eaten in silence, they went as usual into the drawing room, where a fire had been lit. To preserve its precious wooden panelling most of the castle was unheated, and Peg went gratefully to the fire and stood in front of it rubbing her arms. Hubert crouched beside her, a large cigar in his mouth, which he lit with a spill and, when he had it going satisfactorily, he rose and blew a stream of thick smoke into the air.

'You look worried,' he said, turning to her. 'Anything the matter?'

'Addie is going back to Harold,' Peg said. 'After all these years, I can't believe it.'

'What brought that on?' Hubert, not looking unduly concerned, drew heavily on his cigar.

'Jenny, I suppose.'

'Ah.'

It would be Jenny, Hubert seemed to imply. She had caused nothing but trouble since she'd returned home, and he rather wished they'd never found her. Instead he said, 'How can that help? I mean, going back to Harold?'

'Well, he is a schoolteacher and used to young children – not that Jenny's very young, but he seemed keen, according to Addie, to accept the challenge.'

Hubert looked surprised. 'I thought he didn't want her?'

'He is prepared to have her and Arthur in order to have Addie back.'

'I think she's very optimistic if she thinks he'll tame Jenny. That experience of London life seems to have unhinged her.'

It was true that Jenny was difficult. The period after her return had affected them all. She was rude, rebellious, and refused to settle either at home or school, where she was a disruptive influence and scandalized her classmates and teachers with lurid stories of London nightlife. Finally, the school had asked Addie to remove her, and this had prompted her extreme decision to seek a reconciliation with Harold.

'Would you like to listen to the wireless, dear?' Hubert went over to the set and started fiddling with the knobs, a gesture that irritated Peg, whose nerves were on edge.

'Hubert, we're talking about something serious.'

Hubert switched on the set. 'Not for me, I'm afraid. I have done my best with Jenny, but she doesn't like me and frankly I don't like her much either, even if she is Lydney's daughter.' He gazed across at Peg. 'That might have been very different if I had been told the truth, and also if she had been told it many years ago; but it is too late. Frankly, what happens to her doesn't concern me one little bit.'

'I think that's a dreadful thing to say.'

'Well, I've said it.' Hubert turned up the volume on the wireless and went across to the table, on which the butler had left a tray, to pour himself coffee.

Peg crossed to the wireless, turned it off and, as Hubert looked up startled, put her hands on her hips and stared at him. 'I think it's time we had a chat, Hubert.'

'A chat?' Looking mystified, Hubert took his coffee over to a chair. 'What sort of chat?'

'About our lives.'

'What's wrong with our lives?'

'Hubert, don't pretend. It's not very satisfactory and hasn't been for some time.'

Hubert studied the tip of his cigar. 'Can I help it?' he said after a while. 'Do you think it's my fault?'

He crossed one leg over the other and relit his cigar. 'I think we've had a difficult couple of years, Peg. We've had to compromise. Marriages change, you know. They can't stay in a white heat of passion for ever. I think your expectations are too high. We've changed; things have changed. Aren't you happy?' He looked at her in some surprise. 'I'm quite happy.'

'Are you really?'

'For heaven's sake,' he cried in alarm, 'you're not about to say you're going to leave me, are you?'

'Oh, no, of course not. I love you, Hubert, but I want us to be as close as we used to be. I know love changes and becomes different, but I thought it grew. Instead, we seem to have grown apart. I think – I may be wrong – my family irritates you. Maybe you sometimes regret marrying a woman who was so low down the social scale that you have lost half your friends.'

'Nonsense,' Hubert said gruffly. 'I've plenty of friends. Heavens, we entertain at least once a week.'

'Mostly local dignitaries; I don't call those friends.'

'Don't forget we lived abroad for a long time. I lost most of my friends then, and so did you.'

'We're getting stale, Hubert. Maybe we should go up to London more often? See some shows, eat out, see your old friends and some of mine, renew acquaintanceships? The London house is there and it's hardly ever used. I'd love to go up to London more often.'

'Then why don't you?' Hubert took up the evening paper

and, shaking it out, buried his face in it. 'I'm perfectly happy here. Do turn the wireless on again, Peg. It's nearly time for the news.'

Jenny sat in the back of the car feeling chastened yet excited. Arthur wriggled beside her and, in front, her mother sat stiffly next to Frank, who was driving them to their new home.

Jenny knew that all this was entirely due to her and what her family felt was her unreasonable, indeed shocking, behaviour; but she didn't care. The future was unknown and leaving the castle was a good thing. She knew running away had been very naughty and she hadn't expected to be welcomed back with open arms. She had naturally anticipated a reprimand, even some sort of punishment. Instead, she had encountered a wall of hostility, awful silences, disapproving looks as though nobody could bear to speak to her any more let alone try to understand what she had done and why she had done it.

Her mother, who had had such a shock, having expected never to see her daughter again, spent a lot of time in tears. Verity, who had returned to Bristol, remained there.

Peg, whom she had always admired, made more of an effort than the others. She had tried to talk to her, reason with her, and had then grown impatient when Jenny had trotted out all her excuses. There were, in fact, two wounded people – herself and Hubert Ryland – whom no one really seemed able to help or even attempt to understand.

In particular, it was very much held against her that she had stolen money from someone who had always been so kind to her, who had done her best to help her: Verity. Fifty pounds was a very large sum, which there was no possibility of her being able to repay. Taking that money, revealing herself as a thief, had been like a slap in the face to a family who were strangers to misdemeanours of that nature.

At school, however, she had compensated. There she had acquired considerable notoriety, even prestige on account of her adventure, which had lost nothing in the telling. Jenny had become the envy of her classmates and the despair of her teachers. She had begun to fail in her schoolwork, play truant, usually with others she had led astray. She had been disruptive in class and, finally, the headteacher who had been a close friend of Addie's, had been forced to advise her that Jenny might be better off elsewhere. The fields and woodlands of rural Devon had now given place to the streets and genteel dwellings of the outskirts of Exeter.

'Well, here we are,' Frank said, looking across at Addie still sitting ramrod straight in front of her. 'You're *sure* you want to go on?' he whispered. 'It's not too late to turn back.'

Addie firmly shook her head and pointed in front of her. 'Turn left there, Frank, and then right. The house is on the left.'

Now that she was here, despite the show of bravado Addie's mouth felt dry; her heart was pounding and yes, she would have given anything to turn round and go home because the place she'd left *was* home. But she knew it was too late. The die was cast, the goodbyes said. She had made up her mind.

When they turned the corner and she saw the house, panic returned again, however. She put a hand on Frank's arm and then withdrew it.

'There,' she said, 'this is the house.'

It was a substantial dwelling of red brick set well back from the road. It had four bedrooms – ample room for the enlarged family – and a garden for Arthur to play in. Addie thought Harold must have had the woodwork newly painted, as everything external gleamed and shone.

As they stopped outside the house, the door opened and Harold, with a broad smile, stood on the threshold waiting to receive them as if he had been inside just listening for the car.

Frank got out first and shook hands, followed by Addie. As if sensing her apprehension, Harold took her hand and kissed her on the cheek.

'Welcome home, Addie,' he said; and then, more softly, 'You have been too long gone.'

Arthur scrambled out of the car, dragging Jenny by the hand. She found that she did, after all, remember Harold quite well, although she had been a little girl when they had last met. 'Uncle Harold' had, she recalled, always seemed rather nice, which was one of the reasons she didn't mind her mother going back to him. Nevertheless, there was an underlying nervousness, because she was sure he must have heard a lot of bad things about her: how naughty she'd been. Indeed, his expression was rather severe as he greeted her with a polite handshake. Jenny, anxious to be wanted by her stepfather, needing his approval, felt a little rebuffed.

'I have tea ready,' Harold said with an expansive gesture of his arm towards the house. 'Our maid, Felicity, has been busy in the kitchen and everything is ready. How nice to see you again, Frank.'

'And you,' Frank said, following Harold into the house. He was impressed. Inside, it had a cosy feel with good carpet on the floor and a large bowl of flowers on a gleaming table in the hall, which in wintertime was no mean achievement. Harold led them into the lounge, which was a long, gracious room running from front to back, with French windows leading to an extensive garden, bare now but with a well-kept lawn.

A large tea table stood in front of the fire with a pretty cloth, china, silver forks and plates of sandwiches and cakes.

'I expect you'll want to see your rooms first,' Harold said with all the enthusiasm of someone springing a pleasant surprise, and indeed, Addie's initial feeling of numbness had started to evaporate. At first all she had been able to think of was the coldness of the house, the awful atmosphere when she had first lived there and the morning she had made her escape after Harold had left for school. Now, somehow, maybe because he was genuinely pleased to have her back, the atmosphere seemed different. Harold was different. All it needed now was for her to change.

They all trooped upstairs, Frank and Harold carrying the suitcases. Jenny's room was the first one they entered. It was a good-sized room overlooking the back garden. Jenny advanced into it slowly, suspiciously. It was very different from her small, cramped room at home. It had pretty floral wallpaper, cretonne curtains, a blue carpet and bedspread on the single bed. There was a dressing table with a double mirror, a chest of drawers, a wardrobe and a table in the corner, in front of which was a chair.

Addie observed that Harold was watching her daughter uneasily.

'It's very nice,' Jenny said appreciatively. 'It's lovely.' Then her face transformed in a look of happiness that Addie had not seen for a very long time as she cried, 'Oh, Mummy, I'm so glad we came.'

Harold looked gratified and they all trooped along into the room next door, which was Arthur's. This was smaller, more functional, boyish, and Arthur, who was a little bewildered by the journey and the whole enterprise of leaving home, which he scarcely understood, crept over to his mother and fearfully put his hand in hers.

'I'll be very close, dear,' she murmured, then with a gulp added, 'Just next door.'

What, oh what, would it be like sharing a bedroom with Harold once again?

The first thing she noticed was the double bed in the centre. Before, they had had twin beds. There had been no physical side to their marriage, because Harold had said her revelations on their honeymoon about her past had disgusted him. Now he was watching her carefully as if he could read her mind. Perhaps he was a little apprehensive too.

70

Jenny returned to her bedroom with Frank. Arthur still clung on to his mother's hand, perhaps to give her courage as much as for himself.

'You'll find it's changed a little, Addie. I had the whole place redecorated for you.'

'So I see,' Addie said, still preoccupied with the bed. She knew that Harold wanted children. He had told her so when they had met at the hotel, and she wondered if this was the real, perhaps the only reason for wanting her back. What would physical intercourse be like with him now after all these years?

She tried to take in the new curtains and carpet, the fresh wallpaper; but it was the bed that remained the focal point for her.

'Very nice,' she said, turning to him with a bleak smile. He put an arm around her waist as though he understood. But could he?

Frank left after tea for the long drive back. Addie felt quite tearful saying goodbye to him and hung on to him for a long time, as if she didn't want to let him go.

'Harold seems much nicer,' Frank whispered in her ear. 'He's trying to make amends for the past. You must give him a chance.' Addie nodded, but she felt cold. What had she done?

'I shall miss you, Frank.'

'And I you.' He squeezed her arm reassuringly. 'I think this is going to work out well, Addie. Harold wanted you back; he needs you. I'm sure he loves you. He has done so much to please you. He was very good with Arthur and Jenny. Did you see how she responded to him? I am sure he will try to understand her, which none of us can. We're too close to her. In a way I feel I've failed her.'

Addie nodded but said nothing. Frank paused, his eyes filling with tears, and kissed her on her brow.

'I think this is a good move, Addie, as far as you and the

children are concerned, if not for me. For you it is definitely a move for the better.'

The evening saw the new family together for the first time. There was a long playtime before supper with Arthur, a game of hide-and-seek, squeals of laughter echoing round the house. Felicity, the rather grim-faced maid, had never seen anything like it in the bleak bachelor household where she had worked for two years. This was an aspect of Mr Smith – the family man – she had not seen before. Indeed, it was difficult for Harold to accustom himself to this new role – to have, as it were, two ready-made children when all he had wanted was his wife back; but that was the price he had to pay, part of the bargain, and in the course of the evening, as he observed Jenny more closely, he was aware of the effort she was making. His reserve started to evaporate as his heart began to warm towards her. Compliant little Arthur, his character not yet formed, was easier to like, but in Jenny he observed not a child but almost a young woman, with a will of her own expressed in the determined, rather stubborn set of her mouth.

After Arthur finally went to bed there was supper, at which Harold paid a lot of attention to Jenny, asking her about school and her friends and never once mentioning that dreaded word: London.

Jenny was chatty and relaxed and, as though sensing the subtle shift in Harold's attitude towards her, became rather proprietorial about him, as though she'd just won a trophy she wanted to show off.

It was the last thing Addie had expected; so different from that scowling discontented face she had got used to. Maybe they had not made enough effort with her, too ready to condemn and blame her for the terrible fright she'd given them. Then all the trouble at school after what she'd caused already had seemed inexcusable.

Jenny was naturally reluctant to go to bed, but the events

of the day had tired her. She kissed her mother and seemed to cling to Harold as though she was afraid he might not be there in the morning.

'See you tomorrow?' she asked with a note of uncertainty in her voice.

'Of course.' Harold smiled reassuringly. 'We'll think of something nice to do during the day. Won't we, Addie?'

'I'm so *glad* we came, Mummy,' Jenny burst out again. 'I think I am going to be very happy here.'

Now, at last, they were alone together. Harold stood in front of the fire filling his pipe. He seemed rather nervous and Addie noticed how his hand shook, pressing tobacco into the bowl. How well Addie recalled that pipe-filling ceremony. It had always been a way, it seemed to her, of gaining time. Perhaps the same was true now. They were both uncertain, nervous. The bed upstairs was a reminder of unfinished business in their marriage. It was funny how, after having been separated for so long, they were free to come together, legally. The law took no notice of the years they'd lived apart. No need to renew vows – just move into the house and they could sleep together without sin. This had not been the case with the men she had truly loved: Lydney Ryland and, much later, Gilbert Youngman, whom she had in fact regarded as a husband even though their state of union was morally sinful and without legality, as he had demonstrated in the end when he had just decamped and left her without support for her and their child.

'They're very nice children,' Harold said, tucking his tobacco pouch back into his pocket.

'Thank you, Harold.'

'A credit to you.'

'Jenny *has* been a worry.'

'So you said. It is strange for me, of course, to acquire a daughter who is nearly grown up. I must tell you, Addie, I had some foreboding about it.'

'Understandable, Harold,' Addie murmured. 'Don't think I'm not grateful.'

Harold joined his fingertips together in schoolmasterly fashion, as if pondering a problem. 'The difficulty is that Jenny does seem so advanced for her age, which makes the job of helping her all the harder, as really she is still a child. But we know how wilful she can be – witness the recent distressing episode, which was really quite extraordinary. However, I think I understand her. I have a lot of experience with young people and will certainly try my best.'

'Thank you, Harold.'

She felt humble, submissive, which was the way she had used to feel until she had rebelled and run away. He was the man in charge; but now she had returned on her own terms, hadn't she?

Unexpectedly, Harold abruptly knocked out his pipe in the hearth, placed it back on the mantelpiece, then came over to Addie and stood for a long time looking down at her until, at last, she raised her eyes and met his.

'Shall we go upstairs?' he asked her gently, holding out his hand.

Six

February 1933

P eg stood at the first-floor drawing-room window of the Ryland London house in South Audley Street, gazing into the back garden, which was surrounded by a high wall. In the centre of the far wall was a fountain in the shape of a gaping lion's mouth, but there was no water gushing from it. Instead, on this cold, dank February day the garden, though neat, looked bedraggled, with a scatter of yellow leaves covering the paving stones.

Peg turned back into the large high-ceilinged room. The floor was polished parquet covered with thick Persian rugs, doubtless brought back from their travels by far-off Ryland relations. An elaborate cornice of fruits and intertwining leaves ran round the ceiling, parts of which were picked out in gold. From the centre hung a magnificent chandelier with hundreds, perhaps thousands, of tiny pieces of shimmering crystal, for it was a dark day and all the house lights were on.

Though the family seldom used the house it was staffed by a housekeeper and her husband who performed the services of the butler. In addition there were two maids and a gardener/handyman who saw to the running repairs of what was a very old house, built in the reign of Queen Anne.

Peg had rarely stayed there, certainly not alone, and she remained in awe of the size and grandeur of the place as by the fact that she was its mistress. It had ten bedrooms, a large, well-stocked library, a drawing room, a dining room, a myriad of smaller rooms on the ground floor, a parlour and a study. The extensive kitchens were in the basement, where there were also larders, wine cellars, the butler's pantry and cook's parlour. In the attic were three servants' bedrooms.

Peg walked slowly round the room, gazing at the portraits of Ryland ancestors covering the green silk-lined walls. She felt that, as far as she was concerned, they were complete strangers, there being no blood linking her to them. Yet there was to her children, half Hubert's as well as half hers. She closely examined some of the paintings, but it was too early to tell whether any of the features of Caspar, Jude or Catherine resembled those of their paternal ancestors.

Along the heavy mahogany sideboard were ranged rows of family photographs in variously ornate or plain, but inevitably solid, silver frames. Some were very faded, in witness to their age. There were men in frock coats and high collars, elaborately coiffured ladies with expressionless faces in long satin or black bombazine dresses.

There were lots of children, some with golden curls and angelic expressions, surely looking their best for the camera? Depending on the age of the photograph it was almost possible to guess the date, from the time of the first faded daguerrotypes in the 1850s almost to the present day.

Peg bent forward to examine one and had no difficulty recognizing the schoolboy Hubert with his sister Violet and brother Lydney, also dressed in school uniform, standing beside their parents. Lydney had the almost-white hair that Jenny had now, strong facial features and a brilliant smile. By contrast Hubert and Violet looked rather glum. Studying the photograph, which pre-dated the war, Peg felt it was impossible to believe that Hubert had not suspected Jenny was his brother's daughter. Why had he never mentioned it to her? Why had they not been honest with each other? Maybe the seeds of the present crisis in their marriage had begun with this mutual lack of trust.

For it was a crisis. Peg selected a cigarette from a silver box on one of the small tables, lit it and restlessly threw herself down on one of the sofas. In the days of Hubert Ryland's father, grandfather, great-grandfather and beyond, the family had made extensive use of the house and visited it several times a year, staying there for three months in the summer for the London season before they went off to the house in Scotland for the shooting.

The house in Scotland, too, remained staffed, and yet they had visited it only once since Hubert had succeeded to the title. Peg was not keen on shooting or blood sports and Hubert didn't want to go without her.

Maybe this year he would go by himself, she thought, as she rose and began once again to prowl round the room. He had been very definite about not wanting to come with her to London. Theatres, art galleries and such had no appeal for him. Their interests diverged. It seemed like a sign of the times.

The door opened; one of the housemaids came in and dropped a bob.

'Telephone call for you, my lady.'

'Thank you,' Peg said. 'Where shall I take it?'

'In the master's study, my lady, on the ground floor.'

Peg ran quickly downstairs and picked up the receiver.

'Peg?' said a familiar voice.

'Alan!' she cried. 'So you got my note?'

'I'm delighted to hear you're in London.'

'I wondered if you were free to come to dinner tomorrow? I'm spending a few days in the house.'

'Is Hubert not with you?'

'No.'

Slight pause at the other end; then, 'Peg, I'd love to come, but let me take you out to dinner.'

'I'd like you to come here. The cook is dying to have the chance to entertain. There is still a skeleton staff here and yet the house is hardly ever used.'

'I'll say yes then. That would be lovely, Peg.'

'Shall we say eight?'

'I can't tell you how much I'm looking forward to seeing you again.'

'Me too,' Peg said and replaced the receiver.

She had once been engaged to Alan Walker, now Assistant Editor of the *South London Gazette*, a serious newspaper of some prestige on a par with the *Manchester Guardian*.

She had been twenty and he two years older when they had met at a Fleet Street news agency where they both worked. For Alan it seemed to have been love at first sight. For Peg, although she had admired and respected him, and he had taught her a lot and influenced her, it had never been love, or had never seemed like it, which was why she had eventually fallen in love with and married Hubert Ryland. Yet between them remained a bond that, in many ways, had deepened with time, though she couldn't quite explain how.

That night she dined early and alone, tired from the journey to town and, after telephoning to make sure that all was well at home, went to bed.

'You don't change,' Peg said to Alan, on opening the door herself to welcome him. 'Except that you look more prosperous.' And indeed, in evening jacket and black tie, he did. Alan had always lacked obvious physical charm and with it the 'sex appeal' of someone like Hubert Ryland, who had gone out of his way to impress women.

'And older,' he added ruefully, running a hand over his head. 'Thinning on top.' In youth his hair had always flopped over his face, but now it was well greased and sleeked back. A pair of imposing black-framed spectacles lent him an air of distinction that went with his considerable height – over six feet.

Peg pressed the flowers he'd brought to her nose, inhaling the perfume. Out of season they must have cost a fortune from a Mayfair florist.

'Beautiful,' she murmured.

'You look just the same, Peg.' Alan had a catch in his voice. 'More beautiful, of course.'

'Flatterer.'

She placed the flowers on the hall table where the maid would see to them, linked an arm through his, and took him up to the drawing room, where a huge fire had been lit. She wore a simple dinner gown of black velvet with a row of pearls at her neck and a diamond cluster pinned to her bosom. She was very tall and gracious, and anyone seeing them walk slowly up the stairs would have thought them a regal couple.

'I say, what a place!' Alan whistled, looking round. 'Do you remember your tiny room in Clerkenwell?'

'Sharing a loo with six others!' Peg burst out laughing.

'You've come a long way, Peg.'

'And you, Alan.' She crossed to the sideboard on which reposed the rows of family photos. 'A drink?'

'Whisky would be nice.'

Peg poured them both a whisky and went over to join him on the large sofa facing the fire. 'I haven't seen you since Catherine was christened.'

'How is she?'

'She's lovely.'

'And the boys? Hubert?'

'All well.' Peg sipped her drink. 'So you still see Violet?'

'A little.' Alan's expression was guarded. 'She lives in Rome, of course.'

'But may be coming back here, I understand.'

'You're very well informed.' Alan smiled mysteriously into his glass. 'Such a lot has changed, Peg,' he said as if wishing to avoid the subject. 'The world has changed dramatically since we first met. We hoped the end of the war would bring a new era, but it has not been the case. The news from Germany is terrible. Hitler becoming Chancellor is a disaster.

But it is no surprise to me. There was so much pressure on
Hindenberg to give in, with political chaos and anarchy in the
streets of Berlin. I used to attend Hitler's rallies, and though
people scoffed at him elsewhere, I saw the power he exercised
over the ordinary German people.' He stopped and saw she
was listening to him intently. 'Still interested in politics, Peg?'

'Of course I'm interested, but that's about all.' She
shrugged her shoulders regretfully. 'I take no active part.'

'As Lady Ryland you couldn't.'

'It's not that so much as that I haven't the time.'

'But the Women's Institute would never tolerate someone
with socialist views. Do you still have those views, Peg?'

'Of course.'

'Well now we have a Labour Prime Minister presiding over
a National Government. I think Ramsay Macdonald has
been a disappointment to a lot of us.' Alan paused. 'Of
course, as Assistant Editor of a Tory paper I have to be
careful. Oliver has made that very plain to me. When I was
European correspondent it was different, because we are all
against the fascists and the communists, but here I must stick
to the middle ground.' Alan took up his glass and finished his
whisky. 'Yes, it is the middle way for both of us, Peg, the path
of compromise.'

There was a discreet tap at the door; the butler entered
and, after bowing politely in Alan's direction, turned to Peg.

'Dinner is served, my lady.'

The dining room was a shade more intimate than the one
at Ryland Castle and the dining table not as long. Consequently it was easier to converse, though as the butler, Mr
Jenkins, never left the room, they stuck mainly to trivialities
or politics. The food was simple but good: soup followed by
sole and roast beef, with syllabub to finish, a Meursault and a
good claret to drink. Mr Jenkins obviously enjoyed his duties
and when Peg thanked him and asked him to compliment
Mrs Jenkins on an excellent meal, he said fervently, 'I wish

you came more often, Lady Ryland. It is strange in this large house with no one to look after.'

'I'm sure it is, Mr Jenkins,' Peg replied. 'I'll speak to my husband about it. I certainly would like to come more often; but I think Miss Violet may well soon take up residence and come to live here on a more or less permanent basis sometime in the future.'

Back in the drawing room, where a maid had finished making up the fire, Peg offered Alan a cigar and, as he sat lighting it, she poured coffee and a brandy for each of them. She felt relaxed and happy in his company. It was so different from the tense atmosphere at the castle – almost like being a couple again, with so many interests in common.

As if reading her thoughts, Alan continued: 'It is very strange when you think of our socialist principles, all those meetings we attended for the betterment of the working classes, and here you sit in a huge house in Mayfair staffed by people who for most of the year have nothing to do. They are here simply to please you.'

Peg was lighting a cigarette and bent forward while she blew out the spill from the fire. Alan was struck by the classic beauty of her profile; her nose slightly retroussé, long black lashes curling up on her pale cheeks, mouth pursed in the act of extinguishing the spill. As if aware of his gaze – maybe she had unconsciously hesitated a little to prolong the moment, conscious of the effect she was making – she turned towards him and he experienced the full force of what, to him, had been and always would be her particular magnetism.

Almost as if it came from someone else, Alan heard himself saying: 'I love you as much as ever, you know, Peg.'

'I thought you were in love with Violet Ryland?'

'I never *said* I was in love.' Alan had met Hubert's sister by chance in Rome, where they had begun an affair. 'She was always second best. I told you at the christening I was not in her league.'

81

'I'm sure she's coming back to be with you. That must mean something.'

'To her, not to me. She's lonely and bored – also, not to put too fine a point on it, getting old.'

Peg grimaced. It was rather as she thought. Violet and Alan made rather an incongruous pair and he had never seemed happy or relaxed when she had seen him in her company.

'But Alan, you can't go on loving me. I'm married to someone else.'

'And in love with him still?'

'Of course.'

'Then why isn't he here?'

'Because he doesn't like town or the theatre or art galleries. I am going to see a lot of shows and some exhibitions while I'm here. Husbands and wives don't have to be together *all* the time, you know.'

'I detect a restlessness about you, Peg – something I wasn't aware of before.'

'Oh you're quite mistaken,' Peg said a little coldly, getting to her feet and disposing of her cigarette.

'Well anyway, as your husband is not here I'm sure he wouldn't mind if I accompanied you to the shows and galleries instead, purely as an escort, of course. That is, if it's agreeable to you?'

It was pleasing to have an escort, but even more so to have one like Alan. He was so cultured and knowledgeable, up to date with all the latest events. He got tickets for shows that were sold out and knew his way about all the galleries and exhibitions, even obscure ones.

He would call for her in a car, using the chauffeur of the *South London Gazette*'s proprietor, Oliver Moodie, who had also given Peg her first chance as a journalist. He had sent flowers and invited them both to dinner, like the couple they had been when they were engaged, as if nothing had changed.

Peg looked forward to seeing Alan each evening and sometimes in the afternoon for a gallery visit, if he could get away. They saw the latest films: Garbo in *Queen Christina* and Noel Coward's *Cavalcade*, which they both thought jingoistic.

Alan always arrived with flowers, so that the house was full of them. They had known each other for ten years, but now that friendship seemed to have deepened, grown stronger. She felt she was being courted all over again, yet it wasn't physical, there was no intimacy, perhaps because that was how their relationship had foundered before.

She wondered sometimes if Alan was attempting a subtle waiting game and if she was being wicked in seeming to encourage him, knowing how he felt about her. Was she also deceitful? She had told Hubert they were seeing each other, but not how often.

When they had first known each other, Alan had taken her to political meetings in an attempt to convert her to socialism and had been successful. Peg, a natural rebel, hadn't needed very much converting.

'We should hear Mosley speaking,' Alan said late one evening when they were discussing what to do the next day over a leisurely supper after the theatre. 'He's very charismatic.'

'Oh, I'd love to,' Peg enthused immediately, 'as long as no one sees us.'

'Well, we'll go heavily disguised. There's a rally on tomorrow night.'

'Oh, it will be fun!' Peg clasped her hands together in rapture. 'Hubert would have a fit . . .'

'That makes it all the nicer' – Alan was suddenly serious – 'doesn't it, I mean? Deceiving your husband?'

'I am *not* deceiving my husband. He knows we see each

other. However' – Peg gave him a prim look – 'I don't think I'll tell him about Mosley.'

They stood cramped at the back of the hall just off the Whitechapel Road, hemmed in by the huge crowd that had braved police cordons, to hear the Blackshirt leader, whose arrival in the East End had already produced a barrage of protest. Even though he had expected it, when Alan had seen the size of the crowds in the streets all converging on the hall, he had wanted to turn back in case Peg came to any harm; but Peg had insisted they stay. She wore a heavy tweed overcoat, a scarf tied round her head and sensible shoes, and she was aware of that same sense of excitement she'd had in the old days when reporting a controversial political meeting for the paper, and which she had felt could never be rekindled.

Yet it had been.

Suddenly the noisy audience fell silent; the pushers and shovers were, for a moment anyway, still, as the fascist leader came striding on to the platform and, arms akimbo, chin thrust out, stood arrogantly surveying his audience as if he knew he had them in his power. Peg felt the same frisson of fear as she sometimes felt when looking at news footage of Hitler addressing the masses. Mosley had the same stare, as if trying to mesmerize his audience.

Suddenly he raised his arm in the fascist salute and half the audience did the same, while the other half booed him. So the seeds of disturbance were apparent before the meeting began. Alan spontaneously put his arm around Peg's shoulder for protection and she could sense the tautness, the instinctive fear in him too; as Mosley harangued the crowd, some of whom grew increasingly restless, he kept on looking at her anxiously and his grip tightened. She felt safe with him and leaned against him, confident of his protection.

'Do you want to go?' he said in her ear. 'I can't stand much more of this filth.'

'We'd never get away,' Peg replied. 'Look at those toughies at the door. If you ask me, no one can get in or out. This will make good copy for your paper tomorrow.'

'We will be a modern dictatorship,' Mosley screamed, 'created for the good of the people, with powers to act for the benefit of the people. A fascist government will be armed with powers to overcome the problems the people want overcome.'

'Bloody dictator,' boomed a voice from the audience, half of whom wore the black shirts and leather belts of the British Union of Fascists. The voice came from near Peg and Alan and suddenly there was a surge from behind as the black-shirted stewards at the door streamed menacingly along the aisle to stifle the dissent; but now on his feet the agitator, shaking his fists, continued to berate Mosley, who was making every effort to drown the dissenting voice by raising his own to a bellow. The six or seven stewards reached the agitator, who had now been joined by several of his friends, amounting to a mob, probably carefully planted by the Communist Party, strong in this part of London, all shaking clenched fists in unison at the platform:

'Down with fascism! Down with fascism!'

Then the threatened violence, which had been so heavily in the air, erupted. Missiles thrown from the audience began to hit the platform, several narrowly missing the speaker, who, forced to curtail his speech, was hurried away surrounded by his henchmen while the platform became a mass of rotten fruit and vegetables.

'We must get out of here,' Alan muttered, an arm remaining tightly round Peg; but their way was barred by a stream of people who wanted to go one way into the mêlée, confronted by another stream who wanted to get out.

Suddenly Peg felt Alan's grip slacken, wrenched away from her, and she was thrown violently to the ground while people fell willy-nilly on top of her. Raising her eyes in terror, she saw a mass of bodies above her head, and in an attempt to shield her face she had, to her horror, a vision of a similar incident that had occurred many years before on her first assignment as a junior reporter covering a political meeting in this very same part of London: White-chapel.

Then, miraculously, the same source of rescue came as before. With a superhuman effort Alan thrust his way back through the mêlée that had separated him from Peg and, almost diving into the crowd and using considerable force, began attempting to drag her to the surface before she was stifled. Her head already lolled backwards and her eyes were closed. Her scarf had fallen, or been wrenched, from her head. When she felt his strong grasp on her hand, she opened her eyes and saw his terrified face staring down at her. She tried to struggle towards him, hanging on, but her legs were trapped under the bodies of a mass of people who had fallen on top of her.

Whistles started to blow as the police stormed in, the noise, panic and confusion reaching a climax. Alan clung on to Peg, but he felt her grasp grow weaker, and in desperation he called to a man beside him: 'A woman is *dying* down here. You've *got* to help.'

The burly man, his face covered with sweat, immediately divined the gravity of the situation and called for reinforcements from his companions, who had probably been among the agitators who had initiated the riot. Forming themselves by brute force into a circle, they cleared an area that allowed those underneath to breathe, and there were a number of writhing bodies besides Peg's. Policemen blowing whistles rushed across to help prevent a possible massacre and Alan was able at last to find the space to kneel by Peg's side. Alarmed by her pallor, her closed eyelids, he took her head in his hands and cradled her against his face, which was wet with tears.

'Peg,' he murmured, 'Peg . . .'

Then, to his great joy, he heard her through the din, just managing to make out the words, saying feebly:

'I think I've broken my leg. The pain is absolutely excruciating,' and with that she fainted.

Alan sat by Peg's bedside, his elbow resting on his chair, chin in hand, watching her: every twitching muscle, every involuntary movement of her dear, dear face as she slept. He felt crushed by a terrible sense of responsibility for what had happened. He had nearly killed her.

Yet Peg had not been the only victim and one man was at death's door in the same hospital where Peg had a private room.

The Mosley riot was in all the papers, which lay by his side in a heap on the floor:

'Peer's Wife Injured in Crowd Disaster' was one of the headlines, and then came an account of what had happened.

Many years before, Peg had made similar headlines because after she'd been rushed to hospital she had insisted on filing her copy, that first report of the riot. That time she'd broken an arm.

It was so extraordinary how history had repeated itself.

'I don't learn, do I?' she muttered, opening her eyes and giving him a wan smile.

'Oh, darling . . .' Alan leaped to his feet, rushed over and gently stroked her brow. 'I thought you'd died. How *could* you do that to me?'

'You're a silly old sausage,' she said, equally tenderly, reaching up to try to wipe the tears from his face. 'What did *I* do to you? It was your idea to go to the meeting.'

'We should never have gone.' Alan straightened up, vigorously blowing his nose. 'Your husband will kill me.'

'Did someone tell him?'

'I rang him last night from the hospital and he will be here later today.' Alan looked at her ruefully. 'I suppose I'd better be gone when he is.'

'Don't be silly.' Peg put out a hand. 'He can't possibly mind. I'm of an age at which I can do what I like, go where I like. I'm a reporter, a trained journalist. It's high time Hubert realized that. After that awful scene last night I think we must be prepared to stand up and be counted.'

Peg's clasp was cool and strong. Alan felt like weeping again with the enormous realization of his loss. 'Oh, Peg, I wish we could undo the past, go back to as we were and be together again. I do, Peg, I really do. I can't bear to be separated from you again. Despite the disaster of last night, which I'd give anything to undo, it's been such a wonderful week with you and . . . you'll go back to the castle while you recuperate and I feel I might never see you again.'

As if to comfort him, she tightly squeezed his hand, but said nothing.

'Do you really and truly love him, Peg?'

'It's not really Hubert,' she replied slowly, as she was already steps ahead of him.

'What do you mean by that?' Alan, though puzzled, experienced a rash and ecstatic, perhaps forlorn moment of hope; but Peg was shaking her head.

'I shall never leave Hubert, Alan, whatever happens. I love my children too much ever to contemplate such a thing.'

Seven

Maisie took another look at the pie she'd put in the oven – taken so much trouble to get just right, mixing the dough, making the filling according to the recipe book – sighed and closed the door carefully. It was not yet cooked and sagged in the middle, not like the beautiful pie in the illustration, which was round and golden and crispy. The colour of this was a curious grey; but then, she consoled herself, Ed hadn't married her for her cooking abilities, which, at the time of their marriage, had been nil and had not improved much since.

Maisie adored her husband, but had not taken to domesticity. She had left school and home at fourteen and her life, until she had married, had been lived in a series of rented rooms, many of them in insalubrious parts of London.

Ed had offered her the chance of a new life of respectability and she had grabbed it, but from time to time she missed the old days, and her feet tapped in time to the music on the wireless as she peeled the vegetables, laid the table and had another dispirited look at the flat pie. Ed wouldn't mind – he never did – though she knew she tested his patience; maybe because he had a very good lunch at the officer's mess, so that his evening meal was less important.

Maisie also hated housework. They had rented a very nice three-storey terraced Georgian house in the Stoke area of Plymouth where, from their bedroom window at the top, they could see the sea. It had a small front garden and a yard at the back, with a door in the wall that led on to a narrow street.

Maisie had hoped for a maid or, at least, assistance with the housework, but Ed came from a family of capable, hard-working women who expected to look after their men, and this was one of the few things he had insisted on. She had nothing to do all day, surely . . . Besides, a naval lieutenant's pay wasn't a fortune and they had no savings or anything else to live on.

For the first few months of their marriage they'd lived on love, and even the evening meal had been forgotten while they had dashed upstairs to bed.

In the eight months they'd lived in Plymouth Maisie had made few friends, mainly because she hadn't tried very hard. Most of the naval wives, besides being rather snobbish, were preoccupied with their children, their schools, their activities, their bridge and whist afternoons and so on. Maisie had no children and didn't play cards. She felt she would have been happier with the wives of the ratings, who were more the sort of people she was used to.

Ed had crossed the class barrier by virtue of his education and personal achievement, but even he didn't seem entirely happy among his peers, didn't play golf, own a yacht or a horse, so they were thrust a great deal on each other's company. Maisie read a lot of women's magazines and every afternoon without fail she went out, either to the cinema or the shops, or she'd wander along the Hoe, looking at the ships in the Sound. Occasionally, men loitering around would try to pick her up, either in the cinema or on the Hoe, completely misunderstanding her intentions on account of her striking looks and her excessive use of make-up. Maisie never went anywhere without her 'face', as she put it, and even strolls were taken in very high-heeled shoes, which was how she felt comfortable.

There were occasional mess dances, and here she came into

her own; frequently the other dancers – usually naval officers and their prim wives – stopped in some bemusement, mingled perhaps with admiration, to watch her.

Maisie completed her preparations, poured herself a gin and tonic, lit a cigarette and stood by the window, waiting for Ed's car to draw up outside: the highlight of her day.

Ed usually came home at six thirty – you could set your clock by it – so by seven thirty this evening she began to feel agitated, mainly about the condition the meal would be in when she finally came to serve it: the pie now overcooked, some of the vegetables almost done to a crisp. Ed never complained, despite the fact that he'd grown up in this perfect household full of women who gave a high priority to domesticity, looked after him hand and foot, gave him good nourishing meals served on time and kept his room and the rest of the house spotless. As a man, he had not been expected to raise a hand.

Maisie knew she was – well, careless. Maybe she'd have another go with him about getting a maid.

Ed was still not home at eight; Maisie had begun to worry seriously and had poured herself another large gin when she heard the car draw up outside. There was the sound of the garden gate opening and closing and Ed hurrying along the path. Maisie flew to the door, flung it open before he could get his key in the lock and threw her arms round his neck.

'Ed, where have you been? I was *ever* so worried!'

'Sorry, darling.' Ed gently disengaged himself from her embrace and, as she stood aside for him to enter, took off his hat and threw it on to the table in the hall. Maisie could see the tension in his face.

'Bad day, darling?' She went over to pour him a drink.

'Not exactly.' He took his cigarette case from his pocket. 'In fact, I've been promoted.'

'Oh, Ed! That's wonderful! So why the miserable face?'

He offered her a cigarette, which she accepted as she gave him his drink.

He looked at her suspiciously. 'How many have you had?'

'Oh, *Ed*!' Maisie retorted angrily. 'What else was I supposed to do when you were an hour and a half late? Anyway, I only had a couple. And I might as well tell you now: the dinner is ruined.'

'I'm not very hungry anyway.' Ed flopped down, took off his tie and undid his shirt. He closely examined the tip of his cigarette, tasted his drink and then stubbed out his cigarette. Stony-faced, Maisie sat down opposite him.

Ed ran his hand over his face. 'Look, darling, I'm sorry to be in a mood, sorry about everything.' He rose abruptly and went over to her and kissed her. 'Maisie, I love you very much and I'm sorry about the dinner. Do you want to go out?'

'I want to know what's the matter,' she said, reaching for his hand. 'You say you have just been promoted, so what the hell is wrong?'

'I'm being sent abroad next week for manoeuvres in the Far East – Singapore and Malaya. I shall be away for months, maybe a year.'

'Oh, Ed.' Maisie crumpled in her chair. 'You said if you were sent away it wouldn't be for long.'

'I have been promoted to gunnery officer on a new ship. It's an important career move for me. I should be feeling pleased, but the thought of leaving you for so long . . .' – he looked sadly at her – '. . . is more than I can bear. Honestly, Maisie, I feel like absconding.'

'No, you don't.' She let his hand fall. 'Your career is too important to you. Can't I . . .' She looked around desperately. 'Can't I come out too?'

'No.' His reply was unequivocal. 'Wives are not expected to join their husbands. It's not like the army, where a regiment can sometimes be posted abroad for years.'

'What am I supposed to do for a year, for heaven's sake?'

Ed looked at her wryly. 'What other wives do. You could also try learning to cook.'

In fact some of the vegetables had been salvaged, the remnants of pie quite tasty, and Ed said that the meal wasn't as bad as he'd expected; but they had little appetite for food and after a few more drinks they went to bed. Even their lovemaking was inadequate, however, and after a while Ed stopped trying, flopped on to his back and lit a cigarette.

'Maybe I had too much to drink. Sorry.'

Maisie, frustrated and angry, turned on her side. 'You don't have to go,' she muttered.

'I do, I'd be court-martialled if I refused. Besides, you knew when you married me what it would be like.'

'*No one* knows what it will be like!' Maisie turned over on her back. 'Stuck at home all day with nothing to do. I had a job, Ed. I used to work. What can I do here?'

'I don't want my wife to work and that's that. We have a position to keep up. Besides' – trying to make a joke of it, he looked at her sideways – 'you can hardly do the sort of work you used to do.'

'You have got hoity-toity.'

'Maisie, I am just stating a fact. I'm serious about learning to cook. You'll find, if you give them a chance, that the wives are very supportive. When the men go to sea, they're all in the same boat.'

'Stuck up snobs,' she retorted.

'When did they ever do anything to you?'

'I can see they're stuck up the way they look at me.'

'They don't know what you did in London.'

'Are you ashamed of me, Ed?'

'Not at all. I was *never* ashamed of you.'

'You never told your family I was a stripper.'

'I told them you were a dancer.'

93

'But not that I took all my clothes off in front of a bunch of leering men.'

'Why bring all this up now, Maisie?' Ed wriggled angrily in the bed.

'Because it's true, isn't it?'

'It was true. It's not now.'

'Oh, I see; I'm respectable and married to a respectable officer in His Majesty's Navy.'

Maisie stared grimly at the ceiling. Months – a year maybe. What an interminable time it seemed. Beside her she could feel Ed's hurt. This time next week he would be at sea and all he'd remember would be this night of bitterness. She reached for his hand beside her and he grasped hers tightly.

'I'll be all right,' she said meekly. 'The time will pass. I'll be nice to the wives. I'll take cookery classes.'

'If we had a baby . . .' Ed began, but Maisie turned to him, her voice ringing with determination.

'I don't want a baby without a father, Ed. I couldn't go through a pregnancy, let alone have the kid, without you.'

'A call for you, my lady,' Cyril the butler announced, having entered the drawing room after a discreet tap at the door. 'Mr Walker.'

Hubert looked up sharply from his paper. 'Say she is not in.'

The butler, having faced this situation before, looked nervously from one to the other.

'Don't be silly, Hubert,' Peg said, attempting to rise. 'You can't keep saying that! Give me your arm, will you, Cyril, and please pass me my crutches.'

'I tell you' – Hubert also got up – 'I will not allow it.' He looked across at Cyril. 'Do as I say, Cyril. Don't keep the gentleman waiting.'

'Very good, my lord.' The butler hovered for a moment, still unsure where his loyalty should lie. 'Shall I say her ladyship will call back?'

'Say she is *not* here. That's quite sufficient. You don't know, obviously, if she is not here, whether she will call back or not.' Hubert sat down again, resuming his perusal of the paper, as though to signify the matter was now closed.

As Cyril withdrew, Peg was staring at her husband as if speechless with indignation.

At last she found her voice. 'How dare you speak like that to me in front of a servant.'

'Everyone knows who Mr Walker is,' said Hubert angrily. 'It was all over the papers. You think Cyril doesn't know and it won't get round the servant's hall, then all over the village? Probably already has: the wretched man has hardly stopped ringing. If he does it once more, I shall go and speak to him myself and tell him exactly where to get off.'

'But Hubert, we did nothing *wrong*,' Peg protested.

'You did something very foolish and made a fool of me into the bargain: "Socialist Wife of Tory Peer Caught Up in a Riot", "Peeress Breaks her Leg in Fascist Scuffle", and so on.'

'I was merely there as a reporter, a journalist.'

'But you are *not* a journalist, are you? You gave that up years ago when you married me. By attending that meeting you're declaring yourself either a journalist or a fascist and I don't like either of them.'

'I made it *quite* clear I was not a fascist in the interviews I gave,' Peg said heatedly; '– was *forced* to give so as to avoid misinterpretation. I said how I deplored Mosley and all the BUP stands for.'

'And clearly, if you were also not there as a journalist, you were there as the companion of Alan Walker. Not a few people knew that you were once engaged to him, and now a lot more do. Several papers have taken care of that!'

'I think this is all about jealousy.' Wearily Peg sat back. Her leg, in plaster, was resting on a stool and she was still in a good deal of pain despite the painkillers the doctor had given her.

'Call it what you like. As long as I am in charge I am not asking that man here and I am not having him call you. In fact, you will do me a very great favour if you never set eyes on him again.'

'What do you mean, "in charge"?' Peg demanded. 'I thought we were partners – equals? You once said I had no need to ask your permission for anything, as this was my home.'

'The context of that was different. I think a man is entitled to protect his marriage, the mother of his children, from someone whose presence can only cause scandal of the most objectionable nature,' Hubert shouted and, throwing aside his paper as if he could stand no more, he got up and stamped out of the room.

The scene had made Peg feel nervous and she was very close to tears. She had been home from hospital a week and Alan, who was obviously concerned about her, always got the same answer; either she was not there, which he would know was not the case, as she couldn't walk very far – certainly not to leave the house – or she was unable to speak to him. What would he think? What must be going through his mind, frantic, as she knew he would be, with worry?

Hopefully he would understand, knowing how angry Hubert was, how humiliated by the whole situation, which had been highlighted in the press. The implication was that Lady Ryland was carrying on with her ex-fiancé. However many denials were made, it was alleged that there was no smoke without fire etc., etc.

Peg had agreed – wanted – to come home rather than stay in London. She needed to be home with her children and at the time she had given little thought to Alan besides telling him and everyone else how much she owed to him. Once again he had probably saved her life; but they had seen little of each other after Hubert had arrived to take her home. There had been a chilly meeting in the hospital corridor as she was being taken to the car in a wheelchair, a perfunctory doffing of gentlemen's hats, a warm handshake from her, the suspicion of tears in her eyes because she did not dare attempt a kiss. Now Peg decided she would have to write to him, and yet somehow the idea didn't appeal to her. The whole incident had certainly been her fault, not Alan's. She had insisted on staying and once again he had come to her rescue, as he had many years before.

Despite his position on the *South London Gazette* they ran the story for all they were worth, reprinting Peg's article that had appeared in the paper ten years before describing her adventures at a political meeting, which she had attended as a brash young reporter. This had been almost a twin of the Mosley meeting, except that in 1923 it had been on behalf of the Communist Party.

In a way it was a romantic story, which made the front pages of all the newspapers, and that was what Hubert so objected to, because so many asked what a peer's wife was doing there in the company of her ex-fiancé, and innuendos abounded.

The story of her engagement to Alan Walker and subsequent marriage to Hubert Ryland was also explored at great length and the relevant announcements in the newspaper columns at the time reproduced:

The engagement is announced between Alan Walker, son of . . . and Miss Margaret (Peg) Hallam, daughter of . . .

The marriage arranged between . . . will not now take place.

The marriage between the Honourable Hubert Ryland, son of Lord and Lady Ryland and Miss Margaret (Peg) Hallam, daughter of . . . took place quietly in France on . . .

Peg knew that what Hubert hated most was the publicity and also, maybe, in his heart of hearts he wondered how much Peg had been seeing of Alan while she was in London and if that was why she had gone.

Certainly the atmosphere since her return home had been frosty and she felt more alienated from her husband than ever. Her sisters had been very concerned. Verity had come buzzing over from Bristol and Stella from the lodge. Addie had rung several times, but it was her family that had gathered round to support her, not his. No word from his mother to Violet, who probably also wondered what Peg had been doing in London with the man she considered her lover.

After a while Peg rose slowly; with the help of the crutches the hospital had provided, she painfully made her way into the hall and then to Hubert's study, where the telephone stood on his desk. After a moment's reflection she dialled the paper where, she supposed, Alan would be at work. But he was not there. The switchboard girl asked if she could take a message, but Peg said she would telephone again later.

As Peg thoughtfully replaced the receiver, she looked up to see Hubert standing in the doorway.

'What are you doing?' he asked.

'Making a telephone call,' Peg replied. 'What does it look like? If you want to know – and I expect you do – I was trying to contact Alan to apologize for my rudeness. He has rung several times this week and his calls have been ignored. I think that's rude.'

'That's your opinion.' Hubert folded his arms and leaned against the wall.

'Alan is an old friend,' Peg went on. 'It's true I was once engaged to him, but if you remember, I left him for you. I may have behaved very badly in his eyes and the eyes of other people, but I loved you, Hubert, and I love you now, but you are making things very difficult for me, for us.' As he tried to interrupt her, she held up a hand. 'This is not the beginning,

98

is it Hubert? Our relationship has been deteriorating for some time. I trace it to Ed's wedding. I may be wrong, but I think it has something to do with that. Too many things happened that you didn't like. That brought everything to a head: my family – Maisie's family – were not the sort of people you were used to; the castle had been thrown open to everyone in a way it had not been before.' She paused. 'Talking of Ed, by the way, he wrote to say he is being transferred to a new ship and they leave very soon for the Far East. Poor Maisie, I wonder what she will do?'

'Well, she must have known what she was doing when she married a sailor. They don't stay on land all the time.' Hubert's tone was dismissive, sarcastic. 'I suppose you want to ask her here?'

Peg looked surprised. 'Not at all. Why should I? I'd like to see her – she is my sister-in-law – but she has her own life to lead. I imagine they've got plenty of friends.'

'I shouldn't be surprised if she went back to London,' Hubert said, 'and resumed her old career. Basically the woman's a tramp.'

Peg looked at him in amazement. 'I thought you liked Maisie?'

'Oh, I liked her, but she is still a tramp.'

'I don't know how you can say such a thing.'

'Well, I can and I mean it. You mark my words: while your brother's away she'll be up to her old tricks. I bet she's found living in Plymouth hell.'

That night Peg found it almost impossible to sleep. Since she had returned home it had been decided she would sleep in one of the spare rooms so that both she and her husband could have a better night's rest. It had seemed a sensible idea, but one Peg had agreed to almost with a feeling of relief, and she thought it was a situation that could possibly be permanent. Their intimate life had not been satisfactory for some time now. There had been a break in their relationship all round. Maybe a little space would improve it? So it was the state of her marriage rather than the pain of her broken leg that kept her awake.

There had been a time when she could never bear to be parted for a second from Hubert; a night apart would have been unthinkable, and in those hot Umbrian nights they had enjoyed many moments of rapture together. All that had gone.

She wondered if the change in Hubert had been inevitable, even predictable? They had had four incredibly happy years in Italy. She had loved him, as she hadn't thought it possible to love anybody. In Italy he had been fulfilled and relaxed, a family man, a father, and above all a lover.

Neither of them had expected him to succeed to the title so soon, but at first they had coped with it well. Hubert had decided on reforms to the estate and the way it was managed; he had made it more up to date. But gradually he himself had changed. He had become a magistrate, joined many of his father's clubs and associations and taken up many of the duties his father had had in the local community. In short, he had become a member of the Establishment.

And then, living back in Ryland Castle, he had become involved with her relations in a way he had not been before; there was no more deference, no touching of forelocks. Yet Frank, her stepfather, was still his chauffeur and all-round handyman. Her sisters had still occasionally helped Mrs Capstick in the kitchen.

Then there had been the wedding. Oh happy day! But with what consequences?

Jenny trotted home along the pavement, arm in arm with her best friend, Sylvia Birch, swinging their school satchels and chatting away. In the six months she'd been in her new home Jenny had become a reformed character, or rather she had returned to being the well-behaved, obedient girl she had once been.

100

The source of this transformation was, surprisingly, her stepfather, Harold. Jenny adored him and whereas she could be ambivalent about her mother – still a little cheeky and sometimes even rude – she did everything Harold told her, was crushed when he chided her, triumphant when he praised her.

He had spent hours giving her extra tuition and, always bright though lazy at school, she now strove to be at the top of the class just so that she could bask in his praise. It was almost as though a love affair had developed between them, but it was an affair of the mind, of spirit, and Addie was relieved rather than affronted by it. It had made her return to her husband not only so much easier, but also worthwhile.

Thus, on the whole, it was a contented household. Addie, having made the choice, which had turned out to be a wise one, had settled down to wifely domesticity, the art of pleasing her man. She too found herself doing everything that he told her and consequently, like Jenny, was able to bask in the sunshine of his approval.

Sylvia had been Jenny's best friend since she had joined the private school to which Harold had insisted on sending her without minding that the fees came from his own pocket. Sylvia lived two genteel streets away from Jenny and they now stood at the corner of one of them, continuing the conversation that had started when they left school: trivia about the events of the day, their successes or otherwise, a little gossip about one or two of the girls, sometimes a mistress, but nothing malicious. Sylvia wasn't like that. Addie and Harold were pleased with the friendship, because Sylvia came from a very nice family. Her father was a bank manager and they considered her a good influence on Jenny, in whom regression, not unnaturally, was always a lurking fear.

'Mummy says come to tea tomorrow.' Sylvia was reluctant to be parted from her best friend.

'I'll ask Daddy,' Jenny agreed.

'Why don't you ask your mother?' Sylvia looked at her slyly.

'Mummy always agrees with what Daddy says and refers everything to him, and I'm sure Daddy will say yes.'

Sylvia wasn't clear about the details, exactly, but there had been some talk at the school when Jenny had first joined it about who Jenny was and where she had come from. Most of their parents knew the headmaster, either because they had children at his school or socially. It was known that Mrs Smith was, indeed, his wife, to whom he had been married for some time; but there was a lot of speculation about the children, though it was generally thought that Jenny was Mr Smith's daughter – she was so fond of him; there was so much trust and affection between them.

As for the little boy . . . well, he was a bit of a mystery, but there was a great deal of respect for Mr Smith and now his wife, so that it was swept under the carpet, though from time to time it emerged as a subject of idle speculation.

After saying goodbye to Sylvia Jenny continued along the street, looking forward to seeing her father and showing him her success in a composition called 'My Greatest Adventure', but not mentioning that forbidden trip to London or all the trouble she had caused, which certainly had been the greatest adventure in her young life. Any mention of that was strictly forbidden and never referred to; one really might have thought it had never happened and, in time, she began to wonder if it had.

So her greatest adventure was something she had made up, though she had once heard a story like it. It was an innocuous story about a cow caught in a ditch and how she had helped to rescue it. She had made herself the heroine of this adventure, as she did in other things she wrote. She thought she had fantasized a lot in her life, when she had lived in the lodge, about having a father of her own, a nice home, and both of these things had happened; so her conclusion was that in life, if you had great expectations, they often came true.

Harold's car was in the drive and Jenny ran up to the front door, thrilled with the idea of seeing him again, though they had only parted that morning.

Harold greeted her in the hall, took her satchel from her and enquired about her day. He seemed unusually gentle and solicitous. True to his word to Addie, he had indeed become very fond of his stepdaughter, she was so attractive and intellectually bright. He was proud of her and what, with his help, she had managed to achieve in a comparatively short time.

'I got ten out of ten for my composition.' Jenny tugged it out of her satchel and handed it to him. 'Oh, and Miss Barnes says there is a school party in the summer to France.' She looked at him winsomely. 'I wondered if I might go? Oh, and Sylvia has asked me to tea tomorrow. Is that all right? Oh, and . . .' She stopped abruptly and took a deep breath.

'Not so fast. Not so fast.' Harold put a finger to his lips. 'Please lower your voice; Mummy is lying down.' As he opened the door to the lounge, to her surprise Jenny saw her mother with her feet up on the sofa, looking rather pale.

'Is Mummy not well?' Jenny asked anxiously, but Harold, instead of looking concerned, only smiled.

'There is nothing to worry about, dear. You run upstairs and change and I'll read your compositiom while you're gone. When you come down, we'll all have tea.' He gave her a mysterious smile. 'We've got something rather exciting to tell you.'

Jenny continued to look anxiously at Addie, who merely smiled, waved and blew her a kiss. 'Run along, dear; we'll see you in a minute. It's nothing at all to worry about.' But she lay back and closed her eyes as if she were very tired, while Harold stuck his pipe into his mouth after ringing for tea and sat down with Jenny's composition on his knee.

103

Jenny ran upstairs into her dear little room, where she felt so happy and contented. She had her school books, pencils and rubber on the table where she dutifully did her homework every night supervised by Harold. She took off her navy school uniform and put on a jumper and skirt, ran a comb through her hair and went rushing down the stairs, nearly colliding with Felicity, who was taking a laden tray into the lounge. Jenny politely held the door open for her and skipped in after her.

As usual, there were cake and scones – milk for Arthur, if he was there, which today he wasn't. Sometimes Jenny had milk too, but today she had tea and settled down to a large piece of cake, while Addie threw aside the rug that had been covering her and sat up.

'Feeling better, dear?' Harold enquired solicitously.

'Much better.' Addie gave a weak smile. 'I'd love a cup of tea.'

'A piece of cake, my dear?'

Addie grimaced. 'Just tea, thank you, Harold.'

'What exciting thing have you to tell me?' Jenny asked impatiently. 'Are we going on holiday?'

'Well, not this year, you see . . .' Harold looked solicitously across at Addie. 'Mummy is going to have a baby and although it is not due until the autumn, we thought . . .'

'A *baby*!' Jenny gasped, interrupting him and nearly choking on her cake. '*Mummy* is going to have a *baby*? Another?'

'Well' – Addie looked confused – 'is it such a surprise?'

'Yes, it is a surprise. I thought you were over that sort of thing. We are all so happy together, why do we need a baby?'

While Harold and Addie stared at each other in shock, because Jenny's reaction was so unexpected, Jenny herself felt close to tears, she didn't know why. Well, yes, in fact she did. She looked across at Harold and saw the hurt in his eyes. She wondered if he knew how much she loved him and how she wanted to be the one he loved best and not to have a horrible, loathsome little creature arrive, who, as it would be his own flesh and blood, was sure to come between them and ruin their beautiful, special relationship for ever.

Eight

May 1933

'Do have one of these delicious little cakes, Mrs Hallam?'
Maisie shook her head, smiling politely.

'How restrained of you,' Mrs Walmer-Foster said, her
plump, bejewelled hand poised over the plate as if wishing
she could be so disciplined too; but she couldn't, and with a
guilty, self-deprecating little smile she selected one with lots
of icing and a red cherry on top and popped it into her
mouth.

The gathering of the officers' wives had been called a few
weeks after Ed's ship had put to sea. After all, there had been
no urgency. Sailors' wives were not supposed to pine, but to
get on with their lives, as their men got on with theirs. Stiff
upper lips were the order of the day: no tears, no recrimina-
tion, never mind how many children you were left to cope
with on your own – maybe with another one on the way – or
however little money you had to spend.

Most of the wives lived in naval quarters, but Maisie was
one of the few who did not. She had not wanted to and nor
had Ed. Having so little in common with his fellow officers,
Ed didn't see why he should have to socialize with them as
well. He didn't belong to their clubs or share most of their
pastimes, though he did like a game of rugby or cricket in
season.

Accordingly, he and Maisie led their own lives and when he
left she scarcely knew any of the wives, except Mrs Walmer-

Foster who, with her husband, the Ship's Captain, had entertained them to dinner just before the ship had sailed.

Doubtless owing to her fondness for fairy cakes, Mrs Walmer-Foster was an ample lady, in her mid-forties, but most of the wives were younger.

Maisie had been late getting to the tea party and she was aware of all eyes swivelling towards her as she entered the room and stood uncertainly for a moment, looking around her. She did, indeed, feel very nervous – had taken a long time with her make-up and deciding what she should wear. She'd selected a red-silk dress with a white-linen three-quarter-length coat over it and very high-heeled white shoes. The dress was a simple shirt style with a deeply pleated skirt, which was innocent enough; but the belt, tightly fastened, accentuated her slim waist and full bust. In fact, the buttons strained to fasten across it. She wore her gleaming silvery-blonde hair shoulder length and, as usual, was heavily made up with mascara, eye-shadow and a slash of scarlet lipstick to emphasize her full, sensual mouth.

Maisie realized immediately that, judging by the glances that greeted her, some considered her overdressed, and by the standards of most of the ladies present she was. There were frosty, rather than friendly smiles as each of the women – there were ten in all – was introduced. It was quite bewildering; she would never remember all the names: Mary, Gwen, Priscilla – there were two Priscillas – as well as a Pat, Frances, Sarah, Henrietta, and all of them looked identical in cotton dresses, not dissimilar in style to her own. But her flamboyant, vibrant red stood out amidst a sea of nondescript colours: white, beige, pale blue or pale pink, some patterned, some floral, some not, but all making their wearers seem genteel, conventional, smug.

As it was a coolish spring day, some wore cardigans, flat shoes or sandals. Hairstyles were crimped in neat permanent waves or worn straight and secured by a hairgrip. Some

107

looked young for officers' wives, as though they were not long out of the schoolroom. Some wore no make-up at all and others very little. However, one or two, slightly older, were elegant and smartly dressed. The Chief Engineer's wife and the wife of the Ship's Doctor – Mavis Pratt and Henrietta Marsden – had a dash of spirit to them and they both greeted her with more relaxed, friendly smiles.

Conversation to start with was stilted, as Maisie sat down uneasily, accepting a cup of tea but declining Mrs Walmer-Foster's offer of sandwiches or a cake.

There was no talk of the men who had gone – her man, for whom she ached – but a lot about children, recipes and also a great deal about pets: horse and cat stories, and so on.

'Have you children?' Mrs Marsden, the doctor's wife, asked in a friendly fashion. Maisie shook her head. 'Not yet. We'd like to eventually when Ed –' she corrected herself – 'my husband returns.'

'My husband speaks very well of yours,' Mrs Walmer-Foster (Henrietta) added kindly. 'He says he is a great asset to the ship's crew.'

Maisie brightened immediately. 'Oh yes, he will be. He is very clever.'

'Was he at Dartmouth?' one of the Priscillas enquired.

'He was at Durham University.' Maisie giggled nervously. 'He was going to enter the ministry – you know, to be a priest – and then changed his mind.'

'What made him change his mind?' Mavis Pratt enquired.

'He lost his faith in God. As good a reason as any.'

Sarah Fletcher, who was a devout churchgoer, pursed her lips. 'How did that happen?'

'Well, of course, I didn't know Ed then, but he told me that he was seriously ill and he felt that his creator didn't care about him, so he decided to be an engineer and then he joined the Navy.'

The women absorbed this information, sipping their tea

thoughtfully. One of them – Maisie couldn't take in all the names, but thought it was Gwen – eventually got up and said she must go: she had to attend a cookery class.

'Oh,' Maisie said. 'I'd love to learn to cook properly. It was something my husband suggested. He gets ever so tired of bangers and mash.'

'I could let you have the details.' Gwen sounded reluctant, but added, 'I've got them in my bag, which I left in the hall. I'll just pop out and get them.' She looked at Mrs Walmer-Foster and said in a whisper, 'Where is the little girls' room?' Their hostess led the way out of the lounge followed by Gwen and Maisie, who waited in the hall while the other two disappeared upstairs. The door to the sitting room remained partly open and from the other side came a buzz of voices.

'That accent –' Maisie heard someone say, 'so common. Where on earth does she come from?'

'I wonder what her husband's like? I'm amazed they allow people like that to be officers.'

Yet a third piped up, 'I'm afraid the standards in the Navy are slipping. They only used to take men from public schools; now it appears anyone will do. My husband will be horrified.'

Maisie's cheeks flamed and she turned abruptly to the front door, anxious to make an exit, when Henrietta came bustling down the stairs.

'She won't be a minute, dear.' She looked enquiringly at Maisie. 'Would you like to go after her?'

'No, thank you,' Maisie said coldly. 'I really think I'd better be off.'

'Nonsense,' her hostess said brusquely, taking her arm; 'you've hardly been here any time at all.'

At that moment Gwen came down the stairs and, after rummaging in her handbag, produced a card, which she handed to Maisie. 'I think you'll find the details here. It's run by a woman from her home. If you give her a call, mention my name . . .'

'Thank you.' Maisie dropped the card into her handbag and, propelled by her hostess, found herself back in the lounge, where the conversation had now turned to that all-important subject of babies.

Maisie stood trying to identify the ones who had criticized her, but as well as looking alike they all seemed to share those polished vowels of the upper-middle class. None of them so much as glanced again at her. In the hall she heard Henrietta saying goodbye to Gwen and then she returned to the lounge crying out, 'Anyone for more tea?' She looked around. 'Or would anyone prefer a drink?' Then she glanced at the clock and added doubtfully, 'The sun is not *quite* over the yard-arm.'

'Whisky would be very nice.' Maisie sat down and, taking a cigarette packet from her handbag, passed it around, saying in an exaggerated cockney accent, 'Anyone like a fag?'

Almost in unison they all shook their heads. They also declined a drink, so Mrs Walmer-Foster said in a slightly strained tone of voice, 'Oh, it's just me and Maisie then.'

She went across to the drinks table, took the stopper out of the whisky decanter and poured a shot into each of two glasses, one of which she handed to Maisie.

'Cheers,' she said, raising her glass.

'Cheers,' Maisie replied; 'here's mud in your eye, Henrietta.'

There followed an uneasy silence until the one called Pat, as if in an effort to make conversation, asked innocently, 'Did you work before you were married, Maisie?'

'I was a dancer.' Maisie, still boiling with anger, flicked ash into a nearby ashtray.

'At the Wells?' Another looked interested.

'A nightclub in Soho.' Maisie took a big gulp from her glass. 'I was a stripper.'

'A . . .' Mrs Walmer-Foster, her own glass halfway to her lips, looked as though she couldn't believe her ears.

Maisie, now on a high, assumed her best cockney accent again. 'Stripper. You know – took my clothes off. You must have heard of strippers. I'm sure your husbands, sainted creatures that you think they are, know all about them when they're on leave or abroad. That's how I met my husband; he was there with a group of naval friends having a good night out. Shouldn't wonder if some of your husbands weren't with him.' Maisie gave a knowing wink and looked round with satisfaction as the faces of the people around her registered the various degrees of consternation she had caused. The silence around her was electric.

'Yes, a stripper,' she continued, warming to her task, emboldened a little now by a second measure of whisky that a nervous hostess had quietly tipped into her glass, and by the glazed expressions on the faces of her companions. 'I expect most of you were nicely brought up – boarding schools and the like; but I grew up in the East End of London and there wasn't much choice for a girl, especially if she was nice-looking as I was, other than becoming a dancer or going on the streets. Well' – she paused and looked into the eyes of those surrounding her – 'which would *you* choose?'

One of the Priscillas got up. 'I really must go,' she said. 'I didn't realize it was so late.'

'Me too.' Mavis hopped up, looking at her watch.

'Oh, and me.'

There were perfunctory nods in Maisie's direction, followed by a stampede for the door.

Soon the room was empty except for Maisie, left staring into her by now empty glass. She rose and helped herself to another measure, making sure it was a generous one.

She lit a cigarette and looked round the empty room, at the plates and cups scattered about on the small occasional tables. Mrs Walmer-Foster had a nice house; almost certainly it was paid for. With a name like Henrietta she was sure to have come from a good family and doubtless the Captain had too.

There was a buzz of voices in the hall as the women collected their things and, no doubt, made faces in the direction of the room where she sat by herself, an outcast. She had definitely blown it. She began to feel uncomfortable and, as she heard the front door finally close, Mrs Walmer-Foster came slowly into the room, looking exhausted and staring at Maisie.

'Did you have to do that?' she asked. 'I have never known a crowd of women leave so quickly; people didn't know where to put their faces.'

Maisie thought of Ed, looking so smart in his naval officer's uniform. He was so proud and she was proud of him. She recalled the night they had been asked to dinner by the Walmer-Fosters. She had been on her best behaviour and the Captain and his wife had been very nice to her. She knew she didn't talk posh, and she could exaggerate the cockney when she chose, but that night, because of Ed, she had done her very best to modulate her vowels.

She had worn a plain black dinner dress, and Ed told her she looked lovely and was a credit to him. It had seemed such a promising start to his new career.

That night they'd made love beautifully.

'I apologize,' Maisie said at last contritely; 'I embarrassed you. You see, I thought they looked so smug and I'd heard them talking about me when I was in the hall. They said I was common.'

'I'm sorry about that.' Mrs Walmer-Foster's tone was still cold. 'But what you did just now in my home was still unpardonable. If they called you common – and it was very wrong – rather than descend to their level you should have shown you were not. I liked you, and my husband did. We thought nothing of the sort. I'm sure you're much smarter than they are. On the whole they are ordinary women and you might despise them. They are not very smart, not very pretty, rather conventional, but there was no need to go out of your way, as you obviously did, to shock and upset them; and you completely ruined my tea party, but that's by the by. It's not really the point. Every one of those women is married to a colleague of your husband. They write letters; they will tell them about today.

'Whatever smug sense of satisfaction you might feel at getting your own back, it's the harm you've done to your husband and his standing among his colleagues, his future in the Service, that really bothers me. Did you ever think of that?'

As Maisie, eyes on the ground, remained silent, Mrs Walmer-Foster became increasingly heated. 'To imply that these women's husbands went to that sort of place is disgraceful.'

Maisie then raised her head, her fine eyes flashing. 'Well, they do!'

'I'm sure my husband doesn't.'

'Don't be so sure,' Maisie retorted. 'To me he seemed a human being, just like the rest.'

Maisie sat in the corner of the third-class compartment, watching the countryside flash by as the train roared along on its way to London. She was taking flight, leaving a place where she knew she didn't belong – never had belonged. She had never been happy as the wife of a naval officer, however much she loved Ed. She was a Londoner and her life was in London, above all on the stage. The stripping was a sideline, unimportant except to snobbish little prudes like the naval wives. She was a good dancer and she loved the excitement and glitter of show business.

She might even have been a ballet dancer if she'd set her mind to it, except that she had grown far too tall. But that was one aspect of her life; the other was that, as a wife, she'd miserably failed her husband – let him down badly.

Why had she behaved like a street urchin? As the Captain's wife had said, it was the harm she'd done Ed that mattered. There he would be, thousands of miles away, with a mess full of condescending officers, who would have had a full report from their wives about the disastrous tea party with his wife, who was not only common, but a stripper!

The idea produced a faint smile on Maisie's lips, but it was not really at all amusing, so why had she done it? Why had she not told the ladies present, all those horrible snobs, that her sister-in-law was married to a lord? That she, herself, was at home in a castle, knew the ropes and was quite capable of hobnobbing with the aristocracy and behaving herself? Was it her background that had let her down? Hubert Ryland would undoubtedly have called it her lack of breeding, the facts that her mother had run a market stall in Leather Lane, her father was unknown and she hadn't been brought up properly. In short, she was not a lady and never would be, whereas Ed seemed to have made the transition from working-class lad to naval officer in the Senior Service quite successfully.

Maisie had had no regrets when she had shut the door on the Plymouth house, not knowing whether or not she would ever return. She would go on paying the rent – well, Ed had taken care of that – but apart from that she would be glad to turn her back on the very boring life of a housewife, producing nice meals, or trying to produce them; waiting aimlessly for her man to come home and eat them; doing housework, which she hated, and, above all, attending more tea parties like the one at Mrs Walmer-Foster's or being patronized by people like her.

The best thing about her marriage had been the sex and now that comfort was denied her, possibly for a whole year. The tea party in a way had been a blessing, by offering release. That had decided her. There was no point in even trying to be nice to these people; you couldn't mix with them. They were not her sort and she was certainly not theirs.

Maisie wearily leaned her head back against the seat and tried to imagine the sort of life that lay ahead of her now.

June 1933

The news from abroad was very grave. Hitler had banned all opposition parties. German Jews and liberals feared for their lives and reports of Nazi excesses were coming into the newsroom all the time. In many ways Alan wished he had never left Rome, where he had been at the centre of events. Sitting at his desk all day, he felt he was only on the fringe of the place where everything was happening.

Alan Walker, Assistant Editor of the *South London Gazette* and influential man of affairs, sat back in his chair and gazed at the huge, gleaming cross on the top of the dome of St Paul's Cathedral, a London landmark that was just discernible above the rooftops of Farringdon Street. He got up and restlessly began to pace up and down.

He missed Peg. He always would miss Peg. He thought of her night and day; her face haunted him; but he had stopped telephoning her home. It was demeaning, and it was obvious that she didn't wish to see him or speak to him, either because she hadn't forgiven him for taking her to the Mosley meeting or, more probably, because she was determined to make her marriage and her life with Hubert Ryland work. There was something single-minded about Peg and she would see it that way. Only a woman with a well-developed streak of ruthlessness would have treated him the way she had over their engagement, or got as far as she had in Fleet Street. Then why did he love her and remain obsessed with her? There was no explanation for this folly.

His secretary had once told him that a woman had rung, but had left no name. Instinct told him it must have been Peg. Violet rang him a lot and she always left her name and usually a message. Violet Ryland had returned to England

115

soon after the disastrous Mosley meeting and had taken up residence at the family home in South Audley Street. Alan spent most of his nights there.

Violet was an attractive, highly sexed woman and they got on well in bed, one thing that he and Peg never had – never had the chance, really. The one single occasion had been a disaster. She'd been too young and he too inexperienced.

He didn't love Violet, but she was a woman of the world who was witty, amusing, cultured, abrasive at times, but also charming and a great lover of the arts. She carried a torch for him in the way Peg never had. He knew that Peg had never loved him, but during the days they'd spent together in February he had begun to wonder if she was beginning to. Just a little more time and maybe . . . crash! They'd gone to that fateful meeting.

It was, he knew, rather despicable to love one woman and make love with another, but he was a man with a man's needs and instincts and he never tried to pretend with Violet; he didn't need to.

The telephone rang and he crossed the room to pick it up, always hopeful that, at last, it might be . . .

It was Violet.

'Don't forget, darling, we're dining tonight at the Beauchamps.'

'I've remembered,' he said, flicking over the pages of his diary.

'Will you be picking me up?'

'Of course.'

'About eight, or come earlier if you like for a drink?'

'See you then.'

'Goodbye, darling.'

'Goodbye.'

Tessa Beauchamp was a childhood friend of Violet. She too was an honourable and her husband, Charles, was a captain of industry, head of an old family firm. They had a house in Eaton Place and there were six other couples for dinner.

It was the sort of evening Alan enjoyed: intelligent, well-informed people discussing, for the most part, serious issues. When the ladies left the dinner table after dessert, the men lit cigars, passed round the port and got down to a discussion of business. They were all very worried about Hitler and the effect of the German revival on the European economy; but in the United States President Roosevelt had signed the National Industry Recovery Act, known as the New Deal, in an effort to beat the Depression.

The world economic conference currently being held in London had drawn up a plan to stabilize currencies, and these subjects provoked much discussion among men of affairs, but with differing points of view.

Besides himself and Charles Beauchamp there were present around the table, drinking excellent port and smoking fine Havana cigars, a Harley Street specialist, two lawyers and the son of a duke, who was a man of independent means.

A well-heeled bunch, Alan thought, far removed in every way from the inequalities of the world they were dissecting. He remembered his once strongly held socialist convictions and felt rather ashamed of himself.

'I am a man,' he told Violet on the way home, 'who has betrayed the working classes.'

'Don't be so silly, darling,' Violet said dismissively; 'you don't want everyone to be poor.'

She had a point. They stopped outside the South Audley Street house.

'Coming in for a nightcap, sweetie?' This was an invitation to stay the night, a little bit of play-acting that amused them both.

Alan smiled and pulled on the handbrake, got out of the car and held the door open for Violet.

Then he locked the doors and followed her into the house.

It was every bit as splendid as the one in which they'd dined. It was late and the staff had all gone to bed, but lights had been left on in the hall and in the drawing room, where there were also a plate of sandwiches and decanters of red wine and whisky. This was always the case when they had been out, in the event that they should feel peckish even when they had eaten so well.

Alan thought of the starving masses in Europe and the destitute he would see even now in London if he walked in the streets around Whitechapel or the Old Kent Road.

'Penny for your thoughts, darling?' Violet said teasingly, head on one side. 'Wine or whisky?'

'I think a small whisky.' Alan undid his black tie and threw it on to a chair.

'A sandwich?'

'No, thank you. I was thinking of the gap between the people who were round that table this evening and the starving masses, victims of the war, the current worldwide depression. We don't know how lucky we are, Violet.'

'No, we don't.' Violet, refusing to be drawn – Alan was such a bore about the working classes and she avoided political discussion when she could – passed him a glass of whisky, put a couple of sandwiches on a plate and, with a glass of wine for herself in her other hand, sat down beside him.

'Did you know, by the way, that Peg was expecting another baby?'

'No, I didn't.' Alan experienced a sudden shock, as if someone had hit him right in the middle of his solar plexus.

'Apparently they want four – makes a nice round number, I suppose. Have you seen her recently?' Violet looked at him innocently.

Alan, trying to maintain an appearance of nonchalance, shook his head. 'Not since that Mosley business; I think Hubert was none to happy about it.'

'Hubert was furious! I think he hates you, actually.'

'Oh, dear.' Alan stroked his chin, a habit of his when caught off his guard or embarrassed. 'There is no need at all for that.'

'But do you love Peg? Still?' Violet studied his face carefully.

Aware of her scrutiny Alan slowly sipped his whisky. 'Must we discuss this, Violet?' he said at last.

'Not really.' She gave a tight smile, seemed about to say something, but changed her mind. She quickly finished her wine and jumped up. 'Shall we go to bed, darling?'

He followed her out, turning off the lights, as usual, as they went.

In her bedroom Violet's night things had been laid out for her by the maid and, more discreetly, Alan's pyjamas were in the dressing room together with slippers and a dressing gown. His shaving things were there and a change of clothes, suits in the wardrobe, underwear neatly folded in various drawers. It was almost as though he had two homes with a fresh change of clothing in each. In many ways it was a comfortable life, Alan thought, taking off his trousers and folding them in the trouser press while next door Violet went to the bathroom. He sat down and began to pull off his socks, then paused and looked about him. He was really very well set up here; he had everything he wanted, needed or could ever need, but he was in no way a kept man. He was financially independent, a careful man who over the years had saved much of his salary, which he had invested wisely.

Tonight, however, he had looked at Violet across the dinner table and thought that she really was a very handsome woman: tall, slim, blonde and elegant, carefully made up and, as always, beautifully dressed. At nearly forty years of age she was an imposing woman, with a slightly lined face and an air of world-weariness that was not unattractive. It had a certain allure for someone who had been around as much, and had travelled as widely, as Alan, who was seven years her junior.

There was a tap on the door and Violet called out, 'What's taking you so long, darling?' She popped her head round and saw Alan sitting in his shirt and underpants in the act of taking off his socks.

'Just thinking,' he said, getting to his feet; 'shan't be a minute.'

Violet withdrew and he finished undressing, put on his pyjamas and robe and went back to the bedroom.

Violet was sitting on the bed smoking a cigarette.

'Aren't you sleepy?' Alan asked, looking at the clock. 'It's nearly one.'

Violet stubbed out her cigarette, seemed agitated and, nervously rubbing her hands together, looked up at him.

'Alan, darling, there's something I want to ask you. I . . .' She hesitated. 'I was going to bring it up downstairs, but somehow I lacked the nerve – still do.' She laughed shakily.

Alan sat down by her side. 'Ask away,' he said encouragingly.

'Sure you're not too tired? Perhaps it will wait until morning.'

'It's entirely up to you.' Alan yawned. 'I am a little tired, but if there is something on your mind, you'd better get rid of it.'

'Alan, I wanted to ask you to marry me.' Violet paused as a deep flush suffused her face. 'I know you don't love me and it's a cheek anyway – the man should do the asking – but I don't suppose you ever will: it has never crossed your mind.' She paused again, perhaps in the hope that Alan would help her out, but he remained silent.

'I know you love Peg,' Violet went on. 'You always have, but you are never ever going to get her because she would never leave her family. You must realize that, now that she's going to have another baby. And you and I do seem to get on. Don't we?'

'Oh, yes.' Alan at last found his tongue.

'It's not just my imagination, is it, Alan?'

'Oh no,' he reassured her. 'We do get on and I'm—'

Violet held up a hand. 'Don't say it: that you're very fond of me.'

'But I am, honestly.'

'You see, I would very much like children. I'm nearly forty and time is passing me by. I feel I do love you or, at least, I like you very much.'

'And I like you.' Alan, perhaps moved by her candour, took her hand and kissed it.

'I'd like to *be* married as well.' There was no stopping Violet's confessorial mood now. 'You know – be a married woman; but I shan't make too many demands on you, I promise. Well . . .' She looked at him nervously, appealingly. 'Will you think about it, Alan? I don't expect you to make up your mind now, but I had to speak to you and if you don't actually *want* to get married, if you think it's false and hypocritical, well then . . .' – she gave a wan smile – '. . . we can go on as we are. You see, I'd rather have you this way than not at all. But if we *did* get married, I think . . . well I think we'd make a very good pair.'

There followed a long silence while Alan sat on the side of the bed next to the woman who had just proposed marriage to him, thoughtfully stroking his chin.

'Perhaps we would,' he said at last.

'Is that "yes" then, Alan?' Violet spoke breathlessly.

'I suppose it is,' he mused as if he were conducting some sort of internal dialogue; 'in a way, yes, it is.'

Nine

Jenny pushed open the door of the lounge and looked reproachfully at her stepfather, sitting in his chair reading the paper while her mother lay, as usual, on the sofa.

'I thought you were coming to help me with my composition?' she demanded, referring to her holiday work. 'I've been waiting ages.'

Harold put down his paper and looked at her wearily. 'Jenny, it is high time you learned to work on your own. I can't be at your beck and call all the time, you know. Your mother needs me much more.'

'Oh Harold, really, I don't mind.' Addie attempted to rise, but her husband got up quickly and gently pushed her back.

'Now, Addie, you know you have to rest and I am here to see you do. That child is fit and well, which you are not, and she is quite capable of looking after herself.'

Fit and well! In a burst of temper Jenny slammed the door and ran upstairs, hurling herself on to the bed in a torrent of weeping.

Downstairs, Addie looked at her husband with concern. 'Really, dear, I think you should go and help her. I am perfectly all right lying here quietly.'

'But my dear, Jenny does need to learn independence. She is fifteen; it's in her own interests. I feel I have indulged her too much in an effort to win her affection.'

'Which you have undoubtedly succeeded in doing, Harold.'

122

Addie looked at him fondly. 'She loves you more than she loves me.'

'Nonsense!' Harold resumed his seat and shook out his paper.

'It's true,' Addie insisted, 'and I'm very happy about it. This is the girl who, only a year ago, was so out of control we didn't know what to do with her. You have made a wonderful difference to Jenny. She respects and admires you and I am so grateful to you.'

'And I'm grateful to you, Addie.' Harold's tone was emotional. 'I am grateful to you for forgiving me for having been so uncaring and unthinking all those years ago. What a lot of time we lost.'

Addie nodded: it was true. In the last few months Harold had seemed to grow more affectionate every day, more like the man she'd married, until she'd lost him at the end of their honeymoon when he'd discovered the truth about Jenny. He had been quite unforgiving about that.

Harold crossed the room and sat by her side, his hand resting lightly on her stomach. 'Now you are giving me something I have always wanted: a child of my own; but I will not love Jenny or little Arthur any the less.'

'Thank you, Harold.' Addie raised her face to be kissed. 'Now, why don't you go up and help Jenny? She so likes being with you.'

Harold went upstairs and, knocking on Jenny's door, received no answer. He pushed it open and found her still lying on her bed. She was no longer crying, but her face was heavily tear-stained.

'Jenny, Jenny,' he said, patting her shoulder. 'This is a very silly way to behave.'

'Tisn't,' Jenny said. 'You do nothing but fuss about Mummy all day and don't care at all about me, or Arthur.'

'Of course I care about you both' – he continued to pat her shoulder – 'but Arthur is in the care of his nursemaid and, as

I said, you are old enough to look after yourself, be with your friends more, prepare yourself for the new term, as you are so diligently doing.' He looked with approval at the open exercise book on her desk. 'May I see?'

'If you like,' Jenny said grudgingly.

'I'll take it away with me.' Harold crossed to the desk, closed the book and tucked it under his arm. 'Why don't you go and see one of your schoolfriends? How about Sylvia?'

'Couldn't *we* go for a walk?' Jenny begged, getting sulkily to her feet. 'You promised to identify some more of the wild flowers in the wood for me.'

Harold glanced at his watch. 'Not now. While I think it is very commendable for you to prefer a botanical excursion to play, I am expecting the doctor to see Mummy and I want to talk to him. We may go later on.'

'What *exactly* is wrong with Mummy?' Jenny enquired. 'She was never ill when she was expecting Arthur.'

'She has high blood pressure and this is very dangerous, especially if it is not checked as the pregnancy advances; that is why she lies down such a lot. The last thing we want to do is lose our precious baby.'

Precious baby! As Harold left the room Jenny flung herself down on the bed again. Precious baby indeed!

'I hate that baby,' Jenny confided to her friend Sylvia, 'and it is not even born. You know the whole thing makes me feel that I'd really like to run away again.'

'*Again?*' Sylvia exclaimed, startled.

'Oh, yes, I've done it before.'

Jenny had followed up Harold's suggestion and gone to see her friend Sylvia, and the two girls sat in the garden, heads close together, while Mrs Birch, wearing a straw hat and green apron, gardened in the background. Every now and then she would look across at the two girls, heads together, sharing secrets, and she couldn't help wondering what those secrets were. Jenny made her feel uncomfortable, mainly because she seemed in every way superior to Sylvia and was clearly the dominant partner in this schoolgirl relationship, which, to her conventional way of thinking, was not quite normal.

Even though Mrs Birch was a good hundred yards away, Jenny, aware of her scrutiny, lowered her voice. 'I ran away to London and that's why we came down here. I was brought back by a policeman,' she concluded with relish.

'How long were you away?'

'A week.'

'London!' Sylvia exclaimed, clearly impressed. 'But how did you know where to go?'

'I met someone at my brother Ed's wedding who thought I was much older than I was and said he'd like to see me again.'

Sylvia looked even more impressed and Jenny gave a self-conscious giggle, fully aware of the effect she was making. 'He worked at a nightclub and I got on a train and went to see him. I'm not supposed to tell; Daddy would be furious if he knew. Anyway, that made Mummy, who had lived apart from Daddy for years, decide to come home and I'm very glad she did. The year has been wonderful . . . until now. I didn't really expect the baby to happen. You see' – she leaned forward confidentially – 'I am really the daughter of a lord.'

It was all too much for Sylvia, who began to think Jenny was making it up. It was not for nothing that she always came top of the class in English composition. 'Then why do you call Mr Smith Daddy?' Sylvia looked even more perplexed.

'Well, he is my stepfather; my real daddy was killed in the war. I only learned that last year and it made me so angry and unhappy that everyone had lied to me that I decided to run away.

'I was brought up by my grandmother, not knowing that Addie was my mother. You see – and you must *promise* not to tell anyone this – my mother and real father weren't married.'

125

Sylvia put her hand to her mouth, too shocked to say anything, and looked furtively towards her mother to be sure she couldn't hear. She certainly didn't need the warning Jenny gave her, because she was sure that if her parents knew all this they would forbid her to have anything to do with her best friend again.

At that point Mrs Birch did look up from her gardening, put a hand on her aching back and took off her gardening gloves.

'Time for tea, girls,' she called. 'What are you two so engrossed about?'

'Nothing,' Sylvia said, but her cheeks were pink and her eyes suspiciously bright as she hopped down from the wall on which they'd been sitting.

Jenny hopped down too, dusting her hands. 'I can't stay to tea, thank you, Mrs Birch,' she said politely. 'Daddy is going to take me into the woods to look for wild flowers.'

'I wish Sylvia would take an interest in wild flowers.' Mrs Birch looked reproachfully at her daughter. 'She seems to be interested in nothing.'

'Well, nothing is what we were talking about.' Jenny thought her rejoinder rather smart, but Mrs Birch flushed angrily and, without another word but making her displeasure clear, turned to go into the house, beckoning for Sylvia to follow her.

'I'm not sure that Jenny is a very good influence on you,' she said to her daughter a few moments later as she handed her a cup of tea. 'She can be cheeky and she is so secretive, which hitherto you have not been. For instance, I would very much like to know what was engrossing you so in the garden.'

'Mummy, it really was nothing,' Sylvia said ingratiatingly, helping herself to a piece of cake. 'In fact, I can't remember now what it was about,' and she turned on her mother a pair of innocent eyes.

Mrs Birch was not deceived, however. Jenny was too knowing, too smart for her much simpler daughter, who did not shine in class, was not particularly pretty – while Jenny was a stunner – and could be easily led, so that what shone out of her eyes was hero-worship of Jenny rather than an equal friendship.

Jenny ran all the way home, determined not to be late for the excursion, but when she arrived, Harold was closeted with the doctor. When at last they emerged, he was offhand, as though he had forgotten all about it, and said that it was too late to go to the woods, anyway, as it would soon be dark.

'But you promised,' Jenny said, stamping her foot.

'I promised, but it is too late,' Harold said firmly. 'However, you will be delighted to hear that the news about your mother is good: her blood pressure has stabilized and—'

'In that case there was no need for him to stay for so long and for you to disappoint me.' Rudely interrupting her stepfather, Jenny suddenly felt an explosion of rage at the complacent, even sanctimonious expression on his face. 'You don't care for me at all. You are *horrible* and I *hate* you! I wish we'd never come here.'

Harold's composure evaporated at once in the face of this onslaught, which, in his opinion, was quite unjustified. He shook his finger at her. 'And *you*, my girl, really are a horrible, rude, ungrateful and selfish person, caring nothing for your mother or the welfare of your unborn sibling. I believe the other day you were asked to look after Arthur while Betty had a headache, and refused. What happened? Your mother had to do it and the effort sapped her strength. Do you know what, Jenny? You say you wish you hadn't come here; sometimes – and I say this regretfully – I wish that too. You can be an angel, but at times you have a streak of the devil in you and I fear for your future, believe me, I do.'

Harold peremptorily turned his back on her and went into

127

the lounge, closing the door firmly in Jenny's face, another act of exclusion that hurt her.

Addie, who had been listening to the row from her usual place on the sofa, looked at him anxiously. 'What on earth was that all about?'

Harold shook his head, then mopped his brow with a large white handkerchief. 'No one is more devoted to Jenny than I am, Addie, but sadly I fear she's getting out of control again, just as she was with you last year. There's bad blood somewhere in Jenny.' He gave his wife a dark look. 'Oh, not from your side, dear, I'm quite sure of that. The aristocracy is notorious for its black sheep and I'm sure the Rylands have their fair share; some throwback to one of Jenny's ancestors.'

'But Harold, she adores you and I thought' – Addie's lower lip trembled – 'I thought you were very fond of her.'

'But I am.' Harold sighed and sat down, as though he carried a great weight. 'I have found this holiday rather difficult; I'll be honest with you. Jenny needs to be constantly entertained; if she is not, she flies into a rage or sulks. She doesn't care about her little brother. How will she be with our baby? She has a jealous disposition and a constant need to be noticed. Bright she may be, but who wants a clever woman?' He looked across at Addie, shaking his head. 'Most men I know want someone who is going to be a good wife and mother, not someone who is restless and dissatisfied, and always putting them in their place. No, I tell you, Addie, I fear for that young lady's future.'

He stooped and patted Addie's hand – Addie, who had become so obedient and docile since she had returned to him. 'Don't let this upset you, my dear. The doctor says that your blood pressure is nearly back to normal and all's well.'

'But I *am* upset.' Addie clutched at his hand. 'How can I not be?' She fell silent, not caring, or daring, to add that the

128

only reason she had come back to Harold was for the sake of her daughter.

Had that sacrifice been in vain?

Sylvia sat, white-faced, in front of her parents, staring at her father, who had just finished speaking. 'Boarding school,' she cried; 'you're sending me to a boarding school?'

'We think it's in your best interests,' her father said. 'Your school report was very bad and we do not think that Jenny Smith is at all a good influence on you.'

'But she *is* a good influence,' Sylvia insisted. 'She is the brightest girl in the class; everyone admires her.'

'Bright she might be, but none of it seems to be rubbing off on you. There is a side to Jenny we are not at all happy about; it has grown more noticeable during this holiday. Your mother says that every time she is here you slip away together, rather furtively, in her opinion, and start whispering. It does not seem to us particularly healthy.'

'But Jenny is my *best* friend,' Sylvia wailed, tears springing to her eyes.

'It is not only that,' Mrs Birch chipped in; 'nor are we happy about the family. There are all sorts of rumours, which need not concern you, but which make us think she might not be a suitable companion for you.'

'Well, her father is a *lord*,' Sylvia cried, beside herself. 'What do you think of that? Don't you think *that* makes her a suitable companion?'

Her parents exchanged glances. 'Jenny told you that, did she?'

'Yes.' Sylvia faltered, suddenly remembering her promise.

'Well then, I'm afraid she's also a liar, which makes her even less fit as a companion for our daughter. We happen to know that her family came from very humble circumstances; in fact they were in service and anything else is merely a pipe dream.'

Mrs Birch pursed her lips. 'Now, Sylvia, we are taking you to see the school that your father and I have in mind for you tomorrow. It is not too far away and we both feel *sure* you will be very happy there.'

'And for the time being,' Mr Birch added in a more kindly tone of voice, 'we would rather you kept away from Jenny. You have plenty of other friends we consider much more suitable companions for you, who do not tell lies or make things up and whose origins are quite beyond reproach.'

Sylvia stood furtively by the greenhouse at the back of the Smith house, trying to catch the eyes of Jenny who, in an effort to ingratiate herself once more with her father, was dutifully playing with her small brother and his nursemaid, Betty. She threw the ball and Arthur caught it or, more usually, missed it and burst into tears. It was a very tedious game and when Jenny at last caught sight of Sylvia, she tossed the ball to Arthur and ran over to her with an exclamation of relief.

'Whatever are you doing here?' she cried, throwing her arms around her. 'I thought it was forbidden?'

'It is.' Sylvia put a finger to her mouth. 'I'm not supposed to be here.' She looked towards the house. 'Can we talk somewhere? Is your mother in?'

'She's still in bed. The doctor says she must take as much rest as she can.'

Jenny took her into the house through the kitchen door and led the way to the lounge. Once inside, she quietly closed the door.

'Daddy's gone to school to prepare for the new term. I got your note,' she said, referring to the scribbled message Sylvia had sent her. 'What happened? Whatever is the matter?'

Sylvia, pale-faced, flopped into a chair. 'I'm to be banished, sent to boarding school. We went and looked at it yesterday. It is absolutely horrible, like a prison; even the uniform is a drab grey.' Sylvia reached out for her friend's hands and spoke with a breathless sense of urgency. 'Jenny, you know what you told me the other day about . . .' She paused, her voice hoarse. 'I absolutely *don't* want to go to that school. I hated it and well . . . I want to run away!'

Jenny's face assumed an expression of rapture and, hands still clasped, she swung their arms from side to side. 'Oh yes, *let's*,' she cried. 'How soon do you think we can get away?'

'Good Lord!' Hubert exclaimed, bringing the page of the paper he was reading closer as though he couldn't believe his eyes. 'Violet has got married.'

This news was exciting enough for Peg, who was knitting a matinée jacket for her new baby, to drop some stitches.

'*Violet* has got married? Without telling you?'

Hubert nodded, folded the paper and passed it across to Peg. 'To Alan Walker. Does that surprise you?'

Wordlessly Peg took the paper and read the announcement:

> Quietly in Rome on August 23, Mr Alan Walker to the Honourable Violet Ryland.

No 'son of', or 'daughter of', just a bald announcement.

'Well.' Peg handed the paper back to Hubert and, in her confusion, began clumsily to rescue her dropped stitches. 'I hope that will reassure you about Alan's intentions towards me.'

Hubert shook his head emphatically. 'He doesn't love Violet. He's after her money and position.'

Gritting her teeth, Peg carefully counted her stitches. Hubert was trying to provoke her and, in her condition, reacting to this provocation was something she tried hard to avoid.

'I wasn't aware that Violet had all that much money, and

anyway, Alan, I'm sure, has plenty tucked away; he was always careful. As for her position, I don't think he could care tuppence about it. I'm happy for him – happy for them both,' she finished, insincerely. Peg looked at her watch, folded away her knitting and got to her feet. 'I must go and see about dinner.'

Dinner was just an excuse. Peg didn't even go into the kitchen, but walked agitatedly out into the garden to be alone with her thoughts. She was conscious of a deep sense of loss, as though something terrible had happened; but what right had she had to expect that Alan would remain faithful to her when there was no question of a physical relationship between them and she had not only returned to her husband but also, soon after, become pregnant by him?

She smiled grimly to herself. It didn't need to be an act of love to make a baby.

Was it fair to expect Alan to remain a devoted swain for the rest of his life? She had not returned his calls; she had, after all, not written to him. She had been somehow paralysed by the whole experience; but looking at it from Alan's viewpoint she had behaved extremely badly.

But Violet Ryland, her sister-in-law! Did that make Alan some sort of relation after all, a brother-in-law by marriage, perhaps? Were they fated always to be thrown together? She was wandering down towards the lake when she heard a call from the castle and, looking round, saw Hubert frantically waving from a downstairs window.

'A call for you,' he cried, 'something very important.'

Peg hurried indoors to the study where she found Hubert in the act of replacing the receiver.

'It was Harold,' he said. 'He was in a hurry.' He paused for a moment and pointed to a chair. 'Do sit down, dear.'

Involuntarily Peg clutched her breast. 'Something's wrong with Addie?' She sank slowly into a chair while Hubert drew up another and sat facing her.

'Addie is all right, but Jenny's run away again. Addie's all right, but she has gone into premature labour because the news was such a shock. You see, Jenny took a friend with her and the mother has had hysterics and a doctor had to be called.'

'Oh my God.' Peg's expression was agonized as she looked at Hubert. 'What on earth can we do?' She made as if to get up. 'I must go to Addie.'

'Yes, of course. I'll ask Frank to drive you over. Harold was phoning from the hospital, where he says Addie is getting the best attention possible.' He looked at her earnestly. 'Peg, I know it's a terrible shock for you. I want to do all I can to help.'

'That's terribly kind of you, Hubert.' Peg looked at him gratefully, feeling guilty now for all the negative thoughts she'd harboured about him only a short while ago.

'Of course I do, Peg,' he said earnestly. 'Of course I want to do everything I can. I thought, as they seemed to think she must have gone to London, that I would go up and see what I can do. We do have a few clues so, hopefully, she won't be very hard to find.'

His expression suddenly took on an extraordinary tenderness as he leaned across and took her hand. 'After all, my dear, I'm your husband and your family is my family. Nothing changes that.'

Ten

The area round King's Cross station was one of the less salubrious areas of London. It was surrounded by a warren of tiny streets criss-crossing one another and filled with rather mean houses, most of which gave shelter to the flotsam and jetsam of humanity, many of whom had arrived on Britain's hospitable shores without money, nationality or any visible means of support. The area was also notorious not only for its grime and a sense of all-pervading hopelessness, but also for the many women who roamed its streets at night in search of clients, whom they either serviced up some dark alleyway or took back to one of the shabby houses, all of which looked the same.

After nearly a year Jenny had some difficulty recognizing not only the street but also the house she was seeking, and at one time she feared she had entered a maze from which she would be unable to escape. All the while Sylvia clung on to her arm, already regretting the rashness that had prompted this escapade and had landed her so far from home in a strange, alien place.

'This is the one,' Jenny said, having gone up and down the streets and stopped at last before a green door with the number 5 on it – a house that, although small, looked in better repair than the rest. 'I'm sure this is it.' She smiled encouragingly at Sylvia, but already she realized that she was going to be a liability. She did not have that spirit of adventure that Jenny had, that ability to take off for pastures

134

new, however insalubrious, or even dangerous, as this might prove to be.

As Sylvia started to snivel, Jenny knocked firmly on the door and waited. There was no reply. She knocked again and stood back, gazing up at the windows. Still no sign of life . . . Then she too was overcome by a sense of despair. If this was not Teresa's house, then she didn't know which one was. She would have to go to the Monkey Club and without doubt she would be bundled back home in no time if she so much as showed her face there.

Sylvia's snivels had swelled to a stream of tears and Jenny was feeling that the only thing to do would be to capitulate and return home, when the door opened a fraction and a bleary-eyed woman gazed out at them.

'Teresa!' Jenny exclaimed, opening wide her arms with joy. 'Thank goodness, it's you.'

Teresa looked at her as if unable to believe her eyes and, pulling her gown round her more firmly, opened the door wide.

'Is it *you*?' she queried, peering through a thick layer of caked mascara that had failed to wash off, even supposing she'd tried.

'Yes, me – Jenny,' Jenny exclaimed in a voice that was a mixture of relief and delight and, turning to Sylvia, 'this is my friend.'

'Then why is she crying?'

'She doesn't feel very well.' She tried to look beyond Teresa. 'Do you think we might come in?'

'Well . . .' Teresa appeared undecided, from which Jenny deduced that her appearance was not very welcome, which was hardly surprising, given the last time they had met. However, she was nothing if not resourceful and decided to throw herself on Teresa's mercy.

'Just for a while,' she wheedled, at which Sylvia, as if on cue, started to give vent to loud sobs.

135

'What on earth is the matter with the girl?' Teresa asked, looking at her more closely. 'She looks very young.'

'She's small for her age,' Jenny explained. 'She's the same age as me.'

'Which as we know is *not* eighteen,' Teresa said severely. 'Do your parents know you're here?'

'Yes . . .' Jenny looked at the weeping girl beside her. 'No.'

'Then go straight back home.' Teresa wrathfully pointed a quivering finger in the direction of the street. 'You know what happened last time you were here. Alfonso lost his job and that meant I lost mine. I want nothing more to do with you.' She was about to close the door when Jenny boldly stuck her foot against it.

'*Please*,' she begged, 'we won't stay long – just so that my friend can have a little rest. We *will* get in touch with our parents. Promise. Besides, we have a little money . . . plenty, really.'

Teresa's eyes brightened at the mention of money, but her expression remained doubtful. Then, after what seemed like an inner debate, she threw open the door and stood aside.

'Come in then, but only for a while.'

'Oh *thank* you, Teresa,' Jenny said gratefully and pushed Sylvia into the gloomy corridor with its brown-papered walls and torn linoleum on the floor. After the bright sunshine outside it was difficult to see where they were, but Teresa led the way to her sitting room with its overstuffed chairs, heavy ornate furniture and dusty flock wallpaper that had seen far better days. It was nearly noon and, from her appearance and apparel, it seemed as though they had woken Teresa up.

'I'll give you a drink and something to eat,' Teresa said, 'and then you must leave. I want nothing to do with you or your family. Because Alfonso lost his job, he was sent home, I was without a partner and have found it very difficult since to find work.' Her face sagged with resentment as she looked at Jenny. 'I don't know how you have the nerve to come back here.' Her glance then strayed to the horse-hair chair where Sylvia, exhausted, had rolled herself up into a ball and seemed to have drifted off to sleep. 'That child looks done in.'

'We didn't have any sleep,' Jenny confessed, 'or not much; a little on the station while we decided what to do.'

'And what made you decide to come to me?' Teresa demanded, her tone still querulous.

'Because you were a friend,' Jenny said unctuously. 'You were so nice to me and I'm really sorry for the trouble I caused. I didn't realize that you had had such a bad time or that Alfonso lost his job, which wasn't fair. Where is he now?'

Teresa shrugged her shoulders indifferently. 'God knows. I think he went back to Spain.' She then seemed to thaw a little – maybe the apology had mollified her – and got to her feet. 'I'll get you some coffee.'

After she'd gone, Jenny could hear preparations from the kitchen and was aware of a sense of relief. She thought progress was being made. It was neither her nor Sylvia's intention to frighten their parents to death, but to make a point. Last time conditions had improved as a result; maybe they would now. It was too much to hope that they would give the baby away, but at least her place in the family hierarchy would be established and Sylvia would surely not be sent to boarding school.

It seemed never to have occurred to her that the status quo might be altered for ever.

Feeling decidedly more cheerful, even optimistic, she went over to Sylvia and put her arms around her.

'We'll be all right,' she said brightly. 'This is an adventure.'

'This place is horrible,' Sylvia moaned. 'I want to go home.'

Jenny remained by the side of her friend and after a while rather felt that she wanted to go home too. Maybe they had made their point? The real adventure had been in the planning: making preparations, the various subterfuges they had

137

both employed and, in Sylvia's case this time, stealing a substantial amount of money from her father, who always, in the security of his home, left the door of his safe unlocked. Yes, the beginning of the adventure had gone well, but now the thrill had started to evaporate. It had been a difficult and at times hazardous train journey, followed by a taxi ride across London to an imprecise destination, which had aroused the suspicions of the cab driver, who had made some comments on their apparent youthfulness before driving off.

Jenny hugged Sylvia closer. 'You'll feel better when you've had something to eat,' she assured her as Teresa returned, bearing a tray from which wafted the welcome smell of coffee.

'We will just have coffee and bread,' Teresa said; 'I have to save the butter. But the bread is fresh and delicious. It will be enough to keep you from starving.'

Jenny viewed the frugal fare before her with some misgiving. The coffee was strong and black and very bitter. Sylvia took one sip and refused to drink any more, nor would she touch the bread, though it was indeed very fresh.

'I bought it myself on the way home this morning.' Teresa bit into her chunk hungrily.

'Oh, you do work then?' Jenny looked at her with interest. 'I thought you'd lost your job?'

'I do other work,' Teresa said mysteriously. 'None of your business.'

The bread was indeed better than nothing and, after a few sips, Jenny got used to the coffee. She glanced thoughtfully at Sylvia, sitting morosely beside her, and then at Teresa, whose circumstances indeed appeared to have deteriorated since they had last met. Her face looked less well cared for and her remarkable eyes were lustreless. There was no longer a sparkle there. She also appeared to have lost some of her voluptuousness and looked extremely tired.

Oh, Happy Day!

Jenny, feeling better for the nourishment, sat forward on her chair. 'Look, Teresa,' she said earnestly, 'we do have money. If we could stay here for a week, we could pay you. We have quite a *lot* of money, actually, as Sylvia's father is a very rich man.'

'How much?' Teresa asked immediately, and Jenny could tell she had aroused her interest.

'Enough,' she replied cautiously. 'Enough to pay you well for a week and maybe,' she added enticingly, 'get some nice things to eat.'

'I don't want to stay here,' Sylvia wailed from the depths of the chair. 'I want to go home.'

'Don't be silly.' Jenny looked at her disparagingly. 'This is a big adventure. We might never get another chance like this: to see the sights of London, live in the heart of a big city. Imagine what our friends will say!'

'They'd say we were stupid,' Sylvia protested.

Jenny glared at her. 'Would you rather be at that awful boarding school?'

Sylvia vigorously shook her head.

'She was about to be sent to boarding school,' Jenny explained to Teresa. 'Her parents thought I was a bad influence.'

'I'm not surprised,' Teresa grunted. 'I wonder any sensible mother lets her children anywhere near you.'

Teresa sat thoughtfully for a while and then appeared to come to some sort of decision: 'Now listen, I've been thinking. You can stay here for a *week*. But you must behave yourself and at night you must *not* leave your room. Do you understand?'

'Of course.' Jenny looked perplexed. 'But . . .'

'No "buts",' Teresa said firmly; '*that* is the condition. I sometimes have guests at night and it would not do for them to know that I took in lodgers.'

'Oh, but we're not lodgers,' Jenny exclaimed. 'We're

friends. However, of course we'll do as you say.' She tapped Sylvia on the side. 'Did you hear that, Sylvia? – that good news? We can stay here for a whole week; our adventure has only just begun.'

Hubert sat at a table at the back of the room at the Monkey Club, smoking a cigarette, a glass of whisky by his side, mesmerized by the row of beautiful, nubile women, their breasts bare, the rest of them very scantily covered, kicking their legs high in the air. In more senses than one he was mesmerized by a particular woman in the middle of the chorus line who, with her blonde hair gleaming in the bright stage lights, her taut, full breasts perfectly contoured, seemed more beautiful, more vivacious, more natural and infinitely more desirable, at least to his eyes, than the rest.

Maisie.

Finally the music stopped, the dance routine came to an end and the audience clapped and cheered. One or two called out bawdy remarks; then the girls exited and the lights went on.

Hubert blinked, and a woman slid into the chair beside him and gazed at him.

'Can I get you another whisky, dear?'

'Not yet,' Hubert said, 'thank you. Will you have a drink?'

'I only drink champagne.' The woman was small and dark-haired, with an attractive, but well-used face – not young. She had on some sort of evening dress with a seductively low neckline, and exuded cheap perfume.

Hubert beckoned to the waiter, ordered the champagne and offered the woman a cigarette.

'Have you been here before?' the woman asked, accepting one and studying him appraisingly. Hubert shook his head. 'In London on business, are you, or do you live here?'

'Business.' Hubert produced his lighter, lit her cigarette and another for himself as, almost by magic, in a remarkably short space of time, the waiter appeared with two glasses and a bottle of champagne on a tray. He deftly removed the cork without any fuss and filled both glasses.

Hubert stifled a gasp when the chit was handed to him, but paid up and added a tip. After all, this was business of a kind.

Hubert passed his companion her glass. 'What's your name?'

'Roxanne.'

'That's an unusual name.'

'What's yours?'

'Frank.'

Roxanne continued her appraisal. 'You don't *look* like a Frank.'

'Well I am.' Hubert gave a nervous smile and raised his glass.

'Cheers, Roxanne.'

'Cheers, Frank.'

'What time is the next show?' Hubert consulted his watch.

'Midnight.'

'And will the same dancers be dancing?'

'I expect so.' Roxanne pouted. 'Did you like one of them especially?'

'I liked them all,' Hubert replied diplomatically. 'Don't you dance?'

'I'm a hostess,' Roxanne answered in sultry tones. 'I'm here to take care of you.' She glanced at him flirtatiously. 'If you like, we can go to my place after the show.'

'That's very nice of you,' Hubert replied, 'but unfortunately I have another engagement.'

'Oh, really?' Roxanne's tone conveyed that she was unconvinced. 'Like that, is it?'

'I'm afraid so. In fact' – Hubert again looked at his watch and rose – 'I think I'd better go now.'

'But you haven't drunk your champagne,' Roxanne said indignantly. 'You haven't even *touched* it.'

'You have it,' Hubert said, pushing the bottle towards her; 'share it with a friend,' and he walked out of the front door of the club and down an alleyway at the side, where he found the back door, presumably the artists' entrance. He was right; he found himself immediately backstage amidst a mêlée of dancers in various stages of dress and undress, raised voices and some laughter.

As he stood looking around, a man with a cigarette dangling from the corner of his mouth approached him suspiciously. 'Looking for someone, was you?' he asked without removing his cigarette.

'Maisie,' Hubert replied. 'Is she still here?'

'I believe so,' the man said. ' 'Oo shall I say is arsking?'

'Frank,' Hubert said.

'Frank 'oo?'

'Just Frank.'

'Right you are.' The man trotted off and Hubert nervously lit another cigarette. After a few minutes he saw a familiar figure walking towards him, wearing a flowing white robe, her hair caught up in a white band as if she had just taken a bath. He was partly concealed by shadow and, as she stood in front of him peering into the dark, she looked as though she didn't recognize him.

'Was it you who were asking for me?' she enquired.

'Yes.' As Hubert emerged from the shadow, Maisie stepped back, her expression one of shock.

'But George the doorman said your name was Frank.'

'Well it is for this evening.'

'You didn't dare say you were Lord Ryland?' Maisie's tone was cold and unfriendly. 'Why are you here, Hubert?'

'Maisie, is there somewhere we can talk?' Hubert said urgently. 'There's something I want to ask you.'

'I have to do the midnight show.' Maisie's tone was still cool. 'What is it you want to talk about?'

'I'd rather tell you in a less public place than this. Something quite serious has happened and I need your help.'

Maisie suddenly looked terrified. 'Is it about Ed?'

Hubert shook his head. 'It's not about Ed; it's about Jenny. She's disappeared again and I thought you might be able to help.'

A couple of hours later they sat in an all-night café in Charlotte Street with a mixed clientele of workmen and diners in evening dress. Maisie was now wearing a short black dress with a string of pearls and was, as usual, perfectly made up. Her blonde hair cascaded on to her shoulders; her wedding ring and a large engagement ring sparkled on one of her long fingers. In short, impeccably groomed, she looked the perfect companion for a lord.

She was tucking with gusto into a steak, but Hubert, having little appetite, had a bowl of shrimps. Mindful of Roxanne, he had asked Maisie if she wanted champagne, a question which, from her expression, seemed to surprise, possibly even offend, her, and she said that she preferred red wine.

Clearly ravenous, Maisie applied herself to her food. Hubert wondered if she were short of money, if she had enough to eat and where she lived. Above all, why had she returned to London without telling her husband or any member of his family? He sat back, watching her, recalling her splendid figure in the near-nude, her magnificent breasts and narrow waist, her long legs. He thought Ed was a very fortunate man.

When she finished he offered her a cigarette and, as he lit it, she said, 'How did you know I was back here? I haven't told anyone, not even Ed.'

'I didn't. I had no idea. I remembered that this was where Jenny came last time and thought she might have come here again.'

Maisie shook her head. 'I haven't seen her. The man who took her in at the time – Alfonso – was deported back to

Spain. The police blamed him for taking her in and he was lucky not to be sent to prison.'

'The family just wanted her back, not to press charges; but wasn't there a woman involved as well? She was staying with a woman, his partner. Was she deported too?'

'No; her name was Teresa. I've no idea what happened to her, though someone told me she was on the job.'

'Pardon?' Hubert leaned forward.

'You know.' Maisie smiled suggestively. 'Surely you don't want me to spell it out?'

'I see. Have you any idea where she lives?'

Maisie shook her head. 'No, but I could find out. How long are you here for?'

'As long as it takes,' Hubert replied. 'I have to find Jenny.'

'Well if you stop by at the club tomorrow night, I'll tell you what I found out.'

It was a long time since Hubert had breakfasted with his sister at the London home in South Audley Street. Their paths in recent years had very seldom crossed. Now she had a husband and it seemed strange to see him at the breakfast table too – Alan Walker, a man he had supplanted in Peg's affections. Or had he?

Hubert had arrived in London late the previous evening after telephoning Violet to say he was coming. They had not seen each other since her wedding and the brief meeting, especially with Alan there, had been rather awkward. Everyone went out of their way to be scrupulously polite and Hubert enquired about a wedding present. He could tell that the situation affected Alan too and, in fact, he had breakfasted early, so that Hubert and Violet were alone.

They had never been close. Violet was two years older than he and their tastes were very different. Hubert was an outdoor man; Violet was into the arts and liked to think of herself as an intellectual, though she was also a very good shot and a horsewoman. She enjoyed all the pursuits of people of her class and in Hubert's opinion her union with Alan was a strange one; but they were not close enough for him to dare to question her about it.

So, at first, the conversation was perfunctory, a trifle stilted. There were also the servants present, the complement of staff having increased since Violet had taken up residence. He asked her when they had got back and the answer was, apparently, only a few days before, as Alan couldn't take any more leave. 'Hardly time for a honeymoon.' Violet's voice was regretful.

After breakfast they went up to the drawing room and lit cigarettes, Hubert opening the morning paper.

'How is Peg?' Violet asked, nervously flicking ash into a tray as though she felt ill at ease.

Hubert looked up. 'She's very well.'

'When is the baby due?'

'Early in the new year.'

'You hope for a girl, I expect, to even the numbers?'

'We don't really care.'

'My marriage, I suppose, was a surprise?'

Hubert put aside his paper. 'Of course.'

'He doesn't really love me, you know. He loves Peg.'

'Then why did you marry him?'

'Because he can never have Peg, can he? I wanted to be married. I'd like a child. Besides, we get on very well. It sounds a rather old-fashioned thing to say, Hubert darling, but Alan is a thoroughly nice, decent fellow.'

Hubert shook his head. 'I hardly know him, but if you're happy, that's the important thing.'

'Never one to show much emotion, were you, Hubert?'

Hubert looked offended. 'How do you mean?'

'One wonders if you really care about anything?'

'Of *course* I care,' Hubert said crossly. 'If you mean, do I care about Alan and you, of course I do! But as you didn't consult me before you married someone you consider doesn't love you, I don't have much to say about it. You can't blame me for that.'

Violet stubbed out her cigarette. 'I suppose we have our parents to thank for that. They never betrayed much emotion either, did they?'

They gazed at each other for a moment, as though each was aware of the lack of a sibling bond between them and in a way regretted it.

'How long will you be staying, do you know, Hubert?'

'I have to try to find this girl. After all, like it or not, she is our niece.'

'I can never think of her as one of the family – so strange.' Violet looked distracted. 'If you ask me, she should be locked up if she keeps on running away.'

'She probably will be. There will certainly be a severe punishment. The trouble is that she has gone off with a school friend, an utterly blameless, rather immature young girl whose parents already thought Jenny was a bad influence and were about to send her to boarding school.'

Violet shook her head impatiently. 'I can't think why you wanted to get involved.'

'Because it's *our* family. Peg can't go and Adelaide is in hospital having a baby – at least, they hope she will have it and not lose it. So of course Harold can't leave her either; someone has to do it.'

'That's what comes of getting involved with the working classes,' Violet said loftily. 'You should have stuck to Ida. She would never have got the family into this mess.'

Ida had been Hubert's first wife, who had been the daughter of a peer.

Hubert got up and walked across to the window, where he stood for some moments peering out at the garden.

'That is a really unpleasant thing to say, Violet.' He glanced at his watch. 'Unpleasant and unfair. I would have thought your own husband was not exactly out of the top drawer. By the way, I shan't be in for dinner tonight. I shall probably dine at one of my clubs.'

'As you like.' Violet already regretted her remark, but an apology was not in her nature. 'Oh, and good luck with the hunt, although it might be just as well if the wretched girl disappeared for good, and then she wouldn't be able to cause any more trouble.'

'Here again, dear?' Roxanne had seen him as soon as he came in and sauntered across the room.

'Yes,' Hubert replied brusquely, 'and I really don't need you to look after me, thank you, Roxanne, but do have a drink. Not champagne,' he added; 'I'm sure you can also drink gin.'

'Seen someone you like, have you? One of the girls?' Roxanne jealously followed his eyes fixed on the stage.

Hubert waved a hand at her. 'Do buzz off, Roxanne. Tell the waiter to give me the chit for your tipple.'

Roxanne sulkily wandered away in search of a new client to fleece, but Hubert didn't watch her. He couldn't take his eyes off Maisie. In fact he had been looking forward to this all day. He'd wandered about the streets thinking about her; he'd called at his tailors in Savile Row to be measured for some new suits and lunched at his club, where he had also played a few rubbers of bridge just to while away the time.

He went back to South Audley Street to change into a dinner jacket and booked a table at Sans Souci, a nightclub that served dinner, where the membership was exclusive and of a better class than the clientele of the Monkey Club. He'd had drinks with Violet and Alan, who were also eating out, and then he'd wandered slowly towards Soho, savouring the moment when he would see Maisie, a delicious feeling of anticipation such as he hadn't experienced since – well, when he had first fallen in love with Peg. He hadn't felt that way about Ida, because their marriage had come about almost as an agreement between their families, who had known one another almost all their lives. Also, he'd been about to go off to the war and, in view of the carnage on the Western Front, thought he might die and wanted to leave an heir. But that was not to be.

He was still sitting contemplating the sublime Maisie when the waiter came up to him and handed him a piece of paper. Hubert reached into his pocket for some change, but when he opened the paper he saw it was a message. He gave the waiter some coins anyway, waved him away and read it: 'I have some news for you. I am not doing the midnight show so we can slip away early.' There was no name at the bottom, but he knew who it was from; he folded it carefully and tucked it into his breast pocket as though it was a love letter.

The Sans Souci club in Covent Garden was down a narrow street off the market. However, inside it was surprisingly big, with a small dance floor in the centre and tables well spaced out. A long bar ran one length of the room, with two white-coated barmen in attendance and a few men sitting on stools, but no women. All the men wore black ties and the women with their partners scattered round the tables were in evening dress.

'This is quite a classy joint,' Maisie said as they sat down after being shown to their table. 'How long have you been a member?'

'Since the war,' Hubert replied. 'I don't come here very often, but it is useful for late-night eating and the food is good.' As if on cue, a waiter appeared beside him, pad in hand.

'What will you drink?'

'Scotch would be nice.'

Hubert gave the order and produced his cigarette case.

'Did you expect me to ask for champagne?' Maisie sank back in her chair, a half-smile on her face.

'No, why should I? You're welcome to it if you want.'

'I thought that was why you offered it to me last night. It's a tart's drink, isn't it?'

'Don't be silly.' Hubert felt himself flush.

'It's what you think, though, isn't it?'

'No, not at all.'

'I was quite surprised to see you again tonight watching the show. You came early too. What would your wife say?'

'Peg is very broad-minded.'

'But she doesn't know I'm a stripper, does she?'

Hubert lowered his head. 'Perhaps Ed wanted to keep that to himself. You can't blame him in a way.'

'But it doesn't shock you?'

'No.' Hubert began to feel most uncomfortable beneath her fierce scrutiny.

'I suppose that's because, like all men, you enjoy seeing naked women disporting themselves for your entertainment.'

Hubert, who had so looked forward to the evening, sensed that it was teetering on the edge of disaster.

'You know,' Maisie went on when he failed to reply, 'that's why I left Plymouth. I couldn't bear the naval wives, all of whom thought their men were angels. I told them a few home truths, I can assure you.'

'I expect you did.' Hubert gave an involuntary smile. He thought she looked more beautiful than ever – poised and elegant, almost as though she'd made a special effort just for him, though of course this was impossible. She wore a close-fitting green-silk dress with a low neckline, but it wasn't the least bit tarty. He didn't know how he could ever have referred to her – as he had, to Peg – as a tramp.

The waiter returned with their drinks and asked them if they wanted to dine.

'Later,' Hubert said, 'I think, don't you, Maisie; or are you starving?'

'I could eat,' she replied, 'but not just yet.'

Her features were really quite perfect: the moulded lips, the astonishingly deep-blue eyes, the colour of sapphires. His eyes went to the engagement ring on her finger.

'You were thinking it must have cost a lot of money?' she suggested.

'On the contrary, I was thinking it was just like the colour of your eyes.'

'Oh, very gallant.'

'Why are you so prickly with me, Maisie?' Hubert leaned towards her, but she avoided his eyes by looking rather longingly at the small dance floor where about half a dozen couples, pressed close together, were circulating to a smoochy waltz.

'Do you want to dance?' Hubert asked.

'I thought we came to talk about business.'

'We can do that later.'

They were a perfect height and she seemed to fit snugly into his arms, to relax in them as they glided, as best as they could, around the floor. The sensation of her hair against his cheek and the subtle fragrance of her perfume formed a heady mix. He tightened his grip round her waist and she responded, moving closer to him so that her breasts pressed against his chest; for a moment they seemed almost united, as one.

Maisie suddenly broke away and her cool hand became entwined with his. 'I can't really breathe on this floor, can you?' she murmured into his ear; 'there are just too many people.'

They walked back to the table, still hand in hand. Their drinks awaited them untouched and, as Hubert produced his cigarette case and held it towards her, both were silent as though aware that a new dimension had entered their lives.

'So,' Hubert said at last, 'what is the news?'

'I have found out where Teresa lives and, yes, she has taken to the streets, so let's hope your brother's daughter is not holed up in a bordello.'

Jenny lay in bed, staring at the ceiling, unable to sleep. Every now and then there would be the sound of footsteps on the stairs, creaking quite noisily past her room, and a door would shut. After a while it would open, and the floor would creak again as the night people retraced their steps towards the stairs. There might be the sound of muffled voices or there might not. This sort of activity seemed to last all night, as it had the night before. Each night, too, Sylvia had cried herself to sleep and had woken several times with bad dreams.

Jenny was extremely sorry she had brought her. In fact, the whole operation was a disaster and she was wondering how she could get out of it without incurring the most enormous punishment. She couldn't think what had possessed her ever to embark on it. Her mind was now turning to the idea of running away again, doing a double runner, as it were, and leaving Sylvia behind.

Teresa didn't get up until noon, but on the day that had just passed she'd appeared quite cheerful, had looked more relaxed, had dressed carefully and well and sallied forth to Regent's Park with the girls in tow to feed the ducks with pieces of stale bread. It was quite a long walk, but Teresa had appeared to enjoy the outing and had greeted a number of acquaintances. For Jenny and her grumbling, querulous playmate, however, it had been a dismal day. The sunshine was only sporadic, the leaves on the trees were turning yellow and the distinct feel of autumn was in the air. Finally they had trailed back, only pausing for Teresa to buy them all a fish-and-chip supper with some of the money she'd taken from them in the morning. Teresa had also bought a bottle of white wine and drunk most of it. Then she'd fallen asleep in her chair.

They would have to get away. This was no adventure because Teresa, apparently not trusting them at night, locked the door, so it was like being in prison.

Mysteriously, in the morning the door was unlocked and that must have happened when finally Jenny had got to sleep, because she never heard the key turn.

After a fitful sleep Jenny awoke, with no idea of the time except that it was broad daylight. Instead of birdsong, which greeted her at home, all she heard was the sound of the trains shunting into the station; she got out of bed and gazed dolefully out of the grimy window. Sylvia appeared at last to be sleeping soundly. It was cold, Jenny was hungry, so she quickly put on some clothes, tried the door, found it open and crept quietly down the stairs to the kitchen, where the remains of the previous evening's meal were still on the table, unwashed dishes in the sink. Whoever Teresa entertained in the course of a busy night was not offered food, or perhaps she gave them drinks in the seclusion of her sitting room.

Jenny filled the kettle, put it on the stove and hunted for the tea. She was desperately tired, cold, and had a headache. Maybe if Sylvia and Teresa stayed in bed late, today was the day she should make a break for it; but she had no money, Teresa having relieved them of most of their cash.

Suddenly there was a sharp knocking on the front door, which made her nearly drop the tea caddy. It had a brisk, authoritative, somehow unfriendly sound, and her hand holding the caddy started to shake. Then it came again, this time for longer and more stridently.

She went into the hall and saw Teresa clutching her gown tightly around her, standing halfway up the stairs, her face ashen with fright, her hair all over the place. Seeing Jenny, she put a finger to her lips, but the knocking had now turned into a persistent banging.

'Police!' she whispered loudly. 'Answer the door. Say I'm not here,' and she scuttled up the stairs again out of sight. Swallowing hard, Jenny unbolted the door and, opening it a crack, peered out.

What she saw astonished her. Standing staring at her, clearly as surprised as she was, were Maisie, dressed casually in a silk shirt and slacks with a camel-haired coat flung around her shoulders, and her Uncle Hubert in a dinner jacket.

'Hello, Jenny,' Hubert said finally, in a tone of great gentleness; 'I've come to take you home.'

Eleven

Though tiny, she was such a beautiful baby. She was six weeks premature and weighed just five pounds, but otherwise she was healthy and perfectly formed. She was to be called Charlotte and now she lay in her mother's arms, eyes tight shut, with a little upright tuft of bright-gold downy hair making her look like a little pixie.

The two sisters, Stella and Verity, standing on either side of Addie's bed, drooled over her. Peg, who had arrived earlier, sat on a chair watching them, an indulgent smile on her face. Charlotte was the one bright spot, a ray of happiness in an otherwise troubled time, as they waited for news of Jenny and tried to keep at bay a wrathful Mr Birch, who was trying to mobilize the entire police force of the country in an effort to find his missing daughter.

Verity gently pulled back the soft shawl in which she was wrapped in order to get a better look at Charlotte's face. She was engulfed, as always on occasions like this, by a wave of love for the latest relation – she was now an aunt seven times over – but also, as usual, by a sense of sadness that motherhood was something she might never know. This, though, she kept well under control beneath a patina of smiles.

'Harold must love her,' Verity said, reluctantly stepping back after feasting her eyes on the infant.

Addie, who had barely recovered from the trauma of the premature birth, nodded. 'Oh, he does, but I am sorry for his sake she is not a boy. He so wanted a son.'

'Maybe next time,' Verity said encouragingly, but Addie shook her head. 'There won't be a next time, Ver; I don't want another baby. I don't want to go through all that again. Besides, I'm getting old.'

'Nonsense!' Verity said robustly. Still, as a midwife, she understood Addie's predicament. Childbirth was a tricky business, often dangerous, and although Addie had been lucky, many babies who didn't come to full term failed to survive.

'Also,' Addie said, a touch of bitterness in her voice, 'we don't want another girl like Jenny.'

'Oh, that is a *very* unfair thing to say.' Peg's voice came from the background. 'Jenny is a lovely girl. She's going through a bad time.'

'Putting *us* all through a bad time, you mean,' her mother said. 'Jenny had everything she wanted at home with us. Harold adored her and was so good to her; she has thrown all that away through sheer jealousy of the baby. If we let this pass, in future, every time Jenny is thwarted she will want to run away. No – we are going to take very severe steps against this young woman when she does return. She will find no indulgent father and mother; instead it will be a very strict boarding school, probably a convent, where the nuns will take no nonsense. Harold is already writing for prospectuses.'

'That's *providing* you get her back,' Stella observed quietly. 'You can't be sure of that, can you?'

'How do you mean?'

'The way you're speaking you sound as if you don't love her.'

'Oh, I *do* love her.' Addie began to cry, and Verity quickly crossed the room and gently took the baby from her arms. 'I do love her, but I also hate her because of the way she has behaved, the way she has upset poor Harold and made me so ill.'

The three sisters were very silent on the way home, each immersed in her thoughts.

'A birth should be a happy occasion,' Stella said at last. 'This one is so fraught with difficulties it makes you fear for the future. I feel so sorry for darling Addie, just when she had found happiness and, frankly, I do feel irritated with that naughty child. She definitely needs taking in hand.'

'I don't think nuns are the people to do it,' Verity said thoughtfully, 'but I must say I don't know the solution.' She looked at each of her sisters. 'Maybe, in a way, we are all responsible.'

'How do you mean?' Peg stared anxiously out of the window.

'You know what I mean: we were all guilty of contributing to the lie that was her life, and now she doesn't know who she is.'

Frank, who was driving, had been listening to the conversation and glanced at them over his shoulder. 'I think she should come back to the lodge. I'll look after her. I understand our Jenny.'

'Oh, Frank, how *sweet*.' Peg leaned forward and gratefully pressed his shoulder. 'I'm sure Jenny would love that, but you know it is no longer her decision or yours. Addie and Harold will decide what the future holds for Jenny and let's hope they decide wisely for, like Ver, I don't believe that convent discipline is the answer to Jenny's troubles. The problem goes much deeper than that.'

Frank dropped Stella and Verity off at the lodge after Peg had invited them up to the castle for dinner that evening. It had been a tiring day and it was good to be home. For the lodge was home, even though it was now fragmented by the absence of so many who had grown up there. In a way it had changed its nature over the years since Cathy had arrived there with her new husband and children in the year 1909. In that sense it had never been home for Verity, who had been adopted by her aunt

156

and uncle; but it was the place to which she always returned, the place where in many ways she had her roots.

Verity threw her hat on the table and went immediately to make a cup of tea, while Stella sat gratefully down on a chair and leaned forward, rubbing her leg.

'Leg hurting?' Verity asked sympathetically, sitting opposite her.

'Oh no, not at all. It's just become a habit.' But she went on rubbing it and Verity was not sure whether or not her sister was telling the truth. She knew how much Stella had suffered, not only physically, but also mentally and emotionally too, and she was a girl who concealed her feelings, bottled everything up inside her so that one never really knew the extent of her hurt. She had been a vivacious sports-loving girl, in love and about to get married, when she had been struck down so cruelly by poliomyelitis. If anyone's life had changed for ever, Stella's had.

The water boiled; Verity brewed the tea and sat across the table from her sister.

'Stella,' she said, helping herself to a Marie biscuit. 'There is something I have been wanting to ask you.'

Stella, alerted by the gravity in her voice, looked at her. 'What's that?'

'Well, you know I have a big house. I bought it with the family in mind, but they don't come as often as I'd like. Peg and Addie are busy with their lives and the children. I wondered if by any chance you'd like to share it with me? You'd have your own bedroom, naturally, and I could make one of the spare rooms into a sitting room for you if you wished for more privacy. That would leave a guest room or, if necessary, we could double up when the family came. How would that appeal, Stella?'

Verity looked at her diffidently almost as if she dreaded rejection, but Stella's reaction was just the opposite. She clasped her hands together, her eyes shining with pleasure.

'Oh, Ver, I could think of nothing I'd like more! You know I have begun to be very lonely here. As you say, Addie and Peg are busy with their families – not much I can do to help there. Ed is away and Frank is always out. I have nothing to do and, as I am so much better, I've been thinking of looking for a job, but what is there to do round here? Nothing. I thought I might have to go away and live on my own, but with you? Oh Ver, what a *lovely* idea. And I'm sure I can get something in Bristol. There are lots and lots of schools there.'

'That's settled then,' Verity said happily. She went over to her sister, hugging her and kissing her on the cheek. 'I'm so glad. I think we shall be very happy and I shall be glad of the company.'

Suddenly Stella's expression of happiness seemed to evaporate. 'But what about Frank? He will be here on his own.'

'Oh, I expect Hubert will be able to give Frank a smaller house somewhere on the estate. He might be quite glad to have this larger place back for a family. Besides, this house badly needs decorating and doing up. It is such a long time since anything was done to it.'

'How soon may I come?' Stella enquired eagerly.

'Whenever you like. As soon as you can pack up.'

'Two old maids,' Stella said with a giggle. 'We shall grow old gracefully together.'

'Don't be too sure of that.' Verity poured herself another cup of tea. 'I shall almost certainly never marry. I've missed the boat now, but you are a young woman. I don't expect to have you as a lodger for very long.'

Stella ruefully pursed her lips. 'Be realistic, Ver. I should think very few men want a wife who walks with a stick.'

She was interrupted by the sound of the telephone and Verity went into the hall to answer it. She was away for quite some time, during which Stella washed up the cups and saucers and then went and stood at the back door, looking across the garden to the castle on the hill.

She had known this place all her life. She had been born here, grown up here. The only time she'd ever considered leaving was when she had thought it would be as a bride to Ernest Pickering, to whom she had been engaged before her illness had struck with such devastation. He had certainly not wanted a bride with a stick and she didn't think many men would have done.

She turned as Verity came back into the kitchen. 'That was a long call. Anything interesting?'

'Jenny has been found,' Verity exclaimed in a voice full of emotion, 'living, if you please, in a house of ill repute. Hubert is on his way home with her now.'

As a bank manager, Mr Birch felt he should give a lead to society. Even though it was a small branch bank, he was a self-important man who considered himself a pillar of the community. He also felt the same about other people in positions of responsibility and authority: teachers, doctors, members of the cloth and the legal profession. Gerald Birch, in addition to his responsibilities at the bank, was also a churchwarden, a Mason, a member of various worthwhile organizations and the treasurer of some of them.

He also liked to play bowls and tennis and, had he been able to afford it, would have relished being a member of the hunt. That would not only have brought him into contact with the cream of local society, but would also have afforded him the opportunity of acquiring new accounts.

In appearance, Mr Birch was of middling height, balding, clean-shaven, nondescript, and he and his wife complemented each other. Mrs Birch was almost his exact counterpart, the perfect wife for a man like him, a member of almost as many local organizations as her husband, and so busy were they with their various voluntary duties that they scarcely saw each other.

In appearance she was rather plain and homely, a woman

159

who had married relatively late in life and considered herself fortunate to have secured a husband. Sylvia was their only child and it was because of her that they now feared a social catastrophe, possible banishment from a number of worthy organizations.

The Birches lived in a nice house on a street similar to the one where the Smiths lived. It was considered a good area, where the price of houses fetched a premium.

The Birches and the Smiths were acquaintances rather than friends. They met at functions, but had never entertained one another socially. As their concern about Jenny's influence over Sylvia had mounted, they had tried to distance themselves even more. How Mr Birch wished he had spoken to Harold Smith then, before this disaster had befallen them.

As Harold was shown into the Birches' sitting room, he knew he was in for a stormy encounter. Mr Birch stood on the rug in front of the fire, hands behind his back, as though he were about to deliver a stern warning to someone who had exceeded their overdraft, and Mrs Birch sat upright in her chair, hands folded in her lap, lips pursed tightly together. However, both politely shook hands with Harold and he was even offered a drink, which he declined.

'I needn't say how *sorry* I am,' Harold began, but Mr Birch at once interrupted him.

'*Sorry* is not the right word, Mr Smith. What has happened to our daughter is beyond sorrow. It is a catastrophe.'

Harold swallowed hard. 'The whole affair is *lamentable*. Jenny is confined to her bedroom until we decide what to do with her. However, it was apparently *Sylvia* who instigated the idea of running away. She did not want to be sent to boarding school.'

'Nevertheless, if it hadn't been for your daughter's disgraceful example – she had, I understand, already run away before – whatever Sylvia's feeling about boarding school, she would have obeyed our wishes and gone. She didn't want to be sent away because she had, in the opinion of my wife and myself, formed an unnatural attachment to Jenny. She didn't want to leave her friend, your daughter, who exercised such a pernicious influence on her.'

'I think that is putting it too strongly—' Harold began, but again, increasingly exasperated, Mr Birch interrupted him.

'I really don't know how you can stand here and accuse *me* of exaggerating the seriousness of this matter. I have even consulted my solicitor and if there was any way I could sue you for child-abduction and have you sent to prison, believe me I would not hesitate. For my gently reared daughter – not a strong character, I admit – to be taken to a *brothel* is too awful to contemplate. Heaven knows how your daughter had access to such a place! What does that tell you?'

'It was not a brothel as such.' Harold tried to muster as much dignity as he could. 'That is, the woman . . . well, she used to be on the stage. I'm sure the girls came to no harm, nor would have. I am quite sure of that.'

Harold took out his handkerchief and mopped his brow. If they knew about Maisie . . . but then by now they probably knew about everything.

'I repeat, Sylvia went of her own accord,' he concluded lamely.

'She was *seduced*,' Mrs Birch muttered bitterly,' by a very nasty, evil-natured girl who should be in some institution, as I hope she soon will be. She turned our formerly well-behaved, obedient, honest and angelic daughter into not only a delinquent, but also a thief. She stole a considerable sum of money from her father, all of which went to that dreadful woman. Doubtless you intend to punish Jenny most severely?'

'She is already being punished' – Harold was anxious to atone – 'by what she has done. Also the school will not have her back. She was doing well there. She is to lose all her friends. My wife has just had a baby and, frankly, Mr and Mrs Birch, I am at my wits' end.'

161

If he expected sympathy, not a flicker passed over the faces of Sylvia's parents. Instead, Mr Birch, firmly grasping the lapels of his jacket, thrust his chin in the air. 'Mr Smith, what I am about to say to you is not said lightly. I am aware that this is distressing for you and Mrs Smith, but certain things have been brought to my attention that convince my wife and me that you are not a fit person to be the head teacher of our local school.'

'What do you mean?' Harold demanded, finding a firm voice at last.

'I understand that Jenny is not your daughter; am I correct?'

Harold bowed his head. 'She is not my daughter.'

'She is, in fact, illegitimate?'

'Yes.'

'And your wife, mother of an illegitimate child, has the impertinence to present herself as the secretary of the Mothers' Union and an active participant in the Women's Institute. No wonder Jenny has gone to the bad with such an inheritance, such an example! Now' – Mr Birch wagged his finger at Harold – 'it is my intention to inform the local education authority and the governors of your school about what has happened. I have already prepared a document, which I shall show to you, outlining the reasons for your unfitness, in my opinion, to be a head teacher, an arbiter of morals, an example to the young! In short' – Mr Birch paused to take a deep breath – 'I have a great deal of influence, you know. Parents will move their children from your school in droves. You and your wife will be socially ostracized. My suggestion to you, Mr Smith – and I mean this – is that you and Mrs Smith should consider leaving the neighbourhood as soon as possible in order to spare yourselves a great deal of unpleasantness.'

'He can't *possibly* do this to you,' Verity said; 'the whole thing is outrageous.'

'Of course he can't,' Addie concurred. 'We must resist him, Harold. We must carry on as usual. It will soon blow over.'

At first, Harold's account of his interview with the Birches had thrown Addie into a spin and, as usual, her eldest sister was summoned to give her support, but also, above all, her valuable advice. Harold had already had telephone calls from a number of parents and the chairman of governors of the school had asked for an urgent interview.

He seemed to have aged in the days since Jenny had been found and brought back. The story had spread like wildfire in the district and people, although naturally consumed by curiosity, in an area where respectability was the keyword, crossed the street to avoid talking to him. Instead they talked to one another.

What had seemed at first a simple if regrettable case of two girls playing truant had turned into a first-class scandal, as Jenny's origins and something about Addie's past had become known. There had been rumours, whispers, but Ryland Castle was not too far from the outskirts of Exeter; someone had taken the trouble to find out that Addie had lived for some years with a man to whom she was not married and that Arthur was their son.

Addie had only just returned home from hospital, bringing her tiny daughter with her. She looked pale and tired and Verity's concern was for her more than for the situation in which they found themselves. The Hallam family were no strangers to scandal and rumour-mongering; but it was the middle of term and there was no question of taking a holiday.

'Would you like to come back to Bristol with me?' Verity asked Addie, who was feeding baby Charlotte. 'You will have a complete rest and I'll try to get some of the nurses at the hospital to help you on their days off. I shall be there every evening.'

Addie vigorously shook her head. 'Thank you, dear, but I feel my place is with Harold; he needs my support. Besides, I couldn't leave him alone with Jenny. We have Arthur to think of, poor little mite, and Betty can help with the baby, so I shall be able to get some rest.'

Harold suddenly became animated, as an idea seemed to strike him. 'But if you could bear it, Verity, it might be nice if Jenny spent a few days with you. We're at our wits' end what to do with her. I have set her plenty of work until we can find a boarding school willing to take her.'

'Would she come?' Verity looked doubtful. 'And as I can't be with her all the time, how can we guarantee that she won't run away again?'

Jenny had been confined to her room, but was allowed down for meals, which were largely eaten in silence; so upset with her were her parents, they could hardly speak to her. As she showed no signs of repentance, Harold in particular found it hard to forgive a girl on whom he had lavished such affection – Addie likewise, because of the shock Jenny had given her that had undoubtedly brought on the premature birth that could well have cost not only her life, but also the baby's.

Jenny had thus become extremely withdrawn and silent and, in fact, was rather glad to stay upstairs to avoid contact with her parents, above all with her new sister. Jenny knew she had done something really dreadful. Everyone's life had been turned upside down. A man she had adored would hardly speak to her and none of her friends visited, even supposing their parents would have let them.

She was a clever, bookish girl and she consoled herself by reading a lot outside the heavy workload Harold had given her so that she didn't miss out on her schooling. She was lying on her bed reading when there was a tap at the door and she heard a familiar voice say, 'Jenny, may I come in?'

Without waiting for an answer, Verity turned the handle of the door and put her head round. Jenny, not knowing whether to be glad or sorry to see her, simply stared at her. She knew Aunt Ver considered her a thief, someone who had betrayed her trust. She laid her book on her stomach as Verity came over and, to Jenny's surprise, sat on the side of the bed.

'What are you reading?'

Jenny turned the front of the book towards Verity without answering.

'*Little Women* – a favourite of mine, too.' Verity took the book from Jenny's hands and put it on the table by the side of the bed. 'We must have a talk,' she said firmly.

'What about?' Jenny asked sulkily.

'You know what about.'

'Oh, *that*.'

'Yes, *that*. It is very serious, Jenny. I don't think you fully realize how serious. Your parents don't know what to do with you.'

'He's not my father.'

'But I thought you liked him? You got on well.'

'I did like him.'

'Well, you have a funny way of showing it.'

'I hate that baby,' Jenny suddenly burst out. 'Horrible little thing, like a monkey.'

To Jenny's surprise, instead of scolding her, Verity leaned forward and gently took her hand. Rather than a wicked young girl, which everyone called her, Verity saw a deeply disturbed, frightened person badly in need of help and stability. This she could not get at home because of the effect she had had on the lives of her parents. They would forgive her in time, but understandably that was not yet. So she, Verity, had done some deep thinking in the few hours she had been here; she ignored the remark about the baby and, still holding tightly on to Jenny's hand, said: 'Would you like to come and live with me for a while?'

'With you?' Jenny looked startled.

'You liked the house; you liked your room.'

'But I stole from you.' Jenny's cheeks slowly went a deep crimson.

'Yes, but you won't do it again, will you? Or run away? It is a chance for you, Jenny, to make a new beginning. Your parents are at the end of their tether. Your mother has just had a baby and is very weak.'

'They hate me,' Jenny said tremulously.

'They are certainly very displeased with you, which is understandable. You have caused a good deal of pain and real suffering. Harold may lose his job. Did you realize that?'

'How *can* he?' scoffed Jenny.

'Because it has created such a scandal. People want to take their children away from the school. Sylvia's parents are very, very angry and are bent on making trouble.'

'But it wasn't their fault,' Jenny protested, aghast, 'nor my parents'.'

'No, it wasn't, but you are their daughter. You are considered a bad, even dangerous influence. It is especially regrettable that this woman, Teresa, was taking men into her house.'

'We didn't see any men,' Jenny said defensively. 'She was really very kind to us. She didn't want to take us in, but she did.'

'She also, I understand, took all your money, or rather Sylvia's father's money.'

'We offered it to her for food and lodging.'

'Be that as it may, it is a very unhappy situation. Now' – Verity rose and stood looking down at her niece – 'what do you say? We will, hopefully, find you a school in Bristol, but you must behave. You must give me a solemn promise to do as you're told and never, ever attempt to run away again. If you agree and if your parents agree – and I have not yet suggested this long-term plan to them, Jenny – it is your last chance. If you break the rules, you will probably be sent to some sort of institution, where you will be kept under lock and key.'

Stella, her face scarlet with the effort, tried to fasten her trunk while Frank sat on top of it. 'There,' she said, sliding the last bolt into place, 'that does it.' She looked gratefully up at him. 'Thanks, Frank.'

'I hate to see you packing up,' Frank said; 'I shall be very, very lonely without you.'

'Oh, Frank' – Stella rounded the trunk and threw her arms around him – 'and I shall miss *you*.' She gazed into his eyes and plonked a kiss on his cheek. 'But it is a wonderful opportunity for me to live with Ver and get out of a rut. I feel I'm doing nothing useful with my life. I hope you understand.'

'Oh, I understand,' Frank said, stepping back as her arms fell to her sides. 'But still I shall miss you. I shan't know what to do with myself.'

'Well I shan't be going for a bit,' Stella said with forced cheerfulness. 'I just wanted to get some things out of the way.' She looked down at the trunk. 'Can you manage to get it to the storeroom for me, or is it too heavy?'

The trunk was largely full of books; Frank's veins bulged as he lifted it and managed to stagger with it down the stairs and out into the garden shed, which was also used as a storeroom.

Frank was in fact far more upset and affected than he let on. At one time this house had been full of people, grown-ups and children. When he had married Cathy, it had been a great joy for a bachelor in his forties who had never had children of his own. He had become a loving stepfather and felt that they loved him in return, but gradually they had all flown the nest: Ed, Peg, Addie, Jenny, Arthur and now Stella; but the one who had gone first, and whom he missed most, was his beloved wife, Catherine, who had died eight years before, leaving a void in his life that would never be filled.

When he had first got to know Cathy, he had lived in a small cottage on the estate, for which he had worked since he was a raw adolescent, growing in prestige and favour with the Ryland family.

He knew he would be looked after and Peg was not very far away – just up the hill with her children. He had plenty to do; indeed, he enjoyed something of a unique situation among estate workers because of his closeness to the family. Many envied him and some were jealous of him.

Now, though, he would really be alone again and no one would know how much he minded, because he would never tell them. Just because he was a rather burly, bluff, good-natured man, people – even his adopted family – seemed to consider him insensitive; but he wasn't: he felt things deeply. He cared, and life without Stella would be a terrible loss.

As he emerged from the shed, dusting his hands, Frank saw a familiar car come through the castle gates and stop outside the door of the lodge.

'Verity!' he exclaimed crossing to the car and throwing open the door with pleasure. 'What brings you here?'

'Oh, I just came to see you and Stella,' Verity said casually, getting out of the car and kissing his cheek. She was sensibly dressed in a tweed coat with a muffler round her neck and a felt hat sitting squarely on her head. 'Is Stella around?'

'Packing,' Frank grimaced. 'She's got such a lot of stuff. I hope you've plenty of room?'

'Well . . .' Verity paused awkwardly. 'We'll see.'

'I have to go up to the castle to do an urgent job,' Frank said. 'I'll see you when I get back. Does Peg know you're coming?'

'No, I really want a word with Stella. Maybe we'll wander up afterwards?'

Her smile was strained and Frank, a little puzzled, scrutinized her face. 'Nothing wrong is there, Ver? Addie all right?'

'Oh, Addie's fine.' Verity's face broke into a smile. 'You go on up and we'll see you in a while.'

Verity, rather dreading her mission, stood for a time in the back garden, watching him go up the hill. She was not as close to Frank as the others because she had never lived with him as they had, but he was a dear, good man and both qualities would be needed now. She went through the back door into the kitchen, removing her hat and gloves and putting them on the table.

Stella, who had heard the car, was already at the door to welcome her sister. 'Ver,' she cried, 'what a *lovely* surprise! I didn't expect you. You should have said you were coming.' But when she saw Verity's grave expression she, like Frank, became anxious.

'Is everything all right?'

'Well.' Verity sat down heavily at the table. 'I didn't want to worry Frank, but in all honesty, Stella, you could hardly say everything *is* all right. Addie and Harold are in a bad way. Mr Birch, Sylvia's father, is trying to ensure Harold loses his job.'

'But he *can't* do that.' Stella looked appalled. 'How?'

'Well, he's doing his best to freeze him out. There is lot of rumour-mongering going on. People are threatening to take their children away from his school. People have such tiny, narrow minds. Frankly, I think that Harold and Addie will find it impossible to live in the area if this sort of thing doesn't die down.'

'Well, I'm *really* shocked.' Stella flopped down opposite her sister. 'What are they going to do?'

Verity palpably steeled herself. 'Stella, it is very hard for me to tell you this: I know it will be a shock and I am disappointed too, but I have invited Jenny to come and live with me. It is the only way out as, for the moment, she can't stand her parents and they can't stand her. They can't live together, nor can she go to school locally. The situation is unbearable. I have told her she must behave herself with me and I will try to find her a school willing to accept her.' Verity reached across the table and seized Stella's hand. 'So you see, my dear, I shall have to withdraw my invitation to you to make a home for Jenny instead. She is our niece, she's terribly young, and we owe it to her to try to give her some stability. I love Jenny very much – I always have – and I want to do my best for her. Obviously there is not room for you both. I'm terribly, terribly sorry, dear Stella. I couldn't have dreamed it would work out this way.'

Twelve

'The board are ready to see you now, Mr Smith.'

Harold, who had been waiting anxiously in an adjoining room, rose as the headmaster's secretary entered. He had been interviewed the previous afternoon and it had gone so well that he had been asked to return in the morning for a second interview. He felt the job was in the bag. The chairman of governors of his school had promised him a good reference, as had the governors of his previous school.

Despite this, he had not slept well, but that was natural. It had been a period of turmoil. He had resigned from the school, which would take effect at Christmas, so a lot depended on this interview: his very future and that of his family. He examined the secretary's face for clues, but she was giving nothing away.

The post that had been advertised was for the deputy headship of a large mixed school in the north of England, well away from the pettiness and spite of his present location. It was a small town on the edge of the Yorkshire Dales, an environment similar to his present one, but one where nothing was known of his or Addie's past. There would be a blank sheet and they could start again.

Harold was angry that he had to consider such a thing. He had not, after all, committed murder.

Jenny had been found a school in Bristol, where so far she

171

had proved herself a model pupil, as she had before, and Harold was quite content for her to stay there. Time, it was said, healed all things, but it would take a long time to recover from the wound left by Jenny.

The deputy head of this school had unexpectedly been found to be incurably ill and a replacement was urgently needed. Harold thought his chances were good. He followed the secretary out of the room; just before she opened the boardroom door he stopped, straightened his tie, smoothed back his hair and adjusted his spectacles. The secretary smiled bleakly, as if sensing his nervousness, but he did not interpret it as a sign of discouragement. It was an impersonal smile that gave nothing away.

The board consisted of three men: the headmaster and two governors, one of whom, the vicar of the local church, was the chairman. He was a tall, thin man with angular features, a pronounced Adam's apple wobbling above his white clerical collar. Not a glimmer of a smile had appeared on his face when Harold had first been shown into the room, and he was unsmiling now as he pointed to a seat.

Harold somehow felt that the mood, which before had seemed to him favourable, had changed. He adjusted his tie again and sat down, head high, trying to exude a confidence he no longer felt. He noticed that the two other board members were studying the notes in front of them, as if unwilling to meet his eyes. He had an awful feeling that, somehow, the malign influence of Gerald Birch had invaded the proceedings. The vicar, a sheet of paper in his hand as though he were about to deliver a sermon, sat back.

'Well, Mr Smith, obviously you are an excellent candidate, well qualified for the post we are advertising. However, I will not beat about the bush and keep you in suspense: I am sorry to tell you that, after careful consideration, we have decided we are unable to offer you the post.'

Oh, Happy Day!

Harold's mouth went dry. 'May I ask why?'

The chairman glanced to his right and left as though silently communicating with his colleagues.

'Of course I am not obliged to tell you, but I can say it is a matter of personal references, Mr Smith, one of which we rather belatedly received only this morning. Had we received it earlier, I do not think we would have called you for interview. Naturally, we wished to give you the benefit of the doubt, as your candidature was so suitable in every way; indeed, your qualifications are excellent and you stood out among the other applicants. We have discussed the matter long and hard since we saw you yesterday and our decision is unanimous. It concerns family matters. I think you know what I mean.'

'If you refer to my stepdaughter' – Harold stumbled over his words – 'she will not be accompanying us. She has been going through a difficult adolescence and is living with her aunt in Bristol where she is being well taken care of.'

The chairman studied Harold over the rim of his glasses. 'It is not your stepdaughter who concerns us, Mr Smith, but the character of your wife. It would appear that she has two illegitimate children. I ask you: if this were to get around, as it obviously has in your present abode, can you imagine how my parishioners, most of whom send their children to this school, would react? They would be outraged that a person of such loose morals had been introduced into the community. What do you expect the position of Mrs Smith would be? It is not fair to us and it is not fair to you.'

His expression became more severe as he continued: 'I feel I should tell you that, in my opinion and that of my colleagues, with these references I think you would find it hard, if not impossible, to get a senior position in any school in the United Kingdom. Our advice is that you seek a post

173

abroad, where some countries are not as particular as we in England are about certain aspects of moral behaviour.'

Peg could never recall having seen Addie in such a state. She was usually a calm, good-natured person, more like Verity than her, and, despite the many vicissitudes that had afflicted her in life – and there had been an unusual number – she seldom lost control.

Addie had telephoned Peg to say that she wanted to see her urgently, and Frank immediately drove over to collect her, bringing Charlotte as well. The sisters had greeted each other with affection and fussed over the baby, who was then handed to the children's nanny. Peg then took her sister into her sitting room, where coffee stood waiting on a tray, poured her a cup, took her own and sat down. 'Now,' she said, 'I can see you're agitated about something . . .'

'Harold went for this interview,' Addie burst out without waiting for Peg to finish, her distress clearly visible. 'It was at a large school in the north of England, which urgently wanted a deputy head. He got on very well. There were other candidates, but Harold stood out, as naturally he would. They asked him to stay over and return the following day for a second interview.'

Addie gave a little sniff and blew her nose hard. 'Harold felt very confident he had the job, but as soon as he entered the boardroom the next morning he knew that the atmosphere had changed. He was told that, despite being an excellent candidate, he would not be offered the job because the board had received a letter only that morning pertaining to "personal matters".' Addie gulped and the hand clasping her coffee cup shook. 'Well, you know what *that* meant: it meant me. Loose morals, they called it, which would "scandalize" the worthy people of the parish.'

'But that had nothing to do with Harold's suitability for the post,' Peg burst out angrily.

'But it *has*. It's the same thing at home. Harold is blameless. He is a saint, but I am dragging him down now that my past is known. We can only surmise the letter came from Gerald Birch, who had somehow got wind of this application, though so few people knew. His influence is everywhere.

'Poor Harold was doing all he could, resigning from the school, moving from the area, but obviously it wasn't enough for that wicked man, who wants to persecute him. It seems he will go to the ends of the earth to ruin our family.'

'Are you sure it was Birch?'

'Who else could it have been? Harold's chairman is a very nice man, sympathetic to Harold, at least, if not to me. Harold is seen as a victim. His chairman promised him a good reference and the chairman of governors of his previous school the same. It can only be Birch. I wish he was in hell.'

This time Addie gave vent to the tears that she had so far, and with such difficulty, restrained.

Peg let her cry. Tears were often cathartic and she handed Addie a clean hankie when she'd finished.

'The house, you know, belongs to the school,' Addie went on between sniffs. 'They will surely be interviewing for a new head. We have to be out by Christmas and I wondered . . .' Addie blew her nose again. 'I wondered, Peg, if you thought we could come back to the lodge as a temporary measure while we decide what to do. Harold is exhausted and so am I. We badly need time to think.'

Peg bit her lip. 'Well, naturally I can't speak for Stella and Frank, but I can't see that there would be any objection. Stella is, of course, still upset about the collapse of her plans to go to Bristol, but there is a chance that a job might come up locally, which would suit her down to the ground. It would be lovely to have you back here. I would suggest you come to the castle, but – well, the baby is due at any moment and Hubert . . .' Peg paused. 'Well, let's say I don't want to ask him too many favours at the moment.'

175

'Oh, I wouldn't *dream* of suggesting it.' Addie clutched Peg's hand. 'Hubert has done us so many favours.' She paused and the tears once again welled up in her eyes. 'I feel I should offer Harold a divorce so that he can be free of me and able to start his life again. You know I have really come to love that man. There is so much good in him, so much patience. This crisis has shown him at his very best and most generous.'

Addie refused an offer to spend the night because she wanted to get back to Harold. Peg suggested she might talk to Frank on the way home and she would tackle Stella.

After her sister had gone, Peg felt restless and unhappy. Hubert had gone to London, ostensibly on business, but sometimes she wondered if he just wanted to get away. She felt so heavy and lethargic that it was all she could do to walk down to the lodge in the late afternoon, when she judged Stella would be home from school.

She found Stella not only at home, but also busy marking books. She was filling in at the local school, where she herself had been a pupil and where there was the prospect of a permanent post when one of the teachers retired.

Peg flopped on to a chair, her hands clutching her enormous stomach. 'Am I disturbing you?'

'No.' Stella pushed away the books. 'I'm glad of a break.' She peered closely at her sister. 'You look as though you've got something on your mind. Is it the baby?'

Peg shook her head. 'I had a surprise visit from Addie today. She telephoned me this morning and Frank went over to fetch her. She didn't stay long and he has now taken her back.'

'Oh.' Stella looked surprised. 'I'm sorry I missed her. Is there something wrong?'

'Very wrong, I'm afraid.' Peg told her about Harold's interview and their subsequent distress.

'The point is,' Peg concluded, 'they have to get out of the house, as it belongs to the school, and Addie wondered if they could come here for a while?'

'*Here?*' Stella looked startled. 'Back to the lodge?'

'Well, yes.'

'Then why ask you? Why not ask Frank and me? We live here.' Stella sounded really annoyed.

Peg was nonplussed. 'I can't say – well, perhaps she also thought the castle might be an option.'

'And is it?' Peg was surprised by Stella's sharpness.

'Not at the moment.' She patted her stomach. 'We have enough with the baby, but that might change.'

'You mean that it's not convenient, don't you, Peg? Well, I don't think it is here. You don't want a family of four moving in and I don't think we do either, much as I love Addie. How long did she want to come for?'

'Well, who can say? To be quite honest, it might be a long time, if it proves so difficult for Harold to find a job. She even thinks she should offer to divorce him. Of course she won't and he won't agree. I think they realize how much they love each other, which is the one good thing to come out of this whole sorry business.'

Stella's expression remained obstinate. 'Well, of course, I'll have to ask Frank: it is his home too; but speaking for myself, I am not at all happy about the idea. I have just settled down again after my disappointment over Verity. I may get a job at the school. Frank and I have a very peaceful life here and, frankly, much as I love Addie, I am not at all happy about the idea of her coming back here with her family and taking over the reins again.'

Stella's attitude distressed Peg, but she could see the logic of it. After a cup of tea with her sister, in the course of which they avoided the subject of Addie, she walked slowly up the hill again, and by the time she got to her room she felt so exhausted that she put her feet up and lay down on the bed.

177

The problem of what to do about Addie deeply disturbed her. This was a time when the family should all gather round to support her, not make excuses like the wedding guests in the Bible and say it was inconvenient.

Sitting up, she made a resolution. She would, after all, telephone Hubert and see what he thought about a temporary residence. There was plenty of room for Addie and her family, baby or not. She glanced at the clock. It was nearly six and this would not be a good time to telephone. They would all be busy changing to go out. She would do it in the morning, or maybe Hubert would ring later, as he sometimes did.

Feeling better for her decision, but still restless and with time on her hands before dinner, Peg decided to look through some of her frocks for that longed-for time when she would have her figure back again. Some she would discard and some send to the dry-cleaner's. It was a task that took less time than she had expected, and then she thought the same thing could be done with some of Hubert's suits. Though she would throw nothing away until she had consulted him, he wouldn't mind if some went to the dry-cleaner's, so she went into his dressing room and started to go through his wardrobe.

It was quite extensive: the clothes of a wealthy man for all occasions. She left aside dinner jackets, evening suits and informal wear – sporting clothes, jackets and trousers – and concentrated on his suits, of which he had a good number for someone who spent a lot of time out of doors messing about on the estate. Some that she thought could go to the welfare she put on one side, but there were a number of good ones, which she would send with a few of her best frocks to the cleaner's. Of these she started to go through the pockets. There was very little: one or two handkerchiefs, a few coins, a chequebook full of stubs and then, tucked inside one of his breast pockets, there was a piece of paper, carefully folded like a love letter. Peg looked at it, not quite knowing what to do with it.

She could replace it and put the suit back into his wardrobe, but she knew she could never do that; she would think about it and the curiosity would kill her. It was probably, she decided, something quite innocuous, so, smiling to herself for overdramatizing the situation, she opened it. In a bold, distinctive handwriting she read the cryptic message: 'I have some news for you. I am not doing the midnight show so we can slip away early.'

It was unsigned.

'I suppose you sleep with me because your wife is so heavily pregnant.' Maisie turned over in bed and groped for the pack of cigarettes on the bedside table. She extracted two, lit them both and then offered one to Hubert.

'You do think of the nastiest things to say,' Hubert said, taking it from her with, however, a note of amusement in his voice. 'We have such a wonderful time together and you have to try to spoil it. You do it all the time. Why?'

Maisie lay on her back and blew smoke rings into the air. 'I wonder what your motives are.'

'Why does one have to have a motive?' Hubert propped himself on an elbow and gazed at her. 'You are a very beautiful and desirable woman. Isn't that motive enough? A lot of men would like to be in my place. I consider myself very privileged.'

'I thought you were an awful snob when I first knew you.' Maisie reached up and stroked his chin.

'What made you change your mind?'

'Sex.'

'Well, you're very honest.'

'This is pretending, though, isn't it, Hubert?'

'What do you mean?'

'Play-acting.'

179

'Not for me. Is it for you?' He looked at her anxiously.

'I do love Ed. I feel horribly mean.'

'He will never know.'

'Sez you.'

Hubert ran his fingers through her wonderful, pure-gold hair. She was disconcertingly honest. That's what he liked about her – loved, perhaps. Was it possible that he was falling in love with Maisie? In the short time he'd spent with her he found her endlessly fascinating, a woman of great variety; but there was a very earthy side to her, with a style of cockney repartee that he found beguiling. She was clever and witty as well as beautiful and charming. Heads always turned wherever they went and he thought himself a lucky chap. She had so much free time that they were able to spend all of it together; and it was true that a good deal of it was spent in bed.

He watched the show every night at the club, sitting at the back with his cigarettes and whisky, watching her dance and knowing that, because of their intimacy, there were now no mysteries for him about that wonderful body.

Roxanne no longer came near him, because she knew who he came to see.

After the show they dined, usually at the Sans Souci, but not always, and then they went back to her small but comfortable flat in Bedford Square, where they stayed until approximately noon the next day, sometimes longer. They would then lunch, sometimes in town, sometimes further out, like at Richmond or Kew.

They often went to a film, and once Hubert went back to the house for a change of clothes while Maisie waited for him in a taxi round the corner.

It was a wonderful, exotic time and he never wanted it to end; but end it must.

As if reading his thoughts Maisie said, 'When are you going home?'

'It will have to be soon. The baby is nearly due.'

'And then that's the end of us, I suppose?'

'Of course not.' Bending, he planted a light kiss on her brow. 'This is just the beginning.'

Peg had a very restless, disturbed night. She lay awake a long time thinking about the note, and it was useless to try to pretend it meant nothing. He had had an assignation with someone and that someone must be a woman.

Had he a mistress? Is that why he'd gone to London? He had hardly ever used to go and now he went quite often. It had never occurred to her, but then the wife was always the last to suspect, the last to know – naturally.

When she had begun her affair with Hubert, he had been married and she had been engaged to Alan. They had both been guilty of deceit, though they had later found out that Ida Ryland had also had a lover and wanted a divorce, so she had put a detective on her husband's trail. Was that what she should do now? It seemed a horrible, sordid kind of thing to do, and also, she didn't want to divorce him. She wanted their marriage to be restored, as it had used to be when they were in love, during those halcyon years in Italy.

Peg realized then that she would give anything to have Hubert's love back again.

'Where do you suppose Hubert spends the night?' Violet asked her husband over the breakfast table.

'No idea.' Alan, lost in the morning paper, turned a page. Then he looked up at her. 'Why? Hasn't he been here?'

'Darling, you don't notice things, do you?' Chuckling, as though at some amiable eccentricity, Violet carefully spread some of Mrs Capstick's special orange marmalade on a piece of toast.

'Why should I?'

'Well, you are a journalist.' Violet popped the toast into her mouth and wiped her sticky fingers on a napkin. Often breakfast was the only time in their busy lives that she and Alan had to converse or exchange news. They were out most nights, usually surrounded by people and too tired when they eventually climbed into bed. 'I thought journalists noticed things.'

'Only important things,' Alan grunted, his head still inside the news pages of the paper, 'not tittle-tattle.'

Undeterred, Violet went on. 'Well, my precious brother hasn't been in for dinner, he hasn't been in for breakfast and his bed hasn't been slept in. Yet, ostensibly, he's been staying here for a week. Now what do you make of that?'

'Curious.' Alan shook his head, closed the paper, consulted his watch and got up from the table. 'I think it's clearly a case for Sherlock Holmes.'

He went over to her, kissed the top of her head and tucked the paper under his arm. Outside, his chauffeur was waiting to drive him to the office.

'Will you need the car today, Violet?'

'I might.'

'I'll tell Baxter to come back after dropping me.'

'Thank you, darling. Alan . . .' She looked towards him as he made for the door, and he stopped and turned.

'Yes, Violet?'

'Do you love me, just a little bit?'

'Of course I do,' he said and, blowing her a kiss, gently closed the door.

Violet slowly finished her breakfast. As usual, they sat at each end of the long table in the family dining room; and, as usual, since Hubert had arrived at the beginning of the week, three places had been laid.

They all had dined together the first night, before she and Alan had gone to the opera. They had had no idea where Hubert was going, but he'd been wearing a dinner jacket. He had begged a lift and got off with them at Covent Garden. They had had a brief chat in front of the opera house about the opera and who was singing and then, as Alan had taken Violet's arm to lead her inside, Hubert had gone up towards Long Acre.

'Wonder where he's going?' Violet had said.

Violet poured herself a fresh cup of coffee and lit a cigarette. It was a very dull, misty, cold morning and the gas lamps in the street outside were still on, though they afforded very little in the way of light to guide pedestrians on their way. She viewed the day ahead without enthusiasm. She had no fixed engagement and thought she might go to a film. In the evening they were entertaining a foreign journalist and his wife.

Violet, in fact, was very bored. Alan was clever and distinguished, but he was not an amusing or entertaining companion, with little small talk. Tonight there would probably be plenty of intelligent discussion about the situation in Europe, the growing Nazi threat that was exercising Alan and his liberal colleagues. It would not really interest Violet, but hopefully the foreign journalist's wife would be entertaining – the couple were Italian – and they could have a girlish gossip when the men were left to their port.

Violet heard the telephone ring and waited to see who it was – maybe one of her girl friends with an amusing idea to liven up the day. She rather wished she'd asked another couple for the evening and tried to think of someone who would not mind being invited at the last minute.

There was a tap on the door and Mr Jenkins put his head round.

'Lady Ryland on the telephone for you, madam.'

'Ah . . .' Violet thought quickly. If Peg enquired after Hubert, what could she possibly say? 'Would you tell her I've just gone out? I'll ring her later. I'm in a bit of a hurry today.' She paused. 'You didn't say I was in, did you?'

Mr Jenkins's face was imperturbable. 'I said I'd enquire, madam.'

'Good.' Violet sighed with relief.

'Oh, she did first ask for Lord Ryland, madam. I said he wasn't available. Her Ladyship seemed rather surprised and then asked if she could speak to you.'

As the door closed, Violet puffed thoughtfully at her cigarette. She would have to try to discover what that rascal of a brother of hers was up to.

Thirteen

Addie rose from the table and briskly started to clear away the breakfast dishes as Harold strolled out into the garden to smoke his morning pipe, followed by Arthur, who had seemed rather pleased to be back in his old home. On the other side of the kitchen baby Charlotte lay asleep in her pram. Stella remained where she was, sitting at the table, a half-drunk cup of tea in front of her, her eyes following Addie's movements.

'Soon be Christmas,' Addie called out cheerily, up to her elbows in soap suds. 'I shall have to speak to Frank about the tree.' She sighed deeply and looked at Stella as if seeking her sympathy. 'I should have done all my baking by now, but with all this fuss . . .' She gave a gesture of helplessness and turned back to the sink again.

'You might just pass me those few dishes, Stella,' she called over her shoulder, 'then shake the cloth out for me and help dry these few things like a good girl.'

'I am *not* a girl,' Stella said, snatching the tea towel from the rail and picking up one of the dishes. 'I am a grown woman.'

'Oh, sorry.' Addie turned to her apologetically, but there was a hint of sarcasm in her voice. 'I didn't mean to offend, but it's just that – well, Stella, I think you could do a bit more to make yourself helpful in the house. I haven't come here to wait on you, you know. I have enough on my hands as it is . . . Oh, and what time will you be in for tea tonight? I do like to know.'

Nicola Thorne

'I have *no* idea,' Stella said crisply. 'I am perfectly able to get my own tea, thank you, Addie, and I don't like being told what to do with my time in my own home.' She emphasized the word 'own'.

'Oh, really, Stella!' Addie turned to her with an exasperated sigh, 'you *are* being difficult this morning. I'm only trying to be helpful. Get out of the wrong side of the bed, did we?'

'No we did not!' Stella flung the tea towel on to the table and without uttering another word grabbed her stick and left the room, nearly knocking over Frank, who was coming through the door.

'Here, what's the matter?' he asked good-humouredly, but Stella almost pushed him aside without an apology and went as swiftly as she could along the corridor.

'Is she late for school or something?' he enquired of Addie.

'She's in a bad mood, that's what,' Addie said. 'I have no patience with her. She is quite better now, so there is no need to feel sorry for her, yet I've never known Stella so moody as she has been since we got back. It's as though she resents having us here, though why that should be I don't know. There is plenty of room. It was my home as much as hers, yet I suppose it's something to do with that, isn't it, Frank?'

Frank had taken up the tea towel discarded by Stella and continued to dry the dishes. 'Maybe,' he said with a shrug.

'Well, if that's the case, she really has become very selfish. I think we all spoiled her when she was so ill. Just you and she living alone in this large house and she resents giving her own sister a roof over her head.' She looked defensively at Frank. '*You* didn't mind, did you, Frank?'

'Oh, me? Not at all. I love it,' Frank said, wreathed in smiles as he put the dry dishes back in the appropriate places. 'I love having the family about me once again.' He gazed across at Charlotte. 'I never thought we'd see another baby in this house again. There have always been babies, children of

186

all ages, and that's how it should be; but as for Stella' – he shrugged – 'it is a bit of an upheaval for her. You know she is quiet by nature, likes things ordered and just so, and ever since you left we have been alone. I suppose she thinks now that the peace of the place has been destroyed.'

'Well, I think that attitude is a very, very selfish one,' Addie said firmly. 'She won't even say what time she's coming in for tea. You would think she would be glad to have it ready for her, but she's not.'

'It's because you've taken over the running of the place, Addie,' Frank said gently. 'I mean, for me it is wonderful because it is like old times and you were always such a good housekeeper, a wonderful cook.'

'Well, then I wonder Stella doesn't feel that way too,' Addie sniffed resentfully. '*And* I had to give the place a thorough clean when we first arrived. I think Stella had been letting things go. Now, Frank,' she said briskly, tying her apron round her waist, 'I am going to do some baking, so if you have nothing better to do you can take Charlotte and Arthur for a stroll and please send Harold back to me. I've got some little jobs for him to do.'

'I thought I should take Stella to school,' Frank said. 'It's quite frosty underfoot and it will give me the chance to have a little chat with her.'

'What a good idea,' Addie said. 'Talk some sense into her. Teach her to be thankful for small mercies. Oh, in that case, Harold can walk the children, otherwise he'll just be under my feet.'

As Frank went off to talk to Stella, Addie got out the baking dishes, the flour and suet required. She went into the larder and emerged with the ingredients for several kinds of pies. It was true that, when she had had a maid, she had done less cooking and no housework, but for many years she had kept house, and no one was better at it. She had found it quite easy to fall into her old ways again and Peg helped out by sending a woman down from the castle to assist with the cleaning and the washing.

It was true they had not been back long. Harold had left the school a little early, to be replaced by the deputy head. It had been a shock and a humiliation, and Addie had thrown herself almost frenetically into her new life, her new circumstances, to try to forget about the past, put it all behind her.

As far as Addie was concerned, Stella was quite useless, but she had never been as annoyed by her as she was today, because it seemed at once so selfish and also so ungrateful for all she had endeavoured to do since her return.

She went to the door and called Harold, who removed his pipe from his mouth and obediently answered her summons.

'Yes, dear?'

'I want you to take the children for a walk. You've too much time on your hands, Harold. It makes you brood and can't be healthy.'

'I can't help it, Addie. After Christmas I hope something will turn up.'

'I hope so too,' Addie said, 'or my sister and I will have a serious fall-out.'

Harold went in to fetch his coat and hat and put Arthur in a warm coat, with a scarf wound round his neck. By the time he returned to the kitchen Addie had Charlotte all wrapped up and tucked into her pram; she saw them to the gate and stood watching them for a while as Harold, pipe back in his mouth, shoulders hunched, began pushing the pram up the hill while little Arthur, undersized for his age, fell into a trot after him. They looked like a couple of lost souls. Then, shaking her head, she went back into the kitchen, where so many household tasks awaited her.

It had not been an easy time, she had to acknowledge that – and also that at times she lost her patience, particularly with her sister.

With her husband she felt she had to try to be more

patient, though he often got on her nerves too. He seemed to accept defeat so easily, to have lost his sparkle. Not that he'd ever shone or effervesced, but he had been a good deal more forceful, more decisive than he was now. Because of his apathy she made it her business to read the papers and teachers' journals herself and shove advertisements under his nose, almost ordering him to apply for them; but then he'd ask what the point was: he'd been turned down for so many jobs, and most of his applications were rejected without an interview.

Harold, Addie thought, as she sifted the suet and rolled out the pastry, hands covered with flour, really made a meal of their situation. After all, they were not in poverty. Harold had always been careful, with money saved up, but he said that he didn't know how long it would take him to get a job or even if he would ever get one.

It was clear he was in the doldrums. He had lost his job, his home – in a way, his self-respect. He hadn't, she knew, realized just how much he would be affected by it until they were actually here, moving in, back into her old bedroom, which was on the small side, with even less room now, as the baby's crib was with them too.

No, poor Harold really was like a man who had completely lost heart. It was as though the evil influence of Gerald Birch had somehow spread throughout the country, permeating every aspect of their lives.

For a while Stella, hunched beside Frank in the front of the car, said nothing. There was always rather a grand feeling about going to school in one of the Ryland cars, usually the Rolls-Royce because Frank liked to drive it; but how different was the situation between herself and Peg, who had a husband, children, a home – two or three homes, in fact – security, money, besides several expensive cars at her disposal. Stella felt that she had absolutely nothing and was dependent on the generosity and goodwill of other people. The worst thing was their pity and pity her they did, though they tried hard to hide it.

She was sure that Verity had offered her a home out of pity and then thought nothing of rejecting her when something else had come up, because she had no defences, nothing with which to protect herself.

She was aware that Frank kept glancing at her and snuggled deeper into her coat, pulling her muffler tight so that it half-covered her face.

Frank stopped some time before they reached the school. As they were quite early, they had some time to spare. 'Out with it, Stella,' he said.

'Out with what?'

'You know.'

'Addie gets on my nerves. She's taken over.'

'But my dear' – Frank put a hand on her shoulder – 'Addie loves you very much.'

'I know she does and I love her, but that's not the point. She patronizes me; they all do.' Stella turned to Frank with an air of desperation. 'I really want to get out of there, Frank, and make a life of my own.'

'But, Stella' – perturbed, Frank removed his hand – 'they will not be there for ever.'

'They will. They'll be there for a jolly long time. Harold can't get a job. I don't think he's really trying.'

'But he's very depressed.' Frank thought he should at least attempt to make an excuse for Harold. 'I can understand that.'

Stella's expression remained sceptical, completely lacking in the sympathy he expected of her. 'Of course he's depressed; but he won't get a job by sitting around all day smoking that ghastly pipe of his. He gets on my nerves. They both do. They all do. That's what makes me want to lead a life of my own; otherwise I'll spend my whole life as the crippled spinster sister growing bitter and old because no one really wants her.'

She suddenly threw herself against Frank's chest and buried her face in his coat. 'Oh Frank,' she said, 'I feel so unhappy at times, so afraid, so unsure of myself. I try not to let on, but I do.' She raised a tear-stained face towards his.' I have tried so hard to forget Ernest, to pretend I never met him, but I really miss him, I really do. I think repeatedly of the happiness we could have shared, of what might have been, what nearly was but never can be now.' She leaned her face against his chest once again, her tears soaking into his thick serge coat.

'There, there,' he murmured, patting her back, feeling totally inadequate to comfort her; 'there, there.' He paused for a moment, completely at a loss as to what to say, for how could one make up for such unbearable heartache? 'There, there,' he continued, gently, rhythmically patting her back. 'Something will turn up. It always does. I promise you that.'

'Maisie!' Peg cried with delight, making a valiant attempt to heave herself out of her chair. 'What a lovely surprise!'

'Please' – Maisie put out her hand – 'don't get up, but I thought that, as I was passing, I must pop in to see you.'

'It's been such a long time,' Peg said, searching her face.

'I know, I feel very bad about it.' Maisie shyly placed a large and most expensive-looking bunch of flowers on a side table.

'Oh, but you *shouldn't* have.' Peg looked at them appreciatively. 'I'm terribly sorry, but Hubert's not here. He's in London. It was so good of you to help us find Jenny.'

'Well, I was relieved, too.' Maisie sat down, tossing back her hair. As usual she looked beautiful, vibrant and alive, and Peg felt a pang of jealousy when she compared her to her own dumpy, inelegant figure.

'How is Jenny?' Maisie asked cautiously, not knowing how much Hubert had told her about the circumstances in which she had been found.

'Well, she is living in Bristol with Ver, and from all reports making excellent progress.'

'That's good.'

'Hubert will be sorry he missed you.'

'I came primarily to see you,' Maisie said offhandedly, 'and forgive me for not giving you any warning, but there is so much to do. I'm buying a house, a surprise for Ed when he gets back.'

'In Plymouth?' Peg looked surprised.

'Dartmoor – nearby. I hope Ed will like it. We can keep animals and ponies and it will give me something to do when he's away.'

'You must miss him.' Peg looked at her sympathetically.

'Oh, I do.' Maisie's fine eyes suddenly brimmed over. 'I do, very much. But he will be back in the spring.' She sat on the edge of her chair and looked earnestly at Peg. 'How *are* you, Peg?'

'Very well, considering.' Peg suddenly became animated. 'Look, I've just had an idea. We don't see nearly enough of you. Why don't you come and spend Christmas with us? We'll have a full house, but there is plenty of room.'

'I . . .' Maisie looked round as if she were seeking a way of escape, rather like a fox that has caught the scent of the hounds. 'I really should spend it with my mother. She's getting on, you know.'

'Oh, she's not *that* old,' Peg protested.

'No, but hopefully next year – that is, if Ed is back – it will be lovely for us all to spend Christmas together.'

And that, Peg felt, was the end of that.

Maisie stayed for lunch, but Peg thought she was different: edgy, somehow nervous. They did not, after all, know each other very well. Peg was a sociable being, used to all sorts of people, but conversation seemed strained. Maisie told her a lot about her house and where it was and how big and all the things she was doing with it. In fact, Maisie prattled incessantly as if to emphasize the feeling of unease, the artificiality that existed between them. Peg really wished that Hubert were there to help entertain her, until she remembered that Hubert had sometimes been quite nasty about Maisie and once had called her a tramp.

In all, it was a hurried and curiously unsuccessful visit, but Maisie was Ed's wife and Peg was determined that one day she should be a fully integrated member of the family.

In late afternoon she stood on the steps seeing Maisie into her natty sports car, still envying her her figure, her vivacity, her style, her dress sense. In fact, Maisie made her feel a bit dowdy.

'Come again soon!' she cried and Maisie nodded, then waved from the car window as she sped down the drive.

Jenny, hands folded neatly in her lap, sat next to Verity with an angelic expression on her face, drinking in the honeyed words of her new headmistress.

'We're *delighted* with Jennifer,' Miss Carter-Barnes went on. 'She's such a good scholar, such a sweet girl, such an example to others. In the short time that she's been here she has made a very favourable impression, and if this continues, by the summer she will be made a form prefect. Eventually' – the head paused, a triumphant smile on her face – 'I think you might consider sending her to university.'

'University!' Jenny gasped.

'I suppose you'd never thought of it, had you, Jennifer?'

Jenny shook her head.

'I must confess I never thought of it either.' Verity finally found her tongue, almost as stunned by what the head had to say as Jenny herself. Her duckling had turned into a swan.

After some polite chat Jenny and Verity took their leave of the headmistress, who saw them to the door of the school and stood waving them off. She had been made fully aware of Jenny's background and it was with some trepidation that she had agreed to have her at the school, but it was a small private school in a rather poor area of Bristol: fees were an important consideration and not to be sniffed at. To salve her conscience she had agreed, however, to accept her with the proviso that at the smallest sign of disturbance or misbehaviour Jenny would be asked to leave. Such a thing had never happened and it had puzzled the headmistress who, nearing retirement, had a vast store of experience to call on.

Somewhere along the way, in her short life, Jenny had taken a wrong turning, but now she was on the right track again, or so it seemed.

As the car reached the school gates the head shut the door and went to her study to continue writing her end-of-term reports, regretful that they were not all as good as Jennifer Smith's.

Jenny was unusually silent on the way home. She was normally a chatterer who seldom stopped talking, but she hardly said a word, and Verity kept glancing anxiously at her.

'Are you all right?'

Jenny nodded.

'Surprised at such a glowing report?' Verity smiled as she stopped outside the house. Jenny nodded again, turned to collect her school satchel from the back seat and got out of the car. Verity, carrying a few things she'd bought on the way home, followed her. She had taken a half-day off to go to the school, having been full of trepidation when she had received the head's request for an interview; but it had all gone so well she could hardly believe it.

Inside, she removed her coat and hat and took most of the stuff she'd bought to the kitchen, while Jenny went upstairs to change out of her uniform and wash her hands and face.

Usually, when Verity was working, Jenny would then sit down at once at her desk and get on with her homework, but on days when Verity was off, or at weekends, they liked having tea in front of the fire.

Oh, Happy Day!

Since she had lived with Verity, Jenny had become a changed personality as the stresses that had dogged her recent past faded into the background. She was a girl who thrived on security and love. Above all, she liked to be the centre of attention, as Verity had divined, and this she had received in full measure. She was what she wanted to be, the focal point of Verity's life, but she was not spoilt. It had turned out to be an ideal, mutually enhancing relationship.

When Jenny got downstairs, Verity had just carried the tea tray into the sitting room and was drawing the heavy curtains across the French window.

'I hate it when it gets dark so early, don't you?' she asked, crossing the room and beginning to pour the tea.

Jenny shook her head. 'I like the dark.' She accepted tea from her aunt and selected a piece of cake.

'You seem very solemn today, Jenny.' Verity felt slightly worried about her atypical silence. 'I thought you'd be so pleased at what the head had to say about you that you'd be all bubbly. You like it here, don't you? You like the school?'

Jenny nodded vigorously.

'Then what's the matter?'

'I don't want to go home for Christmas. In fact, I don't think of it as "home" at all. This is home.'

Verity felt pleased and flattered. 'Oh, that's it, is it? Don't you think it would be nice to see your mother and stepfather? Give them such a good report?'

Jenny shook her head. 'Not particularly.'

'Is it the baby? Might you feel that you don't like her again?'

'I *don't* like her, that's for sure; but it's not that. I just don't feel comfortable. Mummy and Harold have made no attempt to see me since I've been with you. I feel you're more a parent to me than either of them.'

'I see.' Verity paused thoughtfully, noting the use of the word 'Harold' to replace 'Daddy', the way in which she

195

usually referred to her stepfather. It was true that Jenny had not been contacted by either Addie or Harold and this had both worried and shocked her. She wrote weekly accounts of Jenny's progress and once or twice Addie had telephoned her, but this sense of ostracism continued. It would certainly be a very difficult Christmas back at the lodge, but they were expected and it had to be done.

Finally she said, 'I thought you should go to the lodge, Jenny. Try to build bridges. I'll help all I can.'

'But you'll be at the castle.'

'My dear, it's only two minutes' walk up the hill.'

'Might I not stay at the castle too?' Jenny pleaded.

'I think you should stay with your parents, your little brother and baby sister. Besides, you don't like your Uncle Hubert very much, do you?'

All in all, Verity thought that Christmas could be tricky, a difficult time – not the season of goodwill that ideally one would have liked.

Maisie was playing with her food, uninterestedly pushing it from one side of the plate to the other, making little mounds out of her potatoes and then squashing them flat with her fork like a child building sandcastles. Her task seemed to absorb her.

'What's the matter?' Hubert asked after watching her for a while. 'Aren't you hungry?'

Shaking her head, Maisie put her knife and fork neatly together; then she groped in her bag for a cigarette and lit it.

'Do you feel all right?' Hubert asked anxiously. Usually after the show Maisie was ravenous.

'I went to see Peg,' Maisie said abruptly. 'If you want to know, I feel bad about it.'

'Why on *earth* did you do that?' Looking really angry, Hubert put his knife and fork together, too. Behind them on the dance floor of the Sans Souci couples gyrated, heads close together.

196

'Well, I hadn't seen her for a long time. I felt she might
think something was up – you know, be suspicious.'

'Well, I think it was a very silly thing to do. You might
have consulted me.'

'I was on my way back from Plymouth; I did it on impulse.
Now I wish I hadn't. She looked very pregnant and so
vulnerable. She said she was sorry you weren't there. I didn't
read anything into that and I'm sure she doesn't suspect
anything.'

'Of course she doesn't,' Hubert said impatiently. 'There is
no reason why she should.'

'Still, I feel uneasy.'

'Serves you right. You shouldn't have gone.'

'She asked me to stay at Christmas.'

'Of course you said no.'

Maisie's eyes flashed. 'Supposing I'd said yes, would you
be furious?'

'I'd think that you'd contrived a very sticky situation, but I
can see by the expression on your face that you declined. You
know you're playing a little game with me, Maisie. I don't
know why, but I don't like it.'

'But as Peg said, as a family we've got to get together some
time. Wouldn't you like me there for Christmas, Hubert?'
Her tone was bantering, but Hubert thought he could detect a
rather malicious note in it.

'No, I would not,' Hubert said coldly. 'It would be un-
necessarily complicating. It would be breaking the rules.'

'What rules?' Maisie's eyes narrowed.

'The rules we tacitly accepted when we started this affair:
that we are both married to other people and we should keep
our distance from them.'

'You mean a bit of fun?'

'Well, what else? I don't understand you, Maisie. You
profess yourself madly in love with Ed.'

'And you're keeping the bed warm until he comes home?'

197

'Do you want to dance?' Hubert asked, anxious to change the subject.

Maisie promptly got up and he took her in his arms; but it wasn't the same as usual. There was no rapport, no feeling of passion longing to erupt, and they soon gave up and returned to their seats, where Maisie took a long drink from her glass of whisky like someone dying of thirst.

Hubert frowned. He thought she had been drinking rather a lot. 'I'll take you home,' he said, signalling for the bill. 'If you've come all the way from Plymouth today you must be tired.'

The doorman called a taxi and they sat together silently in the back during the short drive to Bedford Square. When it stopped outside her house, Maisie looked at Hubert as though she expected him to continue the journey, but he got out with her and, after paying the fare, stood on the pavement counting his change.

It was bitterly cold. Maisie put the key in the door and glanced back at him. 'Do you want a nightcap?'

'Look, you're tired. I think I'll walk home,' he said. 'I feel like the exercise.'

He leaned towards her and kissed her on the cheek.

'Right.' With a cold sensation clutching at her heart, Maisie opened the door and it clicked shut behind her.

Hubert walked out of Bedford Square, crossed Tottenham Court Road, continued along Oxford Street as far as the Circus and then through Mayfair towards South Audley Street. There were very few people around; it was foggy and the lamps glowed eerily as he passed. A few houses still had lights in them, though it was two o'clock in the morning. He was angry with Maisie because he felt she was complicating their affair. There had been no need at all to go and see Peg, especially at a time like this, so near Christmas.

What did she want?

So far their affair had been conducted perfectly discreetly.

It had been enjoyable, but now she decided to muddy the waters, and what would happen when at last Ed did come home?

Violet said, 'How *nice* to see you at breakfast, Hubert. That makes a pleasant change.'

'Don't be sarcastic, Violet.' Hubert, plate in hand, lifted the lids of the silver entrée dishes on the sideboard and inspected the contents: porridge, kippers, sausages, bacon and eggs, mushrooms, tomatoes – all beautifully cooked and piping hot.

'What happens to all this food?' he asked as he sat down. 'Is it thrown out?'

'I have no idea.' Violet, who kept an eye on her figure, had only grapefruit and toast.

'Isn't Alan shocked at such waste, with half the population starving?'

Violet looked across at her brother with an expression of amusement. 'Darling, I didn't know you cared.'

'Well, I do care. Where is Alan, by the way?'

'He breakfasted early. He normally does. You know, Hubert, you really should behave more discreetly when you're having an affair.'

Hubert liberally sugared his porridge and poured milk over it. As he had eaten so little the night before he was quite hungry.

'What makes you think I'm having an affair?'

'I should have thought it was quite obvious, but you know it is thoughtless of you. It puts me in a dilemma if Peg phones. I don't know what to say to her. Let us at least know where you are, if not with whom.' She looked at him archly. 'It's inconsiderate and rude. Besides, I think you're taking awful risks with your marriage.'

Hubert finished his porridge and then helped himself to a selection from the sideboard.

'What are you doing for Christmas, Violet?' he asked as he sat down again.

'We're going to Venice.'

'What a very good idea.'

'Were you afraid that we might come to Ryland?'

'My dear, you'd always be welcome. In fact, we really don't see enough of you.'

'We thought Venice might be a last chance for a while. You see . . .' Violet paused, seeming at a loss to know how to convey such momentous, such longed-for news. 'You see, Alan and I are expecting a baby.'

Fourteen

Christmas 1933

'Such wonderful news,' Verity cried, clasping her hands together; 'Jenny's head teacher is so pleased with her progress. She's one of the brightest pupils in the class and the head thinks she might be a suitable candidate for university.'

Addie went pink with pleasure, but Harold seemed less certain.

'University,' he mumbled. 'Well, we'll see. Expensive places, universities.'

'I'm sure there will be no problem about money,' Verity said quickly, 'but that's something we can discuss at a later date.'

Jenny had dreaded this visit and, perhaps hoping to get it off to a good start, Verity had lost no time in making her announcement. They had only just sat down to tea and Jenny's bag was still in the hall.

It had been getting dark when they arrived. The lights were on in the lodge and the Christmas tree, as yet undecorated, was visible through the parlour window. Tea was already laid on the table in the kitchen. Stella had come down from her room and Frank, with baby Charlotte in his arms, was waiting in the hall.

There were kisses and hugs, but it had been an awkward reunion. There had been a sense of strain and, yet again, Jenny wished they had not come but had stayed in Aunt Ver's nice house, just the two of them together. Her mother had kissed her, Harold had not. It seemed to Jenny that a chasm had opened between her stepfather and herself and she wondered now if she minded. Was not fidelity the test of love and had he not failed her in this? Whereas she had come to love Aunt Ver very much.

'Are you excited about Christmas?' Stella asked Jenny, who nodded her head.

'Very,' she said insincerely. She had decided to be nice to everyone, not to argue or contradict, nor be awkward. She just wanted to get this visit over as quickly as possible so as to be able to go home again.

'We have good news too,' Addie said as they settled to their tea. 'Harold has been offered a post at a tutorial college in Yeovil. Not quite the sort of thing he is used to and not as much responsibility, but it's a start.'

'Better than going abroad,' Harold said, tucking his napkin into the top of his shirt.

'That is good news.' Verity expressed genuine pleasure. 'When do you start?'

'After Christmas. It's a temporary appointment and it is only part-time, but it may become permanent. Let's say there is an opportunity there.'

'Will you be moving nearer Yeovil?'

'Well, as long as we can stay here we shall. That is' – Addie looked nervously at her sister – 'if Frank and Stella can put up with us a bit longer. It saves a lot of money and there is the fact that it is a temporary post; nothing is secure.'

'It's really up to Frank,' Stella said. 'In fact, I shall be leaving after Christmas, too.'

There was a shocked silence round the table and for a moment no one spoke.

'How do you mean, you'll be leaving?' Addie, with a glance at Frank, was the first to speak.

'Did you know about this, Frank?'

Frank shook his head, looking numb.

'I only just heard,' Stella explained. 'I decided it was time I flew the nest too, stood on my own feet. I heard of a job through Lorna Marks, whose aunt is the head of a small girls' school in London. I said I was interested and her aunt came down to see me at Lorna's two days ago. This morning I had a letter offering me the job' – and she produced an envelope from the pocket of her cardigan and waved it in the air.

'They don't mind that I'm crippled and use a stick. It is a live-in situation and I shall also have some domestic duties. I am very excited about the whole thing' – her eyes travelled around the table – 'and I hope you all will be too. I also start in January. The school is situated in Hampstead, which everyone says is a lovely part of London.'

'Well, we're happy for you, of course, if it's what you want.' Addie spoke again. 'But it's a shock. I hope it has nothing to do with us?'

'It's an opportunity,' Stella said tactfully, 'which I didn't want to turn down.'

After tea everyone helped with the washing-up except Harold, who went off to smoke his pipe. He was never expected to do anything in the house. It was a tradition that the sisters had grown up with. Frank, who was much more domesticated, also went off to a job at the castle, and Jenny went upstairs to unpack.

Verity, wanting to talk to Stella, suggested they go to help Peg with the Christmas-tree decorations, and the sisters, well wrapped up, trudged slowly up the hill arm in arm.

'Are you *sure* about London?' Verity said. 'It's a long way.'

'You lived there for years, so did Peg. Don't patronize me, Ver.'

'Oh, I'm *not* patronizing you!' Despite the cold Verity felt her face go pink. 'I don't know how you could suggest such a thing. You're so sensitive, Stella. There is no need for it. I just felt that if you incarcerated yourself in a small girls' school in North London you might be there for ever.'

'What's wrong with that?'

'Meeting people, you know.'

'If you mean men, I don't meet any here.' It was quite a steep hill leading up to the castle and she paused to get her breath. 'Anyway, I had to get away.'

'Because of Addie?' Verity looked at her sympathetically.

Stella tucked her arm through Verity's and they proceeded on their way. 'Because of Harold most of all. Addie is bossy and she irritates me, but it's Harold who really gets on my nerves. He is so lazy, so selfish.' She looked despairingly at her sister. 'Frankly, the place isn't the same, Ver. With them around it isn't home any more.'

In an effort to comfort her, Verity pulled Stella very close to her. It was a situation that, in a way, she felt responsible for by having rejected her sister in favour of her niece; but who should really have come first? Right now she didn't know the answer. Or perhaps, to be more truthful, she did: she wanted the young girl to play the part of the daughter she knew she would never have; and Jenny was a joy, no doubt about that.

Yet in her heart of hearts Verity knew that she'd failed Stella, who felt rejected, cast adrift; and for that she did reproach herself.

The following day was Christmas Eve and an atmosphere of bustle and excitement seemed slowly to be invading the castle. Verity was awake early; people were up and moving around, and she guessed that even now Mrs Capstick was at work in the kitchen. One of the maids had already crept in to light a fire in her bedroom and for some time she stayed huddled under the covers until the room heated up, thinking about all the things there were to do today.

Verity got up and quickly washed herself in a basin of cold water. As a nurse in wartime she had been used to Spartan conditions and, besides, she couldn't wait for the hot water to arrive because she was in a hurry to get downstairs.

For Verity, Christmas was an exciting time, redolent of the days when Mum, who had so loved the festive season, had made it a time of fun and enchantment, which was now passed on to her grandchildren, who were sure to be wide awake in their nursery. There would be a big family breakfast and then she would go back into the lodge to help Addie for, although most of the celebrations were taking place at the castle, with dinner this evening and Christmas Day luncheon, there was still plenty to do. Besides, she wanted to see more of her sister, who had gone through such traumas in the last few months, and learn how she really was faring.

Addie was glazing a large piece of ham when Verity arrived after breakfast at the castle. Her first question was to ask where Jenny was, and Addie said that she and Stella had gone to the village to look up some old friends.

'She really seems glad to be home,' Addie added with a smile. 'She's like my old Jenny.' She looked gratefully at her sister. 'Thanks to you, Ver. You were there just when you were needed and we owe you a lot. Both Harold and I noticed the difference and after supper last night she sat and chatted away, telling us all about her school and her friends. She had even brought one of her compositions for Harold to see. He was very pleased.'

'Oh, I'm so glad.' Verity sighed with relief. 'Can I give you a hand?'

Addie put the glazed ham in the larder and emerged with a bowl of potatoes. 'You can help me peel some spuds. Will you be here for lunch?'

'Oh, yes, I'd like to spend the day with you, if I may. It is so lovely to be with you and to know that things are so much better. I do hope Harold likes his new job.'

'Oh, I think he will.' Addie passed Verity a knife and they both began peeling potatoes. The talk turned to their mother and the happy Christmases they'd spent when she'd been alive. How different things had been then.

'Time for coffee,' Addie said at last, sweeping the potato peelings into a bin, from where they would eventually go to the pigs, and putting the peeled potatoes into a pan on the stove.

A pale, wintry sun shone through the kitchen door and Verity thought that really little had changed physically since their mother's day. The house almost seemed caught in a time warp with its gleaming flagstones and the old-fashioned kitchen range.

'Seriously, now that Harold is getting a job, how long do you think you'll stay here?'

'I'd like to stay here for quite a long time.' Addie handed her sister her coffee and sat opposite her. 'I feel very much at home here and it's nice being so near Peg. In a way, I was isolated in our previous place. I had a lot of time on my hands. Now I'm busy all the time and Arthur and Charlotte can grow up with their cousins.'

She looked at Verity and her expression underwent a subtle change. 'Ver,' she began rather hesitantly, 'Harold and I were talking last night about the difference in Jenny and how much more settled she seemed, and we thought we would like to have her home again.'

Verity felt a sharp stab in her chest as though someone had thrust a dagger into it.

'But she is very happy where she is.'

'Yes, Verity, I know and believe me, we don't wish to appear ungrateful for all you've done. Jenny just needed help getting back on her feet, finding her priorities again, and you really have done wonders.'

'Did you tell Jenny about your thoughts?'

'Oh no, not yet. We hoped you might prepare the ground – you know, talk to her about it, see how she feels.'

'That would be very hard for me, Addie.' Verity shifted uneasily in her seat. 'I'll be quite honest with you: I should miss Jenny very much; she has become a real companion to me.'

'Oh, I know that, Ver, and no one would begrudge you your feelings for Jenny. She will come and visit you often, I promise. But there is also the matter of school fees. It is rather a burden and she was happy at the school here. I'm sure they'd take her back with such good reports.'

'If the school fees are all that concerns you,' Verity said quickly, 'I would be more than happy to take care of them.'

'But it is what is in Jenny's best interests, don't you see?' Addie said stubbornly: 'to be with her mother and stepfather, her little brother and sister, leading a normal life.'

'She is leading a perfectly normal life with me,' Verity said with asperity, 'and I think her best interests are served by staying with me and continuing at the school where she is happy and settled. You don't know what is going to happen here, or how long you'll be able, or even want, to stay.'

At that moment a shadow darkened the threshold and Harold came in rubbing his hands.

'It is very cold out there,' he said. 'I think I shall have to have my pipe in the parlour in future. The thing about having one's own home is that one can smoke anywhere.'

His tone querulous, he addressed Verity: 'I only have my pipe in the garden because Stella objects to my smoking indoors. She calls the tune, you know. I shan't say I'll miss her.'

'Coffee, dear?' Addie shot him a warning look.

'Please.'

'I've been telling Verity about our wish to have Jenny back.'

'Oh?' Harold's expression suggested that this was complete news to him. 'And what do you think, Verity?'

'I think it is a very bad idea,' Verity replied bluntly. 'Not only is Jenny doing well at school, she is settled and I have become very attached to her.'

'Oh, yes.' Harold spooned sugar into his coffee. 'But even though we live rent-free and I am about to get a job, during

207

these last few months I have had to dip into my savings. As Stella is leaving, there will be room for Jenny. She is, after all, Addie's daughter. She misses Jenny, who could also be of great help to her mother in the house.'

'But I shall miss her so much and I am sure she will miss me.'

Harold's tone became acerbic. 'I *understand* that, Verity, and you have been wonderful to her; but she is *not* your daughter and I don't think it is altogether healthy for her to be so long away from her real home.'

Verity, her patience by this time severely tested, took a deep breath. 'Be that as it may, Harold, I think it *is* in Jenny's best interests to stay where she is. A change will only distract and possibly disturb her. Furthermore . . .' She paused. '. . . I am not sure she wants to come home again on a permanent basis.'

'Oh, really.' Harold's tone was derisive. 'What makes you say that?'

'Because she is very happy with me. She felt you were not very nice to her, not very understanding.'

'She was not very nice to us!' Harold almost spat out the words. 'She—'

'Let's not talk about the past.' Verity's face had a high colour and she felt she was in a desperate situation. 'She has a large room and the run of the house. She has made friends at the new school. I really am thinking of Jenny first when I say this, and as for the fees, I would be more than happy to take care of them myself. In fact, if you would agree, and she does, I would be delighted to bring up Jenny as my daughter rather as I was brought up by Uncle Stanley and Aunt Maude.'

'I was afraid that was what was behind all this,' Addie said sharply, 'and it is something I very much want to avoid. When you went to live with Aunt Maude and Uncle Stanley, you virtually ceased to be a member of this family and that is the last thing I want for my daughter.'

After this conversation, which ended acrimoniously, Verity decided not to stay for lunch after all and Addie did not try to dissuade her. The matter was left unresolved and they agreed to discuss it later when they had had time to think about it, tempers were not so frayed and they could seek out Jenny's views. But as Verity walked up the hill she realized that a thoroughly bad atmosphere now permeated the situation with her sister and brother-in-law, which threatened not only Christmas, but also the immediate future as well.

Hubert sat in his study, attending to some mundane estate business. Yet he was in a curious frame of mind and found it difficult to concentrate on his work. It was that quiet time of day, early evening, when the children had gone to bed and Peg and Verity were resting in their rooms before dinner. It had been a family day and he had enjoyed it.

He cherished days spent with his family; the boys were getting older and doing more interesting things; Jude was about to go to infant school and already showed an aptitude for sports. Catherine was a mischievous toddler who had delighted in finding her feet – into everything. Even the sight of his pregnant wife was a source of great pleasure and satisfaction to Hubert: a kind of fecund earth-mother about to bring forth their child.

Hubert really liked to see himself in this role of husband, father, landowner, pillar of the Establishment. It was infinitely preferable to that of a middle-aged Romeo inhabiting sleazy London clubs in search of a night's pleasure, prey to a crazy infatuation with a striptease dancer, although really it hadn't been like that at all, though it might be how other people saw it.

At this time of the year he was deeply conscious of Christmases past and how different they had been, with a large house party, guests waited on by twice if not three times as many servants as they had now. A huge amount of food and drink had been consumed. There had been a lot of hunting with a meet on Boxing Day. It had not really changed much after the war because food in the countryside was always plentiful, although there had been a certain degree of austerity and, of course, more importantly, a number of the men who had graced the parties before, including Lydney Ryland, were there no longer.

Hubert, in a nostalgic frame of mind, put aside his papers, lit a cigarette, poured himself a whisky, got some old family photograph albums and looked through them.

He then sat back, thinking of the past – of Jenny, his brother's daughter, whom he hoped one day to understand and befriend; and then suddenly he thought of Maisie. They had parted on a sour note and hadn't spoken since.

On an impulse he dialled her number. It rang for some time and he was about to replace the receiver when he heard her voice.

'Maisie.'

'Hubert,' she said softly, her voice sounding very sexy.

'What are you doing there? Peg said you were going to your mother's.'

'I may go tomorrow,' Maisie said. 'I'm working tonight. Christmas Eve.'

'I miss you, Maisie.'

'I miss you, too. How is the party going?'

'Oh, family, that sort of thing. There's a formal dinner tonight in about an hour's time. I wish you were here.'

'I wish I was, too.' She paused. 'Are we still friends?'

'Of course we're friends. Always will be.'

'After the other night, I thought . . .'

'Well, I was upset.'

'How's Peg?'

'Very pregnant. I must go now, Maisie. I'll call you in the New Year. Goodbye, darling, and happy Christmas.'

'Happy Christmas,' she said, but he thought she didn't sound happy at all. Perhaps she was very lonely.

He was in the act of putting away his albums when Cyril the butler opened the door without knocking.

'Excuse me, My Lord, but Miss Verity says could you come at once. Her Ladyship has started in labour.'

Hubert rushed up the stairs two at a time to find Peg looking in obvious discomfort and Verity bathing her forehead. Peg's personal maid Florence, who had summoned Verity, stood anxiously at the foot of the bed.

'You had better get the doctor, Hubert.' Verity turned to him without taking her eyes off Peg. 'I don't think this labour will be a very long one.'

'Darling, are you all right?' Hubert looked distractedly at his wife, who gave a feeble wave.

'I'm fine. Don't worry; it will soon be over.' Then she grimaced in pain.

'What shall I do about dinner?' Hubert asked.

'Eat it,' Verity commanded briskly, 'but get the doctor first.'

'Thank goodness I have a midwife for a sister,' Peg said.

'You would choose Christmas Eve,' Verity grumbled, but bent and planted a swift, awkward kiss on her brow. 'You'll be all right. With any luck we'll have a Christmas baby. I'd feel happier, though, if you were in hospital.'

'Why? Catherine was born at home.'

'I still think hospital is the best place for a woman to have a baby.'

There was, in fact, something about Peg's condition that made Verity unhappy. Her pulse was weak and the contractions irregular. She was also concerned about Peg's colour as the labour, instead of being swift, as Verity had expected, became prolonged.

She confided her misgivings to the family doctor, Dr

Nicola Thorne

Woolridge, who arrived within an hour of being called. Hubert, instead of obeying instructions to eat, remained with Peg, sensing that something was amiss, and Peg seemed to be losing touch with reality, slipping in and out of consciousness. Verity kept her fingers perpetually on Peg's pulse while the doctor repeatedly took her blood pressure.

Then, without warning, a thin trickle of blood oozed on to the sheet covering the bed. The doctor made a swift internal examination as Peg's face turned ashen, her lips went blue, and Verity had difficulty finding a pulse.

'We must get her to hospital quickly,' the doctor said to Hubert; 'there is absolutely no time to be lost.'

Hubert sat by the side of Peg's bed as he had done for many days past, his eyes hardly ever leaving her face. She was asleep. She slept a great deal, but at least she was alive, and so was the baby, who had been christened soon after he was born on account of his weak condition. He had been given the name Nicholas because he had been born on Christmas Day.

Mother and child were now well on the way to recovery, but Nicholas remained in hospital while Peg, who had now come home, was able to get up for a brief period every day. She had suffered an intra-uterine bleed, which had caused her sudden collapse, but the prompt action of the doctor, the dash to the hospital by ambulance and an immediate emergency caesarean had ensured both her survival and that of her baby.

Death had, in fact, been very close. The doctors said that, but for their timely intervention, the baby could have drowned in his mother's blood and she could have bled to death. Such an emergency was a rare, but not unknown complication of childbirth and Verity had been absolutely right when she had said that the best place for a woman to have a baby was in hospital.

212

Hubert spent most of the day with Peg and during the periods in which she slept he thought a lot about past events, in particular his relationship with Maisie, which he attributed to the temporary breakdown of his marriage. It had not been a glorious episode, not one to be proud of, but it had happened. It took near-death to make one realize one's priorities in life and he knew for certain now that he was a family man rather than a Lothario. He loved his family and, above all, his wife – a fact that had come so poignantly home to him when he had thought she was going to die. In a way, Maisie had always been more realistic than he. She'd called it play-acting and he knew that she was right.

Hubert raised his eyes and saw that Peg's were open, looking at him.

'Penny for them?' she said, raising her head.

'I'm glad you're alive.' Hubert took Peg's hand and held it tightly in his.

'You look very tired,' Peg said. 'I don't think you're taking enough care of yourself. Have you seen baby today?'

'No, I'm going this afternoon. He will be able to come out soon.'

'Oh, I'm so *glad*.' Peg sank back on her pillow. 'Then we shall be united as a family again.'

She looked up and saw Florence standing in the doorway with a huge bunch of flowers clasped in her arms.

'Oh, how lovely!' Peg exclaimed, arms outstretched to receive them. 'I wonder who they're from?'

Florence put the flowers on the bed and Peg opened the card that accompanied them: 'Much love to dearest Peg and darling baby Nicholas. Maisie and Ed.'

There was a row of kisses followed by a postscript: 'PS We have been so worried about you.'

Peg studied the card, above all the bold, distinctive handwriting that seemed to leap out at her, and she remembered with absolute certainty where she'd seen it before. She handed the card over to Hubert.

'It's from Maisie,' she said with a smile. 'How kind.'

Addie stood at the door of Jenny's room, looking at the open suitcase on her bed. 'What are you doing?' she asked.

'Packing,' Jenny said. 'I shall soon have to go home.'

Soon after Peg came out of hospital Verity had gone back to Bristol, leaving Jenny ostensibly to spend the rest of her holiday with her parents. Because of the crisis with Peg, all plans for the future had been shelved; nor had there been any discussion about them. As far as Jenny was concerned, the understanding was that she would return to school in Bristol.

'I see.' Addie perched on the side of the bed. 'I hope it has been a happy time for you here, Jenny?'

'Oh, yes,' Jenny exclaimed, throwing some clothes into the case, shutting it and putting it under the bed; 'except, of course, for what happened to Auntie Peg. But I shall be glad to get home.'

Addie seemed about to say something and then changed her mind. 'Tea's ready when you come downstairs.'

'Right, Mummy; I'll just wash my hands and be right down.'

When she arrived in the kitchen Harold and Addie were already at the table waiting for her.

'Nearly finished,' she said with a smile. 'Packing, I mean.'

Addie looked very nervous and the hand that poured the tea shook a little. 'Jenny, dear,' she said, passing her cup, 'there is something we want to talk to you about.' Addie's nerve seemed to fail her and she looked for help to Harold, who was obviously nervous too.

'Well.' Harold noisily cleared his throat. 'We – your mother and I – have much enjoyed having you here, Jenny, and we wondered if you'd like to stay?'

'*Stay?*' Jenny looked puzzled and began to spread a piece of bread thickly with strawberry jam.

'Permanently. Come home, Jenny. We are your parents and you belong here.'

Jenny looked up in astonishment. 'You mean *never* go back to Aunt Ver?'

'Well, for holidays. Of course you will still see a lot of her.'

'But I thought I was going to stay with her and go to school? You asked me about my work and my friends and . . . well, I thought everything had all been arranged.' Jenny's voice became a little hysterical.

'We would very much like you to stay here.' Addie spoke tremulously. 'We do both love you.'

'You didn't show me very much love before. You were glad to get rid of me.'

'We were not. We did love you, but your behaviour was . . . well, it was difficult at the time to accept it. We are sorry now, but we think this break has benefited us all.'

Addie nodded with approval at Harold's choice of words.

'Have you discussed this with Aunt Ver?' Jenny demanded, her voice rising even more.

'Of course.'

'And what did she say?'

'She said it was up to you.'

'Well, if it's up to me,' Jenny said firmly, 'I want to go back and be with her, and if anyone tries to stop me, I shall run away again and this time *nobody* will ever be able to find me, I can promise you that.'

'How good of you to come, Frank,' Verity said as she alighted from the train and he reached for her overnight bag.

'I could hardly let you travel by car in this weather.'

'Jenny all packed and ready?'

'Yes.' Frank smiled as he opened the car door and Verity climbed in. 'She threatened to run away again. She is a monkey.'

215

'But a very *charming* monkey,' Verity said indulgently. 'I love her so much. I'm flattered and pleased she decided to come back to me. Do you think I'm wrong, Frank?'

'I think it's what Jenny wants,' Frank said. 'She is a very headstrong young lady.'

'She will see lots of her parents.'

'Of course.'

'And she can go back any time.'

'That's understood, too,' Frank said, starting the car.

Verity gazed at the frost-covered countryside through which they were passing, conscious of having won a splendid victory. Jenny had chosen her and now she had someone close to her, a blood relation on whom she could lavish all her love. She would make something of Jenny, as Uncle Stanley and Aunt Maude had made something of her, given her a chance in life. They had been proud of her and everyone would be so proud of Jenny. She would make sure of that.

She and Frank fell into a discussion about Peg and the progress of the baby, who was soon to come home.

'It was such a terrible time.' Verity's voice was full of emotion. 'To think we might have lost Peg. It's just too awful to contemplate, isn't it?'

Frank lightly touched her arm. 'Well it didn't happen, Ver, thanks to you being there.'

'It wasn't just me. Dr Woolridge was excellent.' Verity paused and then went on slowly: 'He reminded me of a surgeon I once worked with who had a similar quality of decisiveness that saved many lives.' She gave a deep sigh as she remembered that sad, furtive romance, which seemed so long ago, with Philip Beaumaurice.

'Anyway, all is well now,' Frank said cheerfully; but then a more sombre note entered his voice. 'I shall miss Stella terribly. She has been part of our lives for so long. When I took her to the station yesterday, she broke down.' His expression was anxious. 'Do you think, Ver, that she has done the right thing?'

'Oh without doubt,' Verity said robustly; 'I am sure that Stella will very much enjoy being in London. It will be the making of her.' Although in her heart she once again experienced that sudden sharp stab of guilt, she turned to Frank with a reassuring, confident smile on her face.

March 1934

Maisie stood on the quay in busy Devonport, searching the deck of the great warship as it drew alongside. Looking very smart, the officers and ratings formed an impressive phalanx and, as the ship got nearer, those on the quayside started waving frantically to the men on deck who, however, did not dare break ranks.

Maisie desperately searched the deck for a sign of Ed, but could not make him out beneath the sea of white caps.

She had earlier spotted Mrs Walmer-Foster and some of the wives further down the quay, and was careful to keep well away from them.

Suddenly, she thought she saw Ed and waved, calling his name; but of course, even if it was him he would not be able to hear.

Finally the ship was secured, the gangplank lowered and as the men began to stream down, there was a surge towards them. For a moment, as partners rushed towards one another, Maisie thought that he had not been on board: lost at sea. Then she saw him, looking rather lonely in the crowd, peering this way and that.

She crept up from behind him, put her hands across his eyes and said in his ear, 'Guess who?'

For a while they sat in the car, looking at the new house. Maisie had left the club just after Christmas and had spent all this time getting it ready. It was their love nest and she had kept sending Ed reports of it so that he almost felt he knew it already. It was a long, low, whitewashed house standing in about half an acre of garden, with an apple orchard, on the edge of a village. Inside, all the walls were white and the furniture was old, but not antique.

'Nice place to bring up kids,' Ed said. 'Shall we go in?' He continued admiringly, 'You're an amazing woman, Maisie, doing all this by yourself.' He looked searchingly at her. 'Were you very lonely?'

'Very.'

Once inside, he inspected everything. Then Maisie opened a bottle of champagne she'd hoarded from the club and splashed it into two tall glasses. She remembered about it being a whore's drink, but it was a drink of celebration, too.

They linked arms and sipped the wine from each other's glass, and then Ed rolled his eyes towards the stairs.

'We can eat later,' he said.

Later – a long time later – they had more champagne in the comfort of their bed. Maisie filled the glasses as Ed lay on his back gazing at the ceiling.

'Were you faithful to me?' he asked her suddenly.

'Of course,' she replied artlessly; 'were you?'

'Of course. But still, we've a lot of catching up to do.' Ed's eyes wandered towards the silver-framed photograph by the side of the bed, which was of them on their wedding day standing on the steps of the castle. He took it between his hands and examined it carefully.

'I can't believe that this was nearly two years ago,' he said, 'that so much time has gone by. You haven't changed at all.'

Maisie leaned languorously across the body of her husband, relishing the feel of his bare flesh against hers, and studied the picture.

'Oh, it was such a happy day, wasn't it, Ed?' she said nostalgically. 'Such a happy, happy day.'